Love's First Light

LOVE'S FIRST LIGHT

a novel

JAMIE CARIE

PUBLISHING GROUP

Nashville, Tennessee

Published by B&H Publishing Group,
Nashville, Tennessee

Dewey Decimal Classification: F
Subject Heading: LOVE STORIES \ FRANCE—
HISTORY—1789-1799, REVOLUTION—FICTION

Scripture quoted from the King James Version.

1 2 3 4 5 6 7 8 • 13 12 11 10 09

Dedicated to Stacy Crays, sister of my heart.
This one is for you . . .

Acknowledgments

To Narelle Mollet, my beautiful Aussie friend! Thank you for the critique of this book. Your perspective on all things Christian fiction and your love for God helped make this story what it is. I am so blessed to have you in my life!

To Dave Bender, my scientific genius neighbor. Thanks for allowing me to ply you with questions about light and color (and a bunch of other topics I can't remember now). I am sure a future book will need your help too!

And finally, to Jordan, Seth, and Nicholas, my three boys. Thanks for being so self-sufficient when I need to work. Thanks for giving up time with me and helping to take care of each other. You are each the light of my life.

Chapter One

1789—Paris, France

They were coming.

They were coming! Christophé shoved his little sister, twelve-year-old Émilie, through a hidden door in the wall, quickly following after her. He held the door open, waiting for the rest of his family, but they didn't appear. The sounds of the soldiers were close. He had no choice. He let the panel fall shut with sudden finality, leaving them in utter darkness.

His sister whimpered and clung to his broad shoulders behind the pearl-paneled, gilt-molded wall. He held her tight against his quivering body, his palm over her ear, pressing her other ear into his chest so that she wouldn't hear their mother's screams. *Too late . . .* His heart felt sick, leaden. They'd captured the rest of the St. Laurent family. He clasped Émilie's filmy sleeved dress in his fist and willed the evil away.

Together they stilled their bodies into stark fear as they heard the rolling wheels of the guillotine. Christophé heard a voice command his mother, the Countess Maria Louisa St. Laurent, to come forward. At twenty-three, Christophé

1

recognized that they'd chosen her first to heighten the horror. He clenched his eyes as the rattle of wooden wheels over the hard floor softened when they met carpet, then stilled. It had reached its place of death and damnation. A heavy thud sounded on the other side of the wall as his mother, shrieking, was locked into place. Wails filled the room. His throat ached with silent screams. A second of shocked silence.

And then the thick thud of the blade.

The eldest son was next. Christophé heard his older brother Louis's heavy grunts as they forced him to the guillotine. He remembered when Louis had sounded like a boy, and then his voice changed. Still, there was the occasional squeak that they weren't to notice. Finally, when his voice no longer squeaked, his brother shot up four inches in a single summer. How proud Christophé had been of that cool, confident young man.

A guttural yell against cloth broke into his thoughts. He closed his eyes and willed it away.

But this nightmare was far from over. Jean Paul would be next—and so he was. The brother who laughed with him and wrestled with him, who ran across fields with him long after Christophé should have outgrown such things. *Jean Paul—brother of my heart*!

Christophé's whole being became stilled screams.

His body jerked as the sound of the blade sliced through the darkness. He nearly lost consciousness. His body grew weak, his breath vanished in terror. He lost the strength to hold Émilie. He could only blink in the dark and feel his eyes flow with tears that seemed never ending. His shirt and Émilie's hair became soaked with his silent grieving.

A sudden sound rang out. A father's cry. He begged and promised things he taught them never to say. The Count of

St. Laurent. *Laurie,* his mother called him. Their father. A husband. Now, in the end, just a man.

Christophé heard threats shouted into his father's face. He pictured him bent for the blade, his hands tied behind his back. "Where are they?" some evil demanded. "You will only prolong their misery."

"We will find them." Another voice, as subtle a threat as a rapier thrust.

This voice sounded familiar. From the few times he had visited their chateau, Christophé could picture a narrow face and wide-set eyes that seemed to see everything. He remembered a cuffing on the chin when he was a child, dark eyes glaring into his as the man stood in the corner of their crowded salon. Christophé would never forget those piercing eyes.

That evil smile.

He couldn't remember the name, but he knew the face. It was as imprinted now as if he'd seen him drop the blade himself.

Christophé vowed he would never forget.

Their father did not give up the hiding place of his two youngest. He said only, over and over, "Don't kill me. Please, don't kill me."

And no matter how hard Christophé pressed his hand against his sister's quivering body, he knew she heard it too. The final *thwack* of a blade . . .

The end to any life they had ever known.

⁓

RUN.

Run from Paris.

It was the one thought that kept him sane while trapped in the room. He had to protect Émilie. *He* had to save her.

They waited in the dark smallness of the space, their ragged breath making the air hot and still. They listened in panting silence while men ran about the room, ransacking and looting, searching for them. They heard the glass break and the fabric rip. Footsteps pounded around the place where they hid—close, causing them to cling together, and then above them and all around them. It seemed a hundred men had come to participate in the fall of the house of St. Laurent. Émilie had not stopped shaking for the first two hours, and then, suddenly, went slack in his arms. He held her tight, knowing she had fallen into an exhaustion of body and emotion. He was thankful for it, hoping she would sleep and that he alone would commit the full horror to memory. The muscles of his arms and back quivered with the strain of endurance. But he wouldn't lay her down; he would not allow the slightest movement that might awaken her.

He didn't know how long to stay hidden. It frightened him, this indecision. He was old enough to be strong for the both of them, but he felt his place as leader slip . . . with two older brothers, he'd never needed to fill that role. He'd been allowed his eccentricities, his head always bent over some experiment or laboring over equations or taking something apart to see the mechanisms. So he continued to wait. Long after all noise had ceased, long after they had both slept and then woke and then slept again, neither saying a word. He was afraid to open the door, afraid of what they were sure to see, but he knew that a full day must have passed and the cover of night was their only hope of escape.

Christophé pulled a handkerchief from his pocket and whispered his first words since they'd entered the room. "I'm to open the door now, Émilie." Then he folded the cloth and put it gently to her eyes. She reared back, afraid, but didn't speak; her breathing grew more rapid as she shook her head. "To protect you," he insisted in a voice meant to soothe. "I don't want you to see whatever is on the other side of that door. I would save you that memory."

Her body stilled. Then she bowed her head and began to cry. She was only twelve, and Christophé could tell that the thought had not yet occurred to her. He allowed her to cry silently into his chest, wetting his shirt, his arms tight around her until she was spent. Then he lifted the cloth and tied the knot behind her head.

The hidden door creaked as he opened it, causing him to stop and listen. Nothing but moonlight spilled in. The air in the room was tainted with the smell of blood, but Christophé could see the illumination of familiar shapes in the light through the long windows. The portable guillotine—the kind they transported to battlefields—and the bodies of his family had been taken away. He kept the blindfold on his sister, though. There was enough blood staining the Persian carpet for a lifetime of nightmares.

Once out of the room, they crept, hand in hand, through the great hall and toward his father's library. Christophé hoped to find his father's gold still hidden there. He remembered how his father had taken his three sons into this room and explained his escape plan to them. After the storming of the Bastille, where a mob had torn the famed prison apart brick by brick, a new wave of panic had struck the nobles. Some fled, some hid their valuables but refused to leave Paris—all watched the new political dealings of the Convention with leaden hearts, angry that King Louis and his queen, Marie Antoinette, were now little more than prisoners, sitting on a barrel of gunpowder, and trying to remain dignified in their palace prison. That is when the Count St. Laurent had called his sons home and made a family plan.

Christophé had been at the Académie Royale des Sciences where he was finally able to immerse himself in his love of mathematics and science. Jean Paul and Louis had moved out of their bachelor lodgings in Paris and taken back residence at the home of their father. All the aristocrats of France were calling home their sons and clinging close to their daughters . . . for no one knew whose head would roll next. Priests, aristocrats, and anyone opposing the new Republic were now the enemies of a nation on fire with the ideals of freedom.

Christophé stopped short upon entering the room. He saw the desk where his father had sat . . . and sudden tears blinded him.

It had been dark that night when the four of them had whispered plans of escape and hiding. They were motioned to seat themselves across from the Count, wondering why their father was so intense and determined. There was only a branch of candelabra sitting on the desk giving them light. The flicker from the candles caught his face, casting it into shadows and then bringing it about again in sharp lines of jaw and hooded brow. The Count sat at his desk, pulled out some papers and then raked his dark, silver-stranded hair away from his forehead. He looked up at the three of them and sighed heavily.

"My sons." He seemed to break and struggle, but the emotion was so quickly extinguished that Christophé couldn't be sure it had ever existed. "This world you have inherited is not the same as any I have ever known." He looked each of them in the eye.

Christophé followed his father's gaze. Louis, rebellious and scoffing, his quick replies sounding throughout the room. Jean Paul, ill at ease, anxious and compliant to any plan that might save them. Christophé didn't know how he appeared to the others, but a great upheaval was radiating from his heart into his quivering limbs and throat. It wasn't fear. It wasn't despair over the old way of life suddenly snatched away. It was an odd mixture of excitement for the future . . . interlaced with despair over the destruction he felt sure was coming. All he knew for certain was that this family—this aristocratic family—would never be the same.

He'd been taught to hate the voice of the people. Who were they? He was supposed to think of them as working-class, ill-bred, uneducated peasants. They were nobodies, he'd been told, that had neither the intelligence, nor the wealth, nor the blue blood flowing through their veins to govern any more than a cow or a field. Perhaps, if they were bright enough, they could ply a trade or run a shop. Still, to have a real voice? To decide on the governing practices of a land so great as France? Never! It wasn't possible.

So he'd been told.

But Christophé lowered his head from his father's intense glare and knew he couldn't echo his father's convictions. He knew he was the only one in the room who thought that, despite it all, they were worthy.

No one need starve in silent, desperate misery.

Christophé looked up into his father's shattered eyes and reminded himself that this man's politics were liberal; he was just and well-liked. Perhaps he . . . they . . . might be spared. But his father's voice echoed around the dark room assuring them that none of the past mattered anymore. They were aristocrats from birth, and the people of France believed they must be annihilated. There was a new invention—the guillotine. And it was created for their necks.

"There are hiding places in the chateau." Their father took up a quill and began to draw. Several rooms appeared on the page, and he wrote their names above the boxes and then marked locations with an X. "Here, in the dining room." He tapped on the paper. "There is a false back in the sideboard table. And here, in the blue salon, behind this painting is a safe."

Christophé and his brothers nodded, their heads bent over the paper as he showed them three more. Then the Count pointed to a spot outside the rooms and drew a long line. "From here"—he pointed to another salon—"is a tunnel leading out into the gardens. You enter it by moving the bookcase. You will see the lever." He looked at Christophé. "Check that it works for me."

"I know the tunnel," Louis admitted. "It works."

His father looked ready to question, but apparently thought better of it. "Very well. There is one more thing."

The three brothers sat up while their father leaned in. "If all else fails, if you have to run, there is an old castle on the southern border of France. In Carcassonne."

"The Trenceval castle?" Jean Paul was the history lover in the family and had spoken of longing to see the castle many times.

"Yes. It's in shambles, a ruin. But it is far from Paris and might be safe for a while."

With that, their father said he was tired, rubbed his temples, and let out a long sigh. "Go to bed, my sons, and don't forget to pray."

Christophé pulled himself from thoughts of that day and led his sister deeper into the library. It was dark, empty, like the thudding feeling of emptiness in his chest. A soundless grate in the fireplace, an echo against the walls that would never again be filled with their happy voices, a darkness that no light could ever penetrate. It was over—*fini*. Their lives as they'd known it. There was only heaviness left. It filled his chest and his shoulders and he bowed his head. He didn't know if he would ever really be able to raise his head again.

Christophé lit a candle on the desk and opened a side drawer where he found a sharp-edged tool. He walked over to a far wall, took firm grasp of either side of the painting's frame, and lowered it to the floor. Behind it was a hidden door, small and disguised by the molding in the paneling. With the tool, he pried it open and plunged his hand inside. *It wasn't there!* Christophé felt a stab of panic. What were they to do?

Turning, he saw that Émilie had sunk to the floor, still blindfolded. She looked so stiff and scared—why hadn't he thought to remove the cloth? As he knelt down beside her, he saw that silent tears were racing down her cheeks. He quickly untied the cloth. She did not look up at him.

Christophé grasped her shoulders and pulled her into his chest, whispering, "I'm sorry." She clung to his shoulders, but did not speak, only kept hold as if in letting go she would dissolve into a million pieces. "We have to go," Christophé finally whispered. "We have to try." He pulled her up, but kept tight hold of her hand.

They crept down a dark hall, the candle a flickering light against the family portraits that hung like ancient memories. Their eyes watched them, demanding, it seemed, justice for the name St. Laurent.

They came into the main hall where the ceiling was high and domed and had always echoed back at their gleeful childish shouts. Christophé lifted the candle a little higher to see into the gloom.

⁂

A SHADOW MOVED with a suddenness that made him rear back, his arms spread to either side to protect his sister. The man that had murdered his family stood in the great hall, so still he might have been another statue.

A name rose to Christophé's conscious—Maximilien Robespierre. Christophé's heart leapt into his throat as their gazes locked. Panic had him backing away, grasping and then pulling Émilie along with him. They ran back the way they had come, booted footsteps right behind them. Christophé threw down the candle and pulled his sister faster, feeling her gasping breaths against his straining wrist.

Several steps and then he felt Émilie jerk as the man grasped her. Christophé swung out with his free hand, catching the man on the side of the head. He heard a surprised grunt, pulled Émilie's hand, hearing her shriek, her cloak falling away as the man grabbed for her.

"Don't give up," he demanded in a hoarse whisper. "Run!" He screamed it through a tight and closed throat. *"Run!"*

Down a narrow flight of stairs, the man just behind them, they reached the door. Christophé twisted the knob with curled, numb fingers. He pulled Émilie through just as Robespierre reached out for her again. He slammed the door hard, catching the thin man again, hearing another grunt and then a curse. He didn't have time to bar the door, nor anything to bar it with, so he pulled hard on his sister's hand and dragged her across the dark street.

The man was soon behind them, but they had gained a few seconds. Weaving into a narrow side street, Christophé guided them by instinct alone. He and his brothers had often explored the city around their palatial chateau. The streets were tight-packed with houses, businesses, and shops. He looked for the red door. The door of his friend.

Robespierre was turning into the side street where Christophé knew they would quickly be discovered. There was no time to find his friend, nor the red door. Émilie was wheezing with the effort to keep up. With a silent plea toward heaven he veered them into some thick bushes, pulled his sister down, and tried to regain his strength. "When he comes by, hold your breath," he whispered into Émilie's ear.

She nodded, her delicate chin catching against his hand.

Christophé watched as the man slowed, looked uncertainly into the deep shadows. He was walking now, winded too, peering from side to side in the dark street. He stopped, turned and turned and turned.

Right in front of them.

Christophé's lungs felt ready to burst. He knew Émilie would not be able to hold her breath much longer. A few more seconds. That was all they had in this life-and-death moment. He looked up and began to pray. His lips moved silently over the words . . .

"Our Father which art in heaven, Hallowed be thy name. Thy kingdom come. Thy will be done in earth, as it is in heaven. Give us this day our daily bread. And forgive us our debts, as we forgive our debtors. And lead us not into temptation, but deliver us from evil: For thine is the kingdom, and the power, and the glory, for ever. Amen."

The man turned again, toward them. Took a step and then another, peering into the bushes. Christophé's heart thudded like the pounding of a drum. Émilie quivered from head to toe, he could almost hear her teeth rattle, but she did not breathe. Her chest was tight against his clasped hands. But she did not breathe!

The man was staring right at them!

Oh, please . . . God in heaven . . . save us!

A loud curse rang from the man as he pulled back and walked a little further down the street, his hand on his head as he searched every shadow on either side.

The sudden noise of horses turning into the street covered the sound of Émilie and Christophé letting out their breath and then gulping in air. Christophé felt dizzy, thinking he might pass out. But he couldn't.

He had to save them. He had to save *her*. It was his duty now. As the last remaining male heir to the house of St. Laurent.

It was his duty to save his family.

Chapter Two

1794—Carcassonne, France

The mist rose above the circle of the earth. The air was crisp, deadly quiet as it always was in the old graveyard at dawn. Christophé St. Laurent grasped his dark cloak against his chest with one fist, the other holding a knurled walking stick. He didn't need it to walk—only to swirl the mist when the mood suited him.

His gaze tripped over the headstones as he passed. *Robert Barret, born 1732, died 1765.* A small stone. A short life, his. Madame Genevieve Montaigne rested on the laurels of goodwife to ten children, and yet not a plant or flower graced that simple edifice. And then there was Captain Fontaine, with a headstone so tall, the etching so old and proud, the moss so thick—a hero in some long-ago history lesson. Christophé's lips grew taut as he contemplated the ghostly eulogies.

A small yellow glow started on the horizon. He stopped his morning walk, stilling the clip of his heels to turn eastward and watch the second-by-second display of a planet's rotation. It never failed to fill him with wonder and he found himself taking a deep breath, feeling the mist move into his mouth and throat and chest.

It was turning pink.

Joy rose from his chest to his throat. "Thy kingdom come," he whispered into the fading mist. "Thy will be done."

He turned, his pace brisk now, knowing the way like a child knows the path home. Energy flowed from the earth, through Newton's gravity, to rise up from his legs and cause a sweat to break between the sharp planes of his shoulders. His legs pumped faster as a sense of power rushed through him.

He could run.

The thought struck him as new. He hadn't allowed himself that freedom in so long. An image flashed across his memory— he and his brothers and sister running through an ornate garden . . . a palatial dream. He saw their bright faces in stark relief. The light was too bright. Something in him wanted to shield it away, but he couldn't. Every blink brought a remembered face. His brother, Louis, with hair so dark and eyes that flashed back a challenge at him. Jean Paul, a year older than Christophé, quiet and solemn, quick and encouraging, quick as moonlight, but willing to forfeit the race to see any one of them smile.

Then he saw Émilie. She reached her hand out toward his, her shorter legs unable to keep up. She was as bright as the braids that had tumbled loose, bouncing upon her shoulders.

Christophé blinked hard several times but could not rid himself of the image of her face, so alight with laughter and . . . life.

"Thy will be done," he choked through sudden tears.

He stopped, realizing he'd been running. He bent over his legs, felt his long hair fall forward like a dark curtain, heard his grievous cry—waves of sound that made no difference. He lifted his head and watched as tears dropped in liquid pools, scattering the dust on the stone path into tiny puffs.

It was like that sometimes. A sudden memory swept away all but this core of grief. No matter how he fought, it knew his weakness. It sought him out in the sane moments when his mind wasn't obsessed with the physics of light and color and the complexities of a mathematic scheme that shouldn't work but, somehow, always did. When his mind was a silent crypt it crept in, an insidious rotting, a ruin, and then simply . . . overwhelmed him.

With nothing short of grace, he pulled himself up and together, took a bracing breath, and continued on this morning-ritual walk of blurted-out prayers and nonsensical thought. It was the only thing that kept the thread holding his mind and soul from snapping.

He turned another way. It was frightening, this varying from routine, but this morning he found himself running. *This* morning, he found he could do anything.

He moved smoothly, his legs and feet pushing against the stone path, up a slow rise, his breathing soft and even. He ran with the cool wind blowing back his hair, the remains of the dead flashing by like glowing stones. He ran and felt he could keep running forever.

He saw her and stopped. She was crouched low, her head down, her shoulders curled within her, stiff and unmoving. He couldn't help but stare at her long, unbound hair. It was dark but alive with color, the pink glow of a morning's glory reflecting in each strand.

Gold and amber and bronze and the color of glowing coals. Bright, white light. He saw the prism in his laboratory. Blinked and saw the split of white into the colors of the rainbow. Saw them reflected on his old castle's walls. Brilliant but cold. So brilliant.

So cold.

He wanted to tell her of it. His chest heaved with the effort not to blurt it out.

She stood suddenly and whirled around—long, dark cape and glorious hair, flowers still clutched in her hand. Christophé's gaze dropped from her frightened face to her rounded stomach and then the gravestone that glared chalk-white in the mist behind her.

"Color," he thought as he stood transfixed. No, not a thought.

Heaven help him, he had said it aloud.

&c∽

SCARLETT STARED AT the tall man on the path before her, hoping he wasn't everything he looked to be. Murderer. Maligner of women everywhere. Dark and dangerous stranger. Everything her mother had warned her might happen on these early morning visits to a husband's grave suddenly rose up as real. She clutched her cloak to her throat, wishing, for once, she had listened to reason and put on something besides her nightgown before leaving the house.

"Stay back," she heard herself whisper and then wished she'd stayed silent. She backed away, slowly, one step after another. The lilies in her hand dropped to the sharp green earth. She turned to run and then heard his deep voice.

"Did you love him?"

She turned her head back toward him and stared. No one had asked her that question. What right did *he* have to ask it? What right to make her feel afresh the guilt in that answer?

She turned fully toward him, felt the flare of her anger and her cape.

"Comment est-il mort?" His eyes were dark and hooded. "How did he die?" He murmured again, this time in English.

She tilted her head into one shoulder and closed her eyes. "For the Révolution. In Paris."

When she opened her eyes . . . she saw nothing but the mist.

Chapter Three

1789—Paris, France

Robespierre walked to the end of the street and then turned. After many more minutes of watching and waiting, Christophé led them out of the bushes. What should they do next? To travel and live in Carcassonne for any length of time would require money. If it were only him, he would run, but he had a sister to think of. He must keep her warm and fed and comfortable. No telling for how long. Months . . . maybe years. Should they become peasants and work? Should they take on new identities?

The questions—and the responsibility they carried—weighed heavy on his heart as he grasped Émilie's hand and pulled her into the shadows of a tall building.

He needed advice. His friend, Jasper Montpelier, lived on this street. Christophé had literally run into the man as a boy. He and Jean Paul had been attempting to fly a kite in this street as the trees were low and they were tired of the harsh eyes of the aristocrats when they'd taken their toy to the formal gardens at Tuileries Palace. That day Jean Paul held the string, letting it out just right, while Christophé ran the length of the street with the homemade diamond-shaped kite. Just as he thrust it into the air, he'd run hard into a man, knocking him down. The man had sprung up on surprisingly spry legs and laughed, righting Christophé with a swift movement. He'd smiled and motioned toward the soaring kite.

"She's a beauty!" He yelled into the wind. They looked up at the fluttering tail that held ripped strips of expensive taffeta and silk for a tail. Christophé was embarrassed by the femininity of it, but it was all to be had in his mother's sewing basket.

The man must have seen his flushed cheeks, for he'd clapped Christophé on the shoulder and let loose a hearty laugh. "Never fear invention, my boy. It is what makes the coming world."

The words struck a chord within him that was alive and stubborn and sure. He smiled, and the three of them flew the kite all afternoon. Tired and thirsty, Jasper invited them to his home for refreshment. He explained to the boys as they walked the long, narrow street that he lived above his apothecary shop.

It was the only shop with a red door.

The shop was small and neat, with a long counter and row upon row of bottles and jars sitting on shelves behind the counter.

"What are in the bottles?"

Jasper answered Christophé with a wink. "My proprietary concoctions." He pulled one down, opened the bottle, and let them sniff it. Jean Paul immediately sneezed and both boys said, "Ohhh, that's horrible."

Jasper chuckled. "Come. I will show you my laboratory."

He led them toward the back of the shop and then into another smaller room. It was rather dark and quite messy, with a shambles of papers, glass bottles, jars of all shapes and sizes with odd things growing in them, and several pestle and mortar sets. It was as though they'd walked into another world. A secret world where the mysteries of the universe could be found.

That proved the first of many visits, and it wasn't long before a love for science took such hold of Christophé that his family despaired what he might do next. He was forever taking apart anything mechanical to find its inner workings, or using rare family heirlooms to put together strange apparatus. He remained locked in his room, scribbling his ideas onto parchment after parchment until there were so many of them they were stacked against the walls of his room.

That day was the beginning of his life.

Jasper was his best friend. There was no one else he would trust so completely to help them. But Christophé needed money, and the only place to find that was back at the chateau. He turned toward Émilie and whispered, "I'm going to take you to a friend's house."

When she immediately cried out and grasped hold of his arm, he took her shoulders and spoke evenly. "It will be fine. I have to go back and get some things. Things that will help us survive." He took her rounded cheeks into his hands and stared into her solemn eyes. "I won't be long. Jasper will protect you." He pointed down the dark street, "The shop with the red door. See? Come."

"Don't leave me! I can't bear it." She was crying again and wouldn't move.

Before he had time to answer, he heard a sound behind him. Émilie screamed as he turned, standing in front of her to protect her. The man was big, but he wasn't Robespierre. Christophé saw the glint of a knife as the man pulled it out and lunged toward him.

"Run!" He pointed to the red door. "Jasper!" He just got the word out as the swing of the knife whooshed through the air. Leaning sideways, he dodged its mark. Christophé balled up his fist and took a swing. His fist connected with the man's chin, and stark surprise painted the man's features as his head jerked backward. Christophé took full advantage, raising both arms up and then slamming them down on the arm that was holding the knife. Lessons from fighting with his brothers rushed back over him. He'd always been taller and leaner than his brothers, but, more often than not, he'd been able to hold his own, surprising them with his wiry strength and quickness.

The man recovered quickly, looking for his knife. Christophé kicked the weapon away and swung again. This time the man caught his forearm in a vise-like grip and charged like a bull into Christophé's body, causing them both to fall to the ground. The man's meaty strength was born of weight and size; Christophé knew he wouldn't last much longer. With a quick look behind he saw that Émilie had indeed run away. He just needed to give her enough time to reach Jasper's door.

"Wait!" Christophé yelled into the man's face, feeling the first real blow to his head, like a swinging lead ball had connected with his skull. "I know your father."

It was an old trick of distraction, but it usually worked. The first time.

The man paused, giving Christophé just enough time to roll and stand. He was off and running before the man could pick himself up.

Christophé ran as fast as he could. Away from Émilie.

Minutes later, he hid in the shadows in his family's garden. It wasn't safe, but he had to get back into the chateau before seeking out Jasper. He'd heard his assailant follow him for a while and then, when Christophé increased his speed, he'd felt more than saw the man slow and stop. Hopefully, the minion had given up the chase and returned to wherever Robespierre told them to go when this night's business was over.

Hopefully, that place wasn't inside the chateau.

He stood for a long time watching the back door for movement. It was still standing open, a dark hole in the stone wall. When nothing moved, no sound was heard, he took a deep breath and crept toward the door. It was now or never. Go in. Find anything of value and get out for good. Émilie would be worrying about him. He rushed inside, then stopped, ears tuned to the slightest sound. When he was sure there was none, he climbed the stairs to his parents' bedchamber.

Everything was dark now. He made his way to a candle and found some flint to light it. With the tiny, flickering light he combed the room, searching for his mother's jewels and feeling a thief. He tore into her wardrobe and found it already ransacked.

Heavy silks, brocades, and satins lay in multicolored piles around his feet. He inspected each one—there might be gold buttons or diamonds and emeralds and sapphires imbedded into skirts and collars and adorning hats and shoes. There was nothing left. His mother's things were ripped apart, looking like a giant pile of colorful rags. Anger and pain like nothing he'd ever known rose to his throat, threatening to choke him. He knew he should hurry, but he couldn't move, could only kneel there among the tattered remains of her things, inhaling her scent and feeling like his heart was failing.

Finally, he wiped the tears from his face and forced himself up. If it were only him, he would lie there in their room all night, not caring if he was caught. But it wasn't. He had to hurry back to Émilie.

Stumbling over the wreckage of the room, he made his way to his father's desk and rummaged through the drawers—nothing, all the papers and important documents were gone. His father's armoire—nothing. They'd even taken his clothing.

He staggered from the room, trying to make his legs hurry but barely able to increase his pace. He searched his brother Louis's bedchamber as silent tears ran down his cheeks. There was little left but the bed and an empty desk and armoire.

With little energy left, he made his way down the hall to Jean Paul's bedchamber. It looked like a tomb in the flickering light of his now-sputtering candle. He would have to find another candle. He couldn't leave until he had something of gain. Walking around the room he gave it a brief inspection and then started to go. Wait. Hadn't Jean Paul always hidden things under his bed?

Walking over, he knelt down and held the candle under the high bed. There was something, a dark form. He reached in and pulled it out. "Oh, God."

It was his brother's shoe. His shoe.

Christophé clutched the shoe to his chest as a sob broke from his tight throat. He bent over it, feeling the leather, remembering the last time he'd seen it on his brother's foot. Had it only been yesterday? He raised the leather up to his forehead and pressed into it. "Jean Paul." His hands roved over the stitching in the leather as if each stitch held a memory that they had shared. As he moved the shoe, he heard a little sound from inside it. He placed his hand inside and brought out a small bag. It was black and soft and as Christophé loosened the cord he heard a clinking noise. Tipping the bag, he poured the contents into his palm. Coins, several of them. The sight drew a little chuckle that quickly turned into a mourner's cry. "Jean Paul, you always did rescue me."

Rising, he stuffed the bag into his pocket and rushed to the library, feeling his energy rise. There were other secret compartments in that room, and in two more rooms: the dining room and the blue salon, his mother's favorite room for entertaining family friends. The library held nothing—the blackguards obviously knew to thoroughly search that room. The blue salon's safe was empty as well. He ran to the dining room, the candle nearly out. The long, heavy sideboard stood on the far wall. Setting the candle on top of it he pulled out all of the drawers. They were empty, all of the fine silverware and dishes gone, but he had figured that would be the case. If only they'd missed the hiding spot . . .

Reaching inside he pulled on four loose nails in the back. It was a false back and held a space between it and the authentic back of the piece. There was a little hole in the middle where Christophé inserted his finger and pulled with all his strength. It popped open, and a clattering sound followed the pop. Something had fallen to the bottom of the piece. Christophé felt with his hand until his fingers wrapped around something solid and metal. He pulled it out and held it up.

Rubies and emeralds sparkled in the dim light of the candle and the silver light of the moon coming in through the window. A golden goblet. He'd heard it existed but had never seen it. Louis claimed their father showed it to him once, saying that it came from their ancestors, the mighty Trencevals. He said that the early kings of France had drunk from it. At the time Christophé and Jean Paul had rejected the idea out of jealousy and knowing how much Louis liked to tease them and lord it over them that he would be the next Count. But now . . .

The cup was heavy in his hands, weighted like a crown, and looked like something from a medieval king's table. The

Trencevals. From Carcassonne. Maybe it was a sign. He shoved it inside his waistcoat and quit the room.

Back out into the cold night, he slunk against the stone edifice that had been his childhood home. Even if Robespierre and his minions weren't still looking for him, it was after curfew and the patrols would be out. He ran, eager now, back into the street where his friend lived. *Please God, I pray Émilie found Jasper's house.*

It didn't take long to find the red door. He knocked softly, pressing himself against the peeling paint on the wood.

After a few moments, Jasper, sleepy-eyed with tousled gray hair pulled open the door.

"Christophé!" He came awake suddenly and pulled him into the room. "What has happened?"

Christophé had a sinking, panicked feeling rise and expand throughout his whole body. "Émilie, my sister"—he stopped, everything in him stopped—"is she not here?" He watched in a kind of sick, slow-motion dread as Jasper shook his head in confusion.

"Your sister?"

Christophé looked around the dark shop. "She didn't come to you? Just under an hour ago?" He stopped and stared, then whispered. "What have I done?"

Jasper pulled him further into the room. "I've not seen her. Did you send her here? What has happened?"

"Robespierre . . . he killed them . . . all." Christophé couldn't get his breath. "All except Émilie and . . . and me. A man attacked me. I sent her here, told her to run to you. I told her to go to the house with the red door while I went back for this." Christophé lifted the heavy goblet from his waistcoat and then let it fall to the floor in a metal clinking thud.

Christophé sank to the floor beside the cup. The events of the day overwhelmed him, like night had come forever. He couldn't think what to do next.

Jasper brought Christophé a cup of water, bade him drink, and then sat down across from him on the floor. "Tell me everything. We will find her."

⁓

THEY COMBED THE street up and down, every tree and bush and shadowed corner. They looked into the streets surrounding them. They quietly called out her name.

"Émilie! Émilie . . ."

"Émilie! Émilie . . ."

"Émilie . . ."

There was no sound.

There was no response.

⁓

DAYS LATER A sudden commotion filled the streets of Paris. Christophé ran to a window and saw that it was a mob of people. "What is it?" he asked Jasper as his friend came up to stand next to him.

"Looks like another execution. Did you see the carts go by?"

"No." Christophé looked over his shoulder at Jasper. "We have to go. They might have . . ." He couldn't finish the sentence.

Jasper pointed to a hook on the wall. "Get your cloak, pull the hood well over your head."

The streets were filled with crowds making their way to the Place de la Révolution where the guillotine stood. Street criers were eager accomplices as they strode through the boulevards and weaved around the chateaus and mansions of what used to be the privileged. The people cheered as news spread of the latest aristocrats to fall.

Unable to wait until they reached the platform, Christophé stopped one of the street criers. "Do you know the identities of the prisoners?"

The man gave him a suspicious look but rattled off several names. "Oh, and Émilie St. Laurent. She's a young one, but they say she is the last of the St. Laurent house. Another aristocratic line ended." The man grinned at Christophé, showing rotten teeth to match his rotten soul.

Christophé turned, his stomach rolling, unable to speak. Jasper grasped his arm and pulled him along. "Hurry."

He felt swept along in the thick crush of people, as if he were one of them. He didn't speak as they did, shouting their victory: "Kill them! Destroy the royals!" He couldn't speak at all, only let himself be jostled along until he neared the front.

They all stilled as the first prisoner was led to the platform. He could feel the hatred around him like a living thing, voracious and feral, as they read the name of a man he was sure he'd seen in his mother's elegant salon. He watched, strangely detached, as they tied him to a long board, lifted him, then slid him under the scaffold and blade.

Christophé's throat thickened as the blade shot down. Gravity. Weight. Steel. Blade. Neck. Friend. Foe. Human. Man. His thoughts were scattered . . . abrupt . . . nauseating.

Then they led another and another. Their heads were taken up by the executioner and held high for the crowd to see and cheer. Some were pierced on a wooden pole. Members of the mob grasped the poles in wild-eyed glee to parade amongst the thronging crowd. The people around him shouted in a murderous, frenzied state that he'd prayed only existed in nightmares. Christophé couldn't imagine that he was still alive. That this was real and terrifying and . . . real.

God! He cried silently. *Oh, God!*

Then they led a girl up to the platform. Christophé saw the long, golden hair. The slight, shaking body. There was a hood over her head, but he knew.

It was Émilie.

He had thought to rescue her. He had thought he might do *something.* Now he knew. There was nothing he could do—except rush, screaming her name, to his own death. Émilie would die this day.

And the only choice he had was to watch or turn away.

⟳

CHRISTOPHÉ BRACED HIS legs. He took long, deep breaths to keep from succumbing to the beckoning blackness. But he stayed. With tears rushing, one after the other. With dread filling him like a blackness taking over his body, with legs that shook with the effort to stand . . . he stayed and he watched and willed with everything in him that God would work a miracle.

He blinked as her body was laid on the wooden platform. He stumbled as the blade swooshed down. He cried out as her head fell into the bloody basket, the honey curls bouncing.

As the crowd cheered he staggered away. Jasper was behind him, supporting him, half carrying him . . . but he couldn't care. He sank to the side of the street and curled into a ball.

"*Noooo* . . ." The cry wrung through him and then out. Jasper hastened to hush him, but he did not care if the hordes of murderers surrounding him noticed. He did not care if they raised him up, stripped him down, and pulled the hood over his head. In that moment he welcomed the mounting of those wooden steps.

There was no one left to care what might happen to the new Count of St. Laurent.

Chapter Four

1794—Carcassonne, France

Scarlett charged through the door. She paused just inside, seeing the shabby furniture, the old carpet that they beat with a stick every other laundry day, the dim light of dawn filtering through the small windows of the cottage. But it smelled of fresh-baked bread and no amount of shabbiness could take away that homey feeling of comfort and, with it, a measure of peace.

She shut the door behind her and leaned back against it . . . who *was* he? Where had he come from? She was still shaking inside as she threw off the cloak, tossing it to a chair, thinking to run upstairs and put on some clothes before her mother found her out.

"Scarlett, is that you?"

Too late. Her mother was already up and in the kitchen. Scarlett took a deep breath, brushed a stray lock of dark hair behind her ear, and entered the hot room, the smells of market day heavy in the air.

"Yes, it's me." She avoided her mother's eyes as she rushed in and tied an apron over her billowing nightgown. She hadn't realized how late it was.

Her mother, Suzanne Bonham, turned and wiped her sweat-soaked hair from her temple with the back of one hand, her eyes assessing. "You were at the gravesite again." She said it low and a little disapproving.

Scarlett looked up and saw the concern in her mother's eyes. "Yes. Time escaped me." She would not apologize.

Scarlett picked up a basket and moved toward the long, golden loaves of baguettes. "I will hurry."

"You should have at least dressed." Her mother started the tirade as she turned back to the fluffy dough she was kneading on a wooden counter. "I'll not have you running about the countryside in slippers and your nightgown. It is bad enough that you have to go at such an ungodly hour, but, saints preserve us, in your nightclothes! What would anyone think if they saw you?"

Scarlett agreed but couldn't force anything but a whiff of air from her tight throat. All she could see was the man. His dark silhouette against the pink of the sunrise. His deep voice resounding against the gravestones. His dark cloak hung loose and yet moved with the breeze as if . . . as if something important was to happen. As if her life was more than grave visiting and guilt assuaging and this eternal waiting. As if . . .

As if that man meant something to her.

And how can that be? she chided herself. *Will you always let yourself fall suddenly for a man? You don't even know his name?*

That's what had happened with Daniel anyway—her falling suddenly. That should have taught her a lesson. She wasn't going to make that mistake again.

Scarlett turned at the sound of her mother's voice, knowing that she'd missed some of the lecture.

"Sorry will not help you should you meet some strange man and he think it an invitation. I've told you time and again it's not safe to be alone at such hours. With everything going on these days you should visit the grave during the daylight hours like any good girl would do. I don't understand why you need to visit it every day. It has nearly been six months."

Scarlett's round stomach bumped into the basket of bread and tipped it over, causing the steaming loaves to fall to the floor. "Oh!"

She bent, an awkward sinking, half-bending motion around her pregnancy, and scrambled to gather them up. Rising with effort, the bread clutched in her hands, she looked up into her mother's stricken eyes. "I'll dust them off."

Her mother pursed her lips together and sighed. "We have no choice. There is not time nor enough flour to make more." She turned back to the dough and began to knead the giant soft ball with her hands. "I do wish they would send more flour. We could sell double what we bake."

Scarlett had heard the argument countless times before. Her husband's uncle, the infamous Maximilien Robespierre, had arranged for them to receive flour from his powerful office in the Committee of the newly established government. He also gave them a small stipend every month to supplement a household of three lone women. But still, it was a struggle to keep the cottage and body and soul together. Becoming bakers had been her little sister's idea. Stacia had her father's entrepreneurial spirit and was always coming up with ideas to increase their bottom line so that she could buy dresses and shoes and fashion papers from Paris. Scarlett and her mother simultaneously despaired over Stacia's reckless streak and admired her sharp business mind.

The baking of bread, though, had turned into a small gold mine. Scarlett's uncle agreed to send what flour he could arrange, it being closely managed by the new French government, and so their business had begun.

As it turned out, all three of them had a knack for baking. The weeks took on a comforting if exhausting routine.

It was an ordered life. A simple life. In the wake of Scarlett's father's death, and then Scarlett's husband . . . with no man to carry them . . . flour, yeast, water, *bread*. That was what sustained them now.

"Scarlett, did you hear me?"

She shook her head, turning from arranging the basket to best display the loaves. She seemed to have a knack for making the bread look more a decoration than something to eat. "I'm sorry. My mind doesn't seem as keen these days. What did you say?"

"About visiting the grave as you do, so late or so early. It's not fitting. Why do you insist on going only when it is dark?"

She would never be able to explain it to her mother. That in dark, it still wasn't quite real. That in the bright light of day she couldn't hide as well from the guilt that she was a little relieved her marriage was over. Had she known Daniel at all? There hadn't been enough time. She would have, after this Révolution was over, been able to make it work between them if he'd lived, wouldn't she?

She turned away, not knowing how to answer her mother, except: "I will try."

"You will try." Her mother put her hands on her rounded hips, making Scarlett sigh internally. *Please, God, let the lecture be finished.*

"What if some evil person comes upon you? What will you do then? I worry so about you." Her mother paused, throwing her hands into the air. "And in your condition." She thrust her hands out toward Scarlett. "You couldn't even run away."

It was true. She could *not* have run away this morning. She looked down and saw the giant mound of her stomach. Her mother was right. There had been a moment when she thought that she should run. Until he spoke . . .

Who *was* he? She could not let her mother learn of him! Their encounter would send her into a worried state of agitation that would last for weeks. Scarlett didn't doubt that her mother would even start to follow her, at a distance, thinking she was successfully spying. She had done it before to both Scarlett and her sister. But Scarlett was a woman grown, and about to be a mother herself. She should be allowed to make her own decisions.

Scarlett turned back to the hot fire, pulling the round, split, sweet-smelling bread from the heat with her flat, wooden paddle. Her cheeks burned from both the blaze and the thoughts of the dark stranger. How could she not recognize him? Carcassonne was such a small community, and being bakers at the market three mornings a week had assured that they knew every reaching hand. But this man, she was certain, had never been in the busy streets on market day, never reached out for their meager sustenance.

The baby kicked hard and then turned, folded, and stretched inside of her. She stilled her hands and then clutched her stomach. She could feel him stretch against the thin barrier of his world and hers. He wanted out . . . and soon. She smiled with the thought, her head down, her body curled into their private world.

"What is it?"

"The babe." Scarlett rose up and motioned her mother over. "I don't believe he likes it when I bend over. It must crowd him."

Her mother took the few steps toward her, her hands dusted with flour. She hesitated. Scarlett took firm hold of her mother's hands and laid them on the round stomach. Scarlett moved them to the place where she could feel the child move. "Here. Can you feel it?"

Scarlett's mother looked up, her round face still unlined, her eyes closing. Her lips curved into a smile. "A baby in the house again." She blinked rapidly, a look on her face that Scarlett seldom saw. Another sudden turn by the babe and both their eyes grew round as Scarlett's entire mound shifted. They burst out laughing. "A strong one!" Her mother leaned in and kissed Scarlett on the forehead, and then waved a hand. "Go and get your slugabed sister up. I will finish down here."

Scarlett ducked her head and smiled.

It wasn't often that her mother kissed her.

❦

CHRISTOPHÉ TUCKED THE curtain around the narrow rectangle of the old castle's window. At one corner he propped up the dusty fabric with an old bottle in the corner of the sill. It allowed a small shaft of light into the vast, stone room. On a table he positioned a prism, hard won and a little stolen; convincing the woman it was but glass. God help him, that had been years ago, soon after he had fled Paris.

Alone.

The memory pained him like a stab in his belly, so that he bent toward the table and the prism. He lifted the triangular glass object toward the beam of light with shaking fingers. He held it steady though. He would stop living before letting this prize shatter on the floor into a hundred useless pieces. His life would not look like that ever again, so help him . . . please, God.

He looked down at the floor. He was standing in one of hundreds of rooms in a crumbling castle. It was a place so large, and in its time, so foreboding, that no army could stand against it. He saw a rusty stain on the floor. He'd heard his ancestral history told to him like a bedtime story. The castle was built in medieval times. It had watched, from this southern border of strength and impregnability, the crushing of the Cathers, a religious sect against the Catholic Church. It had seen the glory of standing firm during the Crusades, thus this floor bore the blood stains of horror stories—stories of the Cathers, the Crusades, the great Trenceval family. And now him.

Up . . . up . . . through the dust motes, through the darkness, to that one place of light. There. Just there. He held the prism steady as it met the beam of light. But it wasn't right. Something was not quite right. The beam was too wide, there was too much light in the room. Christophé held the prism at different angles and variations, but all that showed through was a wash of shadows.

He fell into a nearby chair, frowning, holding the prism in his palms. He stared at it, pondering the mathematical equations springing to his mind. Leaping up, he took up a dry quill, cursed at it, then rummaged around for some ink. Dipping the pen, he scribbled down the numbers swirling in his mind. It always amazed him. This language of time and space and distance and matter. The language of numbers. That it could be put to pen and ink spoke of God. And it could. Somehow, he always knew just what the dripping black point should say. He sighed heavily, his hair hanging in his eyes, his mouth pursed, his jaw clenched until he had the full of his thoughts written out.

But he had to prove those thoughts through experiments. Like Newton and the scientific papers from England that he had studied over and over at school. Mathematics were only numbers until they could *prove* something by sight or sound, touch or smell, taste or even hunch.

He reared back and stared at his calculations. He'd learned all that the university could teach him of mathematics in one year. He'd studied geometry and the newer calculus until his eyes were blurry. He knew what he wrote on paper was sound. Now was the time for experiments. He looked at the calculations again and grinned and then frowned in the next moment. It was impossible. No one would believe him. If what he'd just written—and Newton's experiment—was true, he could place a second prism some distance away and realign the colors.

White light . . . becoming color . . . back to white light. It was white light that held all the colors, not black as they'd thought.

His mind reeled with the implications. A sudden thought struck him as a blow. He breathed through his nostrils with the vision of it. What if God was like light? Pure and white. And what if man was the splitting into a myriad of colors? And then in the realignment with God, they became pure again.

"But how?" he asked aloud, rising suddenly, scattering the dust motes to pace in the echoing room. "How might we become pure and white again?"

He reeled in his agitation, bumped a table and fell. His head knocked against the sharp edge of a wood table. Dazed, he sat up, bracing his hands against the cold, stone floor. Something warm ran down his temple and cheek.

He lifted his hand to the spot, felt the oozing. When he pulled back his hand, it shone with blood.

He stared at the smear on his finger.

Red.

The color of sacrifice.

He rose, looked down at his disheveled dress—his shirt hanging open, his breeches and bare feet. He rushed to the room where he kept his few belongings, threw on clothes, and tied his cravat haphazardly. He shoved his feet into shoes that were worn and tattered from the long walk to this ancient, southern place next to the Pyrenees Mountains. Carcassonne.

He rushed from the crumbling, old castle, where no one dared live for fear the roof would cave in on them in their sleep. His cracked shoes sprang over the bridge to the other side of the Aude River, where civilization flourished—the real living people. Not the ghosts who haunted him.

The actual village frightened him in the full light of morning. Someone might see him, recognize him as the shabby aristocrat he was, and tell the Republic's patrols that roamed to and fro across the land. He pulled his long, dark cape closer, hid his face deeper in the folds of the hood, and kept his eyes downcast.

His steps turned toward the noise of town—the marketplace. The woman's face from the cemetery yesterday morning rose before his mind's eye. He would like to see her face in the full light of the day, to drink it in for a few shadowed moments . . .

His eyes widened at the thought. No. His hiding place and careful routine, these were all he had. He must remember that.

He turned into the busy street of the city market. There were many booths on each side, selling food of all kinds and tapestries and cloth and anything a man confined to an ancient relative's castle might need. But all he could smell was bread.

When had he last eaten? He couldn't recall. Yeasty warm scents led his footsteps deeper into the street, deeper than he'd meant to go. He lifted his chin, the protective hood deep around his face, following his nose. There.

He opened his eyes and saw her.

The impact of her face made him want to shrink back, recoil from such beauty. This world, the world they lived in, didn't deserve her. Her beauty might break all their hearts—certainly his heart—but he didn't turn away. He stood and stared. Soaking in the creamy skin reflected by morning's light. Her eyes were an unusual shade of green, wide and bright with dark, highly arched brows. Her features were perfectly symmetrical, an equal equation. Dark curls lay on either side of the lush display like a frame. She was smiling at a customer. A man.

Before he knew what he was doing he stepped forward, shouldering the man from her view and snatching up a round, still-steaming loaf.

"Oh!"

It was such a feminine squeak of both surprise and then something else—gladness, maybe?—that he pressed his lips together and could only stare at her from his hood. "I need bread." *Ah. That was so wrong!*

A gentle smile made her face glow in the morning's light. It lit so, on her face and in his heart, that sudden equations sprang into his mind. Like the sun. When it ruled the planets. Like rotations. Beauty turning over. *Like starlight forever shining.* But he could only pull deeper within the cloak and nod as she handed him the steaming loaf.

He reached into his pocket, then stilled. He'd not thought to bring money. He thrust the loaf back toward her, turning away.

"Wait."

Her voice was like the power of sound . . . wave after wave after wave . . . resounding in his chest and in his heart. The sound of his own heartbeat roared in his ears.

She held it out to him, leaning in. Her breath fanned across his cheek, sending him reeling back a step or two, clutching the loaf like some gift from heaven.

He looked down at the present thrust into his hands. Regaining his voice, he spoke low, leaning toward her. "My thanks."

It was all he could manage. He didn't know if she heard the low words but didn't turn back. As his footsteps rang over the old stone bridge back to his crumbling castle, he found something inside him that hadn't been present in a very long time.

Hope.

Chapter Five

1789—Paris, France

Jasper pulled Christophé from the middle of the deafending mob to a side street and supported the young man as they half-walked, half-ran from the ghastly scene. Christophé's body shook uncontrollably within his grasp. Jasper saw the silent tears on Christophé's cheeks and felt his own heart break with a thunderous crash. How could this have happened?

Jasper had never married, had no children of his own, and had never grieved a loss. His father, an alchemist with a small shop in one of Paris's business districts, had died several years ago—leaving Jasper his trade, his shop, and all his knowledge. The shop's steady clientele believed their concoctions could cure everything from stomachaches to the plague. He did particularly well when some pestilence struck the city. He was an old man, but happy in his solitude. He had his laboratory, his experiments and books, and the cryptic recipes he reworked and refined. He was content—until the day a ten-year-old boy ran into him, knocking them both down.

Now, as he looked down on the man that boy had become, intense gratitude swelled within. He didn't have much faith in God, had never really needed Him, but even he recognized that it was the hand of fate that brought him and young Christophé together that windy day on a kite's tail. Without the boy, he would have never known the joy of having a child—nor the sorrow. After all they'd witnessed this terrible day, his heart lay broken and heavy, but he knew that was nothing compared with what Christophé must be feeling.

"Come now. Almost there."

Christophé had stopped shaking and was walking beside him, stiff, stilted . . . like the dead upright. Jasper reached his door, fumbled for the key, and ushered the young man inside. "Come, sit by the fire," he ordered his friend in a voice meant to soothe.

Christophé obeyed, collapsed on the floor in front of the small flames, and held out his hands. When he appeared to begin studying the back of one hand in a lost way, Jasper set into motion. He quickly poured Christophé a cup of two-day-old tea, then rummaged around the cupboard until he found a loaf of bread and a crock of butter, setting them side by side on the plate. He sliced the bread into hearty slices then brought the refreshments over to Christophé. He sat the tray down next to the young man with a clatter. The noise had Christophé turning and finally noticing that Jasper was in the room with him. "Here," Jasper held out the glass. "Drink this."

Christophé turned his head away from the offerings.

"If you don't drink it and eat a little, I shall make you a sleeping draught." He might do that anyway, but he wasn't going to say it yet. Let the youth get something warm in his belly and then Jasper would see what had to be done next.

Christophé looked up, a little light of humor sparked in his eyes, then extinguished as quickly as it came. He took up the cup and gulped at it. He coughed a little, looking up at Jasper with an angry blaze. "That's horrible! Are you trying to kill me?"

Jasper offered a grim smile. "No. Trying to save you."

Hurt and confusion darkened Christophé's wide eyes. "What do I do? What do I do now?"

Jasper shook his head and stared into the fire. "You can start by not blaming yourself." He knew it was too soon to be saying such things, but he couldn't help it. Clearly Christophé thought he had brought this on Émilie by sending her to Jasper's door alone.

Christophé's laugh was a harsh cry in the room. "How can I not? When I am alive and she is dead?" He downed the rest of the cup and set it heavily at his side. "It should have been me."

Jasper's eyes filled with tears as they locked onto Christophé's. He couldn't remember the last time he had cried, if ever. Life was so ordered for him. So immersed in compounds and powders and elixirs. His patrons might have problems that they needed solved, but he rarely did.

"Possibly." Arguing would only upset his young friend more. "But don't forget the true enemy, son. You did not do this to your family. It was done to you."

Jasper was of the trade class and should be on the other side. Truly he had wondered what was wrong with him that he felt such antipathy toward the Republic and despair over the reckless-ness of the Crown. He had little patience for politics. He could only credit the fact to his immersion in his own world, and how he had never lacked for anything he wanted.

"Yes. Robespierre." Christophé brought him back to the topic at hand. "Robespierre will pay for this day." Christophé's eyes sparked again, but this time they burned with fire. "I will escape, hide until they are tired of hunting me. And then, when they've given up, I will return and see justice done."

Jasper wasn't sure what he had just unleashed, but for now, it was better than the debilitating grief. Against his better judgment, he nodded. "I will help you leave Paris. You will go to Carcassonne, yes? To the old castle your father told you about. It should be safe there."

Christophé rose and poured another cup of the cold tea. He slung the drink into his throat. "I will sleep now. Tomorrow we will plan it all."

Jasper led Christophé to the spare room where his father had slept. He tucked him into the covers like a child, watched as Christophé pulled the blanket chin high and turned on his side. When Christophé closed his eyes, Jasper turned to leave, but Christophé's hand shot out to grasp his coat. "Thank you."

Jasper ruffled the young man's hair as he might have years ago when Christophé impressed him in the laboratory, which was quite often. "Sleep now."

Christophé let go, his arm falling to the side of the bed. "Yes. For a little while."

❦

THE MORNING LIGHT intruded into the room. It was harsh, and Christophé couldn't remember, at first, why he didn't want it to come. Then, sudden and complete, the previous day's events rushed over him like a death chill.

Émilie! His mind screamed her name. *Why God? Why not leave me her? I don't understand. I can't move . . . out of this bed.* How to make his limbs work? How to make his heart slow to any normalcy? *Why did You leave me here? It should have been me.*

He wanted heaven to answer him. His muscles grew taut against the crisp sheet as he waited. Nothing. Nothing. So much nothing.

Angry, he swung his feet to the floor and stood, his bare chest heaving in the cold air of the room. "Is that all You have for me?" In the continued silence, Christophé turned away and swung his fist into the thin air. "Fine then. Thy will be done." That was the first time he said the phrase, and it was filled with all the pain and hurt and rage that he could muster.

Stretching his tired muscles, which felt like they hadn't any rest or sleep, he reached to the ceiling and then out to the side. He looked at his arms stretched wide. His muscles bulged and flexed as he tested his physical strength. He raised his forearms at a ninety degree angle and bulged out his biceps. He looked down at his chest, saw the muscles swell as he took a deep breath and flexed them. He looked down at his lean belly and chuckled. He was young. He was strong. Maybe he didn't need God and His will.

Maybe he should abandon his faith—little good it had done him—and trust in his own strength. He laughed, knowing his thoughts were foolishness, but feeling a rise of power into his throat. Walking over, he grasped the molding at the top of the door, set his fingers in the groove of the wood, and lifted his body until his chin touched the doorframe. He did this again and again and again, the air from his lungs becoming great whooshes. He did twenty, then thirty, then fifty.

"Exercise is healthy for the mind."

At Jasper's wry voice, he glanced over his shoulder.

"Come. Have some breakfast."

Christophé dropped to his feet. "I'm not leaving today."

"No?"

"No."

Jasper stared at him for a long minute and then smiled. "Very well then. Perhaps you can assist me with a problem I am having."

Christophé grinned, rubbing his stomach. "Some food first. I have a feeling any problem of yours will require an astute mind."

Jasper waved him into the kitchen. "Only a study of Pascal's—some unknown bacteria and the wherewithal to destroy it without killing the good cells. But come, I've made you oatmeal."

As they sat across from each other, Christophé told Jasper his plan. "I can't leave yet. Not while Émilie's final resting place is yet unknown. I have to know where they buried my family before I can leave Paris. I have to pay my last respects." He looked at Jasper, his lips pressed together in a thin line, then voiced his fear. "I don't want to put you in danger. Robespierre is looking for me. If he finds me here . . . you will go to prison, at the very least."

Jasper stared back into Christophé's eyes, equally hard. "You have always been welcome in my home." The old man paused and looked down into his own lap. His voice was low as he revealed the hidden parts of his heart. "You are as close to a son as I will ever have. So never again question my love for you."

Christophé nodded once, then looked down at his bowl and shoved a big spoonful of oatmeal into his mouth so that he wouldn't have to reply. He nearly choked on the giant mouthful, then grabbed his cup and gulped a quick drink of water to help him swallow.

After breakfast the two men entered the sanctuary of the laboratory. It was just a room. A room filled with beakers and books and powders and potions. Jasper kept methodical records of all his experiments, all the concoctions he had invented or improved upon were carefully recorded, sometimes in a secret code that Christophé had helped invent. Christophé's interest had veered from alchemy but he respected it more as an art form.

"Here. Come look at this."

For a moment, being in this place he had loved so as a child, hearing the voice that had led him into the wonders of alchemy and science . . . Christophé was ten years old again. Life was full of promise, not destruction. Life surrounded him.

Death did not exist.

He moved to stand beside Jasper, and they bent their heads, his dark and the other gray, over the latest recipe, which looked more like artistic symbols than text. The familiar symbols filled his mind, drawing his heart and spirit away from terror, into the light of reason.

And there, at his mentor's side, cocooned by symbols and numbers, Christophé was, for a little while, at peace.

A FEW NIGHTS later, just after the eleventh hour struck, a loud banging sounded at the door. Christophé heard Jasper get up and pull on a dressing gown, then pad to the door. Indistinct voices demanding to search the house drifted to his ears. Christophé leapt out of bed. He could hear Jasper trying to put them off, delaying with sarcastic humor and questions. Christophé dressed, shoved a few precious belongings into his bag—the loud and heavy goblet—and then scurried to make up the bed and put the room to rights. In his haste, he backed into the bedside table, tipping it over with a loud thump. He stopped and listened. Heard the voices go quiet. And then . . .

"In there! What was that noise?"

No time! Christophé cursed silently, grabbed up the bag, and slithered through the open window. He didn't even have time to put on his shoes!

Barefoot, he charged across the lawns of Jasper's neighbors.

"There he is!"

A shot rang out and Christophé felt the bullet whiz by his left ear. His heart pounded until he thought it might spring from his chest.

Another shot and then more shouts. Christophé veered into a side street, barely registering the fact that his feet were bleeding from sharp stones in the street. He raced passed shops his mother had taken him to as a boy—the barber, the sweet shop, and—his favorite besides Jasper's laboratory—the general mercantile where he begged her for tools and anything mechanical for his experiments. Now the dark shops passed by in a blur.

The voices behind him seemed to be receding, but he was too afraid to stop. He crossed a bridge to the small island and the medieval beginnings of Paris—Île de la Cité. Then he turned down the winding street that ran behind Notre Dame.

The cathedral loomed massive and imposing as he made his way through the carefully tended trees and bushes that made up the back gardens. He didn't have time for reflection, but something in him pulsed, sad and angry at the state of the cathedral. It had been gutted, looted, turned hostage as a massive storage house for a government that no longer believed in God.

Don't stop . . . don't stop . . .

But he did. He paused, pressing his back into the stone wall that rose so high he could no longer see the shape of the crescent moon. He panted for breath, then held it in for a long moment so that he could hear sounds of pursuit. Nothing. Naught but the sounds of the wind rustling through the branches overhead and the distant lapping of the river.

He'd lost them. Relief weakened his knees, and his body collapsed at the base of the wall. He sat, knees upraised, head hanging down, dragging in long, deep gulps of air. Had the soldiers really given up? Or would they appear at any moment? And even if he escaped now . . .

Would Robespierre ever stop looking for him?

He didn't know. In fact, the only thing he knew for certain was that he had to get out of Paris.

Now.

Chapter Six

1794—Carcassonne, France

It was just before dawn, the time when the stars gave their last twinkle toward a sleeping world and the moon's glow faded through the firmament. Like ghostly arms, the night lights were slowly fading to give way to the sun and day.

Scarlett pulled her warmest dress over her head and stretched her arms back to button it, only managing to get it three-quarters up and then two at the top, leaving a gap in the middle of her upper back. Oh well. Nothing was fitting right these days anyway since she didn't have any clothes for these few short months left in her pregnancy. She scooped up her bonnet and turned toward the door.

Her heart pounded as she grasped the knob to her sister's room. She'd nearly promised her mother she wouldn't go to the cemetery anymore, but she had to. She tried to tell herself she wasn't through grieving Daniel's death, but she knew that wasn't true. Her initial infatuation with the man had soon faded, leaving him forever gone on army business and she . . . lonely. But when she visited the grave, she felt, for reasons she wasn't quite sure, peaceful. As if in remembering him and talking to him, they were finally close. Perhaps it was not so much his death she still mourned, but their distant marriage.

Her room was in the back of the second story—unfortunate for nightly escapades. She had to go through Stacia's room to gain entry to the short hall at the top of the stairs. Thankfully her frail little sister slept like the dead. Her mother, though, was another thing altogether.

Her mother's room, which was much larger and opened directly into the hall, was across from Scarlett's room. Scarlett couldn't make a sound on the stairs or her mother would arise amid tangled covers and come running to discover what crises had her daughter up and about so early on a Saturday. Without market day, they were all supposed to be sleeping later.

It was curious, the way the night seemed to call to her and wake her during this pregnancy. She'd never had trouble sleeping until Daniel's death. Now she only snatched five or six hours before something woke her. Was it loneliness? Anticipation for the babe to come? Fear for a future that looked so hazy and unwritten?

Scarlett shook away the thoughts, bit her lower lip, and crept to the top of the stairs. If only there were some light. Her brow knit together as she took the first step. It creaked a little as she grasped hard on the handrail. Leaning her chest back as she'd seen all pregnant women do when traversing stairs, she crept down them until she was sure she'd reached the bottom, her foot feeling about to ascertain it was, indeed, the last step.

Quicker now, her steps more certain, she made it through the sitting room and into the dark kitchen. One hand reached out in front of her, the other curled protectively around her stomach. My goodness, she was hungry. Reaching for a long baguette, she tore off a hunk, then seeing the leftovers of roast duck from yesterday's supper, she picked up the plate, grabbed some cheese—and then laughed at herself. She might as well pack a basket, eat while sitting at the gravestone, and watch the sun come up.

Thinking of the sunrise brought to mind the dark stranger from the market. He'd acted so odd! As if he hadn't conversed with people in a long time and had forgotten how to comport himself in society. Though his black cloak hid him, she'd seen more of him in the morning light than on their first encounter. He was all tall, lean, tightly wound muscle and had a look as if anything might set him off into some ominous explosion. Despite his deep hood, she'd been able to see glimpses of his face. Longish straight black hair swung over brooding eyes. The memory of his eyes, so intensely blue and filled with fear and pain, brought her thoughts up short as she heaved the basket on her arm. There was a longing in those eyes . . . something she'd not seen before. Some remembered horror shining from them. Those sapphire-rimmed, pale blue eyes had struck her heart like a ghost visiting from a crypt.

Or hell's tunnels.

She turned and made her way back to the sitting room toward her cloak hanging on a hook. She took it down, slipped into the sleeves, and tied the sash firmly above her stomach. With the basket on her arm, she eased open the front door.

Carcassonne was beautiful at dawn. It was two cities in one. Across the Aude River sat the Cité, the ancient town, with its massive, crumbling castle. And then there was the Bastide St. Louis, where the people now lived, where she had grown up. A bridge, made of row after row of stone, connected the two in a graceful rise and fall over the foam of the river. Few people walked it these days, but there was a time when the castle was the stronghold of the southern boundary of France. Now it was mostly mounds of crumbling, fallen, dangerous stone.

She heard her steps ring out as she crossed to the center of the bridge. She paused and stared at the castle. It was still magnificent. Standing there, staring at the shadowy structure rising against the gray-tinged horizon, her breath caught. A shadow of the greatness it once represented, the structure seemed tonight as alone and echoing and mysterious as the man who had stood at the path of her husband's grave.

The graveyard was just to the right of the castle. Vast and deeply interwoven with moonlit headstones among thick green vegetation, it seemed a world all its own. She'd visited her father's grave here, but not so often—not often enough to know every pathway as she did now. Now she knew this place like her own house in the dark—the winding stone path, the brush that wasn't cut back enough and snagged her skirts if she wasn't careful, the names from centuries past, worn by rain and wind so that they were as faint as the memories of the dead. She supposed that was why she'd chosen these early morning visits. Everything here was mystery; a perfect match to her feelings about Daniel and their marriage.

Daniel. How he'd dazzled her when they first met. As her steps continued over the cobbled walk, her own memories rose before her.

Her cousin, the Countess de Beauharnais, was born and raised on a sugar plantation in the French province Trois-Ilets, Martinique, the Caribbean Island that was an overseas department of France. The countess had married well above her station and convinced Scarlett's mother by letter that there were many available alliances to be made for her beautiful daughter. Since Scarlett's father had passed away several years ago, Scarlett's mother was quick to respond that her daughter would travel to Paris to make such a match.

They'd packed her off in a coach on a clear blue day, where the gentle wind blew her thick, dark curls away from her cherry-colored bonnet. Her small, stuffed trunk was secured atop the vehicle with the best clothing, slippers, and jewelry that they could scrounge together. She would never tell her mother the mortification she'd felt when sized up by her benevolent cousin. But Louisa had been generous. She'd commented immediately on Scarlett's lithe form as she evaluated her in an up and down move-ment of her light brown eyes. With a dazzling smile, she pulled Scarlett into a dressing room overflowing with gowns, the fabrics of which were unknown in the backwater of Carcassonne. Silks and brocades; laces and undergarments that had names Scarlett had never heard; overcoats and wraps of fur and satin; and long, glorious gowns of colors she'd never dreamed existed in the world. Louisa had magically, it seemed, summoned a swarm of talented seamstresses, all of whom were more than willing and able to remake a married woman's castoffs into the gowns of a debutante. Louisa was single-minded in her mission to prepare Scarlett to meet the Paris society. But it had all proven unnecessary. It took only that first dinner party, when Scarlett met the tall and hand-some Daniel Robespierre, to strike a match.

Oh, how her heart had jumped when he first looked her way. He'd stopped mid-sentence and stared, a slow smile upon his face. She looked down, her face growing warm, and then stole a quick look at him—only to discover that he was walking toward her. As her aunt made the introductions, Scarlett had to tilt her head back to meet his gaze. Then he bent over her hand, brushed it with a mere whisper of a touch of his lips, and looked up and into her eyes. She stood very still, then smiled. When he smiled back, it brought a thrill to her throat. She opened her mouth to say something clever, but all that came out was, "Oh."

He grinned at her then, one side of his mouth kicking up, his eyes alight with suppressed laughter.

They seated him next to her at the long, lavish table, and she quickly learned that Daniel was a young lawyer, a patriot, and dedicated to the Révolution. He was clearly comfortable in their surroundings, but to Scarlett it was all a foreign world, where crystal glasses clinked in toasts, where dish upon dish was served by a man dressed as richly as any of those seated. Where she watched the others to learn what to do, which elegant fork to raise, when to dip her fingers into the silver bowl of gleaming water, when to laugh.

She knew Daniel saw her ineptitude, but he didn't regard it with any care. Instead he would motion to her when to lift her cloth napkin and dab at her lips, when to lift her glass for another toast.

To the Republic!

It was their cheering cry. She turned to him and whispered the unspeakable. "What do you want . . . the Republic?"

He could have disparaged such naiveté. Instead, he leaned in and whispered something that she hadn't known could ring throughout her entire being. "Freedom."

After the meal they took a walk through the garden of the estate. Daniel left his place in the parlor with the other men as up-and-coming speaker and thinker to take her aside and explain the way of the world outside of Carcassonne.

"But how will you overcome the Crown? The king? Is not such thinking treason?"

"Treason is now siding *with* the king. The Republic believes the king is treasonous to his country. The royal debt, the taxes on the poor, the oppression of a splendorous, decadent crown. They live on their next whim whilst the people starve."

Scarlett nodded. She had seen the suffering. After her father, a mason worker and jack-of-all-trades in Carcassonne, died, she, her sister, and her mother had suffered to pay the tax, selling many family heirlooms to keep their home. It was what propelled Scarlett on this search for a husband.

Daniel took her by the shoulders. "I plan to be one of those who ends the tyranny of the crown. Like my uncle, Maximilien, I will work for, and if need be, die for the Republic."

The weeks that followed held that same enchantment. He took her driving around the city of Paris, showing her the sights and places like the indoor tennis court near Versailles, where the assembly had signed the Tennis Court Oath, and the Bastille. He spoke to her in that same passionate way that overwhelmed crowds and left them shouting and waving their fists in agreement. Her shouts were internal, but she knew when she looked at him, stared into his dark, sure eyes, she had become his greatest supporter. He held her heart in the palm of his hand; all he had to do was ask.

It happened late one night in her aunt's parlor. As if some hidden signal had been given, their elders had filed from the room, exchanging amused glances that had only added to Scarlett's nerves—and anticipation.

As the door clicked shut, Daniel took her hands into both of his. They stood there for a long, silent moment, the crackling of the fire in the background, her nervous smile framing the moment. Waiting . . . waiting for him to speak.

"Scarlett."

She swallowed hard, her brows raised, and held his intense gaze.

"Will you do me the great honor of becoming my wife?"

Glee bubbled up and out her throat. She blinked back the happy tears and nodded. Suddenly shy, she looked down and then back up into the most beautiful male face she'd ever seen. "Yes."

"Yes?"

"*Yes.*" She could feel the smile in her heart spread to her face. She laughed and placed her arms around his neck as he drew her close.

He held her for a long moment and then traced little kisses from her jaw to her cheek, stopping only for a heartbeat when he reached her lips.

At long last he lowered his lips to hers—and Scarlett reveled in her first kiss.

THEIR WEDDING CAME about almost overnight, and before she'd had time to take a real breath, Scarlett was Madame Robespierre. They'd moved into a comfortable apartment on the fashionable Rue Saint-Honoré, near his uncle, the most renowned member of the Jacobin Club and the Committee of Public Safety—Maximilien Robespierre. She had hardly become accustomed to married life before Daniel had left for Nantes and the battle there.

Within weeks Robespierre came himself to tell her the news.

She could still remember pulling the weight of the door open, it swinging wide as she saw Robespierre's face and knew. He never visited her. She looked up at him with dread filling her,

her brows drawn together. She felt all the life and color drain from her face as she asked him in.

He was brisk. No offer of comfort in voice or touch. "He was killed by Royalists. A group of them ambushed his regiment."

She'd wanted to drop to the floor, but commanded her legs to stay strong. "How? Gunshot?" She needed to know.

"Yes. We were victorious. We have rid the city of conspirators. Daniel died with great honor in service for his country."

She wanted to tell him that she needed more time, that the husband she loved for so few days was still a mystery, a stranger to her. That he couldn't really be dead. Daniel would never know he was to be a father! She wanted to tell Robespierre that she'd just discovered she was with child. But she didn't. She only saw him to the door.

He turned toward her in the opening and looked in her eyes for the first time. "If there is anything I can do . . ." He let the phrase hang.

"I would like to take the body back with me. To Carcassonne."

He looked like he might reject her request, and with sudden decision she brought a hand to her stomach. "I will need to go back and be with my family to raise our child. I don't think it is so very much to ask to have his grave near where his son or daughter will be raised."

Robespierre glanced down at the hand covering her stomach and visibly shuddered. A flush filled his cheeks as he looked back up but didn't meet her eyes. "Yes, of course. I will see to it." He turned to go and then turned back. "When will you depart?"

"As soon as it can be arranged." She didn't want to talk to this cold, walking corpse of a man anymore. She wanted him to go so that she could turn aside and let her tears run their course.

Robespierre hesitated, his hat in his hands. "I–I am at your disposal, citizen."

Scarlett bowed her head, her hand on the edge of the door to close it. *"Merci."*

❦

SURPRISINGLY ROBESPIERRE CAME through on his promise. He sent Daniel's body to their border town, where Scarlett saw to the burial. Then he set them up with a weekly supply of flour to support the Bonham women's business as bakers.

Since then, Scarlett's life was built on the routine of visiting Daniel's gravesite daily. It was the only way she found she could really believe Paris happened at all.

Her thoughts returned to the present as her feet turned into the familiar path, the basket weighing on her arm even as her memories weighed on her mind.

She stopped suddenly.

He was there.

The stranger from the market knelt beside Daniel's grave. But rather than facing the grave, he faced the sunrise. His head was uncovered, revealing the choppy cut of shoulder-length, straight hair draped like a curtain around his face.

Her heart beat in her chest. What was he doing there? Was he hoping to see her? She hesitated, ready to slip away before he noticed her, but stilled as his deep voice rang out against the dead ones' stones. "And he took bread, and gave thanks, and brake it, and gave unto them, saying, 'this is my body which is given for you: do this in remembrance of Me.'" He held a piece of the bread she'd given him up into the dawn light, then brought the small lump to his mouth, his head bowed. Next he took up a cup. She gasped at the golden cup, embedded with precious jewels that sparkled in the dim dawn light—and then hoped he hadn't heard her. But he had. He turned, but didn't rise. Instead he held his hand out to her.

She should turn back, run away. He could be dangerous. But she found herself rooted to the path, staring into his eyes. He looked sad, bereft, and so alone.

He dropped his arm back to his side and turned a little away from her. Scarlett took a long breath and a step closer. "What are you doing here, sir?"

He didn't look back at her, only said in his deep voice, "I am taking the sacraments of Communion."

She took another step. "Why?" She had only done so in church, and there weren't any churches open anymore, so it had been a long time. Another part of the Révolution.

He turned then and looked into her eyes. She saw him struggle with an answer and then smile a little. "It helps me remember."

She took another step forward. "Remember what?"

"All that I've lost, I suppose, and all that He lost. I like to think God felt alone for a time, until His Son rose again and then went back to heaven to sit at His right hand." Sadness weighed his smile. "I like to think He has a plan for me too."

Scarlett walked the short distance to her husband's grave, sank down beside the stranger, and set the basket on the ground beside her. She turned her face toward his and saw that there were tear tracks on his lean cheeks.

He repeated the phrase, "This is my body, which is broken for you; do this in remembrance of Me." He tore off a hunk of her mother's bread and held it out to her.

Scarlett reached for it. The man watched her while she placed it into her mouth, knowing how it was made, knowing all the ingredients and the hands that had kneaded it, but feeling that somehow, with this prayer, it had become sacred. She closed her eyes. She chewed and thought of Christ's body. Given for her. There, as they sat together, it was suddenly real.

The man lifted up a golden goblet embedded with gemstones. Scarlett stared at the beauty of the cup and couldn't help the overwhelming feeling that it had once, long ago, belonged to a king.

The man's voice was a little stronger as he recited to her and the dead that seemed to be listening, "This cup is the new covenant in My blood, which is poured out for you."

She watched as he lifted it up and he held it out to her, his gaze intense in the early morning light.

She felt him watch her as she took a sip, then lowered the cup and her gaze, the liquid sloshing over the edge onto her fingers. Scarlett took a deep, long inhale. When she looked back into this stranger's eyes, her breath caught. There was a spark of joy in his eyes now. It made him look, almost, a different person.

"Who are you?" She asked, clutching the heavy, golden goblet in her hands.

"I am Christophé St. Laurent. The last of the house of St. Laurent." He reached out and took the cup from her hands, making her a little afraid again. "And you must tell no one that I am here."

Names and faces and titles rolled through her brain. She'd lived in Paris long enough to know some of the names of the hated aristocrats. This man, as frail and shattered as he was, should not be alive.

Christophé watched the play of emotion on her face and hoped he hadn't made a terrible, deadly mistake. It was just that he needed so badly to tell someone the truth. It was as if he didn't tell her, then he would cease to be, just slip away into nothingness.

Her words slipped out on a solemn whisper. "I won't tell."

He believed her.

Christophé leaned in, his hand coming alongside her cheek in a light caress. She stiffened, and he supposed he couldn't blame her. He must appear half insane. He couldn't remember quite how to act with a woman, not that he'd ever been very good at that anyway. But now, he didn't even remember how to show her how much she meant to him without coming across a lunatic and frightening her away.

As if to prove his point he kept staring at her lips. They were so sweetly made and . . . prominent, heaven help him. Red lips against a pale, serious face and long, thick, curling dark hair. He'd always wondered what was wrong with him concerning women. They were a laughing, silly mystery to him. He always preferred the solitude of his experiments and laboratory work. But now, this woman . . . she had become light to him. She was all he saw in light and its refraction and the splitting of colored rays. She filled his mind almost as often as his calculations. *"Comment t'appelles-tu?"*

She pulled back a little and gazed at him with both fear and fascination. "Scarlett. My name is Scarlett."

A feeling of falling beset him. He shook his head. "Are you certain?"

She laughed, a lilting sound that rang around the stones and brought warmth, true warmth, to his belly. "My mother says I was born with red lips. She wanted to name me Cerise." She smiled, her hand held to her chest. "Cherry. Can you imagine such a name? I am most thankful that father said no, I should be called *Scarlett.*"

He didn't say anything, could only try and still the dizzy rush that assailed him. He must have looked frightening as she looked up uncertainly and rushed out, "It's a silly story."

"No. It is a perfect story."

He watched while she brought a basket forward. "Are you hungry?"

He was always hungry, although he often didn't notice it. "You don't have to share it." He'd sounded harsher than he meant. He tried to fix it. "I meant, you brought that for yourself." He looked down at her round stomach.

Scarlett laughed, low and quiet. "I must look as if I need it." She placed a hand on her stomach. "I *am* eating more these days, but there is plenty for two. I fear my eyes were bigger than my stomach." Then she laughed again, a little louder. "Well, not bigger, that would be frightening, wouldn't it?"

A rush of joy jolted through him and he hardly recognized the emotion. She was so light, so free, laughing at herself. He was truly going to be besotted if he spent another moment with her. If he had any sense, he would leave at once.

"Well, in that case"—his voice was warmer than he remembered it being in a long time—"I'd be happy to share your repast." He felt almost normal, the way he'd been before the ruin of his family.

She handed him a hunk of bread and cheese, and some roast duck. He pulled out a water cask for them to wash down the food. They sat side by side, quietly eating and watching the sun rise above a castle that had withstood Constantinople's army, impenetrable to all except time and God's own elements—both of which had taken a toll.

Then, slowly—as this woman who seemed a dream-gift, became more comfortable with him—Scarlett began to speak of everyday things. The old Cité and its crumbling ruin and history. The marketplace and how she and her mother and sister sold bread three days a week. The coming winter and how it was going to be hard to keep the town from starving.

Christophé responded when necessary, but he was almost too happy to speak. He could barely get the food down his tight throat. It was as if his world was being righted, as if he was coming out of darkness back into the land of the living. He was afraid for her to leave.

Then Scarlett paused. "Where do you live?"

Christophé pointed toward the castle.

"Not in the castle? It can't be safe."

"I am a descendent of the Trencevals. The castle in Carcassonne was where my father directed I go . . . before he was guillotined."

Scarlett stared at him for a long moment. He found he couldn't turn away from her tender gaze. "I am sorry. And the others? Your mother? Your siblings?"

"All guillotined that day. Except for Émilie. My little sister."

Scarlett pressed her lips together, a look of profound sadness on her face. "What became of your sister?"

He shook his head. He couldn't speak of that, not even to her.

Taking the last bite of duck he wiped his hands on the cloth she'd laid between them and stood. He held out a hand to her and helped her rise. She was so round and awkward and . . . beautiful. His hand tentatively reached toward her rounded stomach. New life. All he knew was death and more death. What he wouldn't give to have such a fresh start knowing all that he now knew. He barely touched her, more a skimming of his fingers against her dress. "When will the baby come?"

"About two months." She looked up into his eyes and he saw there a trust growing that he knew he didn't deserve. But he wanted to. He wanted this chance she represented. A place to belong. A family to love and care for.

Someone to need him again.

I'll do better this time!

Chapter Seven

*S*carlett returned home to find her mother crying into a lacy handkerchief, her little sister patting her back.

Alarm filled Scarlett as she pulled off her cloak and tossed it to a chair. "What is it?"

Stacia looked up and pressed her lips together. "A letter arrived. From Robespierre." The name sent a shiver up Scarlett's spine. Robespierre was responsible for much of the terror of this Révolution and, after hearing Christophé's side, she was beginning to truly loathe her husband's uncle.

Stacia rose, strode over with a determined air, and grasped the opened parchment from a round, dark table near the door. She thrust it toward Scarlett. Before she could open it and read the first line, her mother wailed the news. "He's cutting off the flour, Scarlett. Only one more month. What will we do?"

Suzanne Bonham had never been one to accept sudden change with grace. It always came as a shock to her. Somehow, Scarlett just rolled with it. Stacia, though, seemed to thrive in the challenge of it. Between them, they had weathered their father's death, Daniel's death, Scarlett's pregnancy—and now they would have to cope with no means to continue their income.

Scarlett scanned the letter, heart sinking. Their allotment of flour was being brought to an end due to increasing demands in Paris. She felt less like crying than like throttling the man. She knew him as these others in the room did not. He was a clever, manipulative man who, she was certain, could provide them with anything he wanted should he want it badly enough. When Daniel died he assured Scarlett that, as she was carrying the Robespierre heir, he would ensure her future. Even in such turbulent times as these, he'd assured her that when she returned to the safety of the southern countryside, he would provide for her and her family.

She carefully folded the letter and pressed the wax seal against her thumb, then set it back on the table. With slow steps she walked toward her mother and sank down, placing her hands in her mother's lap, gaining the attention of her tear-stained face.

"What will we do?" her mother repeated.

Scarlett stared at her mother and then her sister. An idea formed, and she pressed her lips together, studying her little sister. "We still have one asset."

Stacia raised a single dark brow at her. She tilted back her head, a laugh escaping. "Is it husband hunting time?" She clasped her hands together in dramatic glee. "I have been waiting for the day."

Scarlett gave her sister a serious look. It would have to be Stacia. Not only was Scarlett round with child and in little position to go husband hunting, she feared it was too late for her. Scarlett couldn't tell them that she thought she was in love with a madman, a beggar, someone who needed saving instead of the other way around. It was impossible. She was loathe to put this burden on Stacia. But what choice did they have?

And, to make matters worse, there was only one place to find a good match for Stacia: Paris. In Scarlett's condition, there was little chance she could travel such a distance. They would have to go without her. But how to convince her mother?

She rose and slowly paced the length of the room. "You and mother will go to Paris. I will write a letter for you to give to Robespierre—"even saying the name aloud made her shiver, but she plunged on—"reminding him of his promises to us." She put her hand on her stomach. "He will take you both in, having little choice."

"If only your cousin Louisa was still in Paris," her mother moaned.

"Yes, it is too bad Louisa went back to Martinique. She couldn't stomach the Révolution. Regardless, you must be strong. You have to go."

Her mother stared up at Scarlett, brows wrinkling. "We cannot leave you alone! What will become of you?" Her shoulders slumped. "What will become of us?"

Scarlett sat down beside her mother and took her hand. Since her father's death, her mother had been more the child than the parent when something outside the daily running of the household happened to them. Scarlett had been the one to pick up the role of her father, taking odd jobs before she married Daniel and managing the family's bigger decisions.

She squeezed her mother's hand. "I will be fine. There is a good doctor here, as you know. And you and Stacia will find opportunities for her that she will never have here."

Her mother raised her head, blinked out tears, and blurted out. "I never thought, when I married your father, that he would leave us to do this alone."

Scarlett leaned into her mother's side, their heads touching. "I'm sure he didn't dream of this either." She paused, tearing up herself and catching Stacia's gaze. "God will give us strength for what is to come."

Stacia walked over and knelt down in front of them. "We should pray."

Stacia prayed like no one else Scarlett had ever heard. She prayed the same way she'd always spoken to their father. Like God loved her beyond measure, like she was a valued and precious part of creation. Scarlett had always felt a little afraid of God. What if she asked for something that wasn't His will? What if she made some mistake approaching Him? She loved hearing Stacia's freedom in prayer. If only she could have more of that in her own prayers.

"Yes. Please pray, Stacia. Ask God to supply what we need. He will hear you."

Stacia bent her head and closed her eyes. *"Dear heavenly Father. Dear Creator of all life. Help us as we, as I, go forward as an ambassador of this family. Scarlett must stay behind and have her baby"*—she brushed a hand across Scarlett's knee—*"but we are much afraid and do not know where to turn but to You. Be our guiding light as Mother and I go to Paris. Let me find a husband, if that is Your will."* She laughed. *"And let him be fine in every way. Thank You for Your perfect plan for all our lives. Thank You for Your love for us."*

They all let out a little laugh. Lightness filled the air and their spirits as they opened their eyes and said together, "Amen."

They spent the rest of the evening planning. Stacia went through her wardrobe, and Scarlett went to great lengths to find the perfect dresses for husband lure. They decided that some of Scarlett's elegant Paris clothes could be remade for Stacia, which should only take a few days. Scarlett figured the household accounts and went through each line of numerals with Suzanne. There was enough saved back to keep Scarlett for a few months, as long as she embraced frugality. The rest would be used for traveling expenses.

Finally they all collapsed into bed. Stacia excited. Suzanne exhausted. And Scarlett, as she wrapped the covers around her shoulders and curled into her babe, felt the taut roundness of her stomach and the ache in her back, sad and afraid.

"I miss you," she whispered to Daniel's ghost. And she was glad to feel in that moment that she did.

But she wouldn't show it.

She would not tell them how afraid she was to be left alone.

❧

A WEEK LATER Scarlett woke in the middle of the night. Was it a cramp? A nightmare? She couldn't grasp what had her wide awake and sitting up, swinging her feet over the edge of her bed and reaching for a dressing gown.

She stood awhile, regaining the real world around her. What time was it? Was is early morning and time to visit Daniel's grave?

Before she was even fully awake, Scarlett had her shoes on and was outside taking in the chilly night air. She looked up into the dark sky, studied the placement of the stars, and realized that it must be the middle of the night. She smoothed her hands across her stomach and shook her head. "We should go back to bed," she whispered to the babe, but it didn't move and she was wide awake. Before she knew it, she was walking in the direction of the old Cité.

She watched the dark water of the river, heard it slosh over the stones and ebb against the banks as her feet rang, too loud, against the stone bridge. On the other side she paused. Her footsteps would normally take her to the right and toward the graveyard. But this time . . .

She turned to the ancient castle. The original Carcassonne.

As she neared, the old stones seemed to whisper their legendary past. Built during Roman times, the city saw its greatest glory during the Middle Ages and the dynasty of the Trencevals. Scarlett had heard the tales of troubadours and knights and the grand tournaments held within the castle walls. But soon after, the Cathars—Christians who were viewed as heretics by Pope Innocent III—brought wrath and crusades to the town. Upon their defeat, Carcassonne was given to the French king.

In the years that followed, the second wall was built and Louis IX built a new town across the river. As the new town grew, the Treaty of Pyrenees after the Hundred Years War came into being, changing the southern border and ending the Cité's strategic stronghold. The old Cité fell further and further into ruins. Scarlett couldn't remember hearing of anyone living in the castle for over a hundred years. But as she gazed at it, she could still feel its greatness, its history leaking from the stones.

She trudged through the weed-clogged path toward the crumbling entrance. She passed the two famed walls, an outer wall and a lower inner wall. There used to be a watery moat, but no more. It had been dry, with only river rock to fill it for some time. Her footsteps took her into the inner chamber of the grand hall. Here, she paused, catching her breath, looking up into the dark ceiling. What was she doing? It seemed someone was guiding her tonight. Was it God?

A sound, a spark of light, had her spinning toward a long, narrow hall.

She veered toward it and saw a room where a light was flickering. She came to the door and stood at the threshold, her heartbeat loud in her ears. Slowly, carefully, she pushed the door open. She stood blinking in the darkness. A cold shiver raced up her spine as she took a step forward and looked about the room.

He turned. Dressed in nothing but a pair of ragged breeches, his long, blunt hair fell like a curtain over his intense gaze. He turned further toward her, impaling her with those sapphire-rimmed eyes that seemed to belong to another world—and suddenly Scarlett could neither move, nor think.

∞

CHRISTOPHÉ SPUN AT a sound behind him, knocking off a bottle that flew to the stone floor and shattered. He dove for his pistol, rose up with it, and held it trained on the intruder.

Her features overwhelmed him, made his hand shake as he lowered the weapon. He couldn't seem to get his breath as his mind wove its way back from calculations to this pale, frightened face staring at him with huge eyes. "Scarlett?"

She was gripping her rounded stomach, blinking at him in the dim light of the room, looking like she'd walked out of his dreams so that he woke up to find it was real.

He went to her and cradled her face in his hands. "Scarlett." His lips lifted and he was smiling, glad she was there. "You are shivering. Come. Warm yourself by the fire." In an underbreath he added, "Heaven knows it is the last stick of wood."

A hint of fear shone in her eyes as she followed him toward the tiny fire he'd set up to do his experiments. If only he had something to offer her, other than his scattered wits and dusty home. But he didn't. He hadn't eaten anything in days so that he could buy the wood and candles for this night. He'd barely slept since he last saw her. He'd only worked.

And he was so close! Light's mysteries, the splitting of white light into color and then back into white light with naught but specially cut glass was something that could be expressed with inked-out equations. He knew it. But there was so much yet to be written out mathematically—in calculus. He had to find the answers. Answers were the only thing that could set him free.

"What are you doing?" Scarlett's voice was filled with shock as she gazed about the room.

He shook his head and looked down, not knowing how to explain his life as he now lived it. "It's an experiment."

He looked up to see her reaction to his odd words, afraid she might laugh or run away.

She had her back to the flames. He only just noticed that she stood in her nightgown, a dark cloak, and thick-soled shoes— like that first early morning they met. Her stomach protruded through the cloak, a streak of white against the dark folds. She must have seen his appraisal for she looked down at herself, then looked back at him and in a voice that sounded hesitant and brave at the same time stated, "I should like to see an experiment."

She held tight to the cloak as she took a few steps toward his makeshift work table. "What will you discover?"

It wasn't a question. It was an expectation that his discovery would happen at any moment. Such faith in him caused him to take a long look at her and reach for her hand.

It didn't matter anymore that they were strangers, that any who came upon them now would consider them dressed as husband and wife. It didn't matter that they had only met a short time ago. It didn't matter that she was pregnant with a dead husband's child and he was a runaway aristocrat with no future, no hope for anything aside from these experiments.

The only thing that Christophé was sure of, now that he'd found her, was that he never wanted to let her go.

Chapter Eight

Their heads bent over the crystal prism, so close his forehead almost brushed hers. A combination of fear and exhilaration rose in Scarlett's chest. What was she doing? Letting a man take hold of her mind and heart so sudden and sure, like the last time. With Daniel. Had she learned nothing?

She forced her attention from the man to his experiment. Christophé held a candle high in the air, directing Scarlett to hold the prism up, just so, to isolate the candlelight. The light coming from the long, rectangular window interfered with their attempts to catch a single ray.

As she gazed at the window, she saw the pure, true light from the sun creeping into the room and lighting Christophé's tired eyes and unshaven cheeks. Suddenly she shrieked with an idea.

Christophé turned toward her, clearly alarmed, but she rushed over to him. "What if we designed a curtain, something to block the light coming in?" She pointed toward the window. "Then cut a tiny hole, so that only one beam comes through. What if we held the prism up to that?"

He looked at her, delighted and astonished. "Can you sew?"

"Yes, but I haven't any thread."

Christophé turned away from her, picked up his long, dark cloak. "This is all I have."

She bit her lower lip. If she were home it would be easy to find an old sheet or blanket to use. All she had was what she was wearing. Wait! Her cloak! It lay where she tossed it, across the back of a chair. She rushed to it, held it next to Christophé's cloak and smiled. "This should be enough. Though I must have something to sew with. Do you have a needle and thread?"

He shook his head, then paused. "Wait here." Before she knew what he had in mind, he had disappeared into some other part of the castle. While she waited, she spread the two cloaks onto the floor, side by side. Hers was shorter by several inches so instead she arranged them end to end. The window was long and narrow. It just might work.

She turned as he came into the room, the glinting silver prize pinched between his thumb and finger. "I never throw anything away."

She held out her hand for it. "Now. What shall we do for thread?"

He shook his head. "I don't know." He looked momentarily crestfallen. It made her heart ache to see that look. She looked down . . . and smiled. She lifted the hem of her nightgown and saw the long, white thread holding the hem together. "Do you have a knife?"

He brought her a small knife from the work table, wiping it on his breeches as he walked toward her. She tried not to look at his bare torso as he leaned down to hand it to her. She'd been trying not to notice his shoulders and ribs and back and chest with its light scattering of dark hair, this whole night. He was thin, but muscular and strong in a wiry way. He'd not thought their whole time together to find his shirt.

Oddly enough, that fact didn't disturb her. And she didn't think twice about sitting on the floor and lifting her hem high enough to see over the mound of her babe . . . that is until he stared at her bare, curled legs.

Heat surged into her face. "Turn away, if you please."

He did as asked, but seemed somewhat perplexed by the request. She bent over the tiny stitches, cutting into the thread. Slowly, with painstaking care, she pulled the thread loose from the fabric. It was strong and came free in one long strand.

Christophé looked back at her over his shoulder and grinned. "Are you sure you don't need help? You shouldn't be sitting on that hard floor, you know."

"Oh, *now* you are concerned for my well being." She grinned back at him, flicked down her hem, and held out the long thread. "Come and help me up."

He held out his hand and hauled her into his arms. Her stomach was so large between them that no other part of her touched him. "Are you tired?" Sincerity and sudden worry lit the blue depths of his eyes, turning them as dark as molten silver. "You seem so able. I . . . I forget. You should sit down and rest."

Scarlett pursed her lips together, delight filling her. Once he came out of his intense distraction, he could be quite intuitive and caring. "Now you want to coddle me?" Her gaze held his—and something inside her shifted. This was what marriage was. This sudden longing in her heart to make his passion her own. This feeling that he would watch over her and care for her, that he would leave his world behind if need be, for her. The connection was overwhelming.

Her next words were soft with new conviction and wonder. "I can't rest now, we have light beams to catch."

Christophé stood in front of her looking like a still, frozen painting of a man come alive, like Adam after God breathed into him, when he stood for the first time looking at his Maker and the world He had created for him. Christophé looked at her—and into her—like no man ever had. She didn't pull away when his gentle hands took hold of her shoulders, his touch feather light as if afraid she might break or disappear.

"Scarlett." His hands moved down her arms, a simple caress that left her feeling light-headed. "You will not want me to say it, but I'm glad you are free."

"Free?"

"To love again."

Yes . . . Oh, how she wanted to say it. But the minute she let herself think, guilt overwhelmed her, burying her beneath its cursed weight. She should have felt this way for Daniel.

He leaned close, and again, she didn't withdraw. She caught her breath as his lips touched hers and held there for a long moment. Neither moved as their breath intermingled and their lips barely brushed.

Then Scarlett's sorrow escaped, whispering against his mouth. "Not quite free yet."

∽

HER WORDS HELD such sadness, such grief . . .

Christophé pulled back. He was frightening her. It was just that he had never felt this way before! She brought him bread when he needed it. She brought him thread when he needed that.

She showed up in the middle of the night when he thought he might drown in the darkness. She showed him light, the pinhole of discovery, the source of which he'd sought for years.

His whole being longed to take her rounded, sweet body into his arms. He wanted everything she thought or ever imagined to be in his safekeeping. He wanted her trust.

But he freed her and backed away, putting the distance she needed between them.

She held his gaze for a moment, then turned back to her sewing. "There." She said a few minutes later, holding out the heavy folds of the cloaks sewn together into a dark curtain. "Can you hang it?"

Christophé was sure he would find a way. There was an old ladder he'd found in the castle many days ago. "I will be right back."

As he went into the room where he slept, he looked around at the piles of miscellaneous things he'd found in the castle. Upon arriving, he'd risked life and limb scouring the place for anything worth keeping. He'd found this ladder among the rubble, along with some other tools, things that the thieves of long ago had missed or thought worthless. He'd stacked them into piles in the two rooms he designated for his sleeping quarters and laboratory. It was a hodgepodge of items. Weren't there some iron nails too?

Digging in an old wooden pail, he found the nails. They were large and heavy. A hammer or sledge was not among his treasures, so he picked up a large stone, one of many that lay all over the floor of the crumbling edifice, and made his way back to the laboratory.

Scarlett was sitting on a chair, the cloaks draped over her lap, her eyes closed. She looked to have drifted off to sleep, her head leaning against the back of the chair. Christophé crept over and slid the cloak from her slack fingers. He paused for a moment to take in her creamy skin, the dark waving hair that framed her face. He found himself bending toward her, studying her red, red lips—a color that couldn't be matched or mixed with pigment and oil to dash across a canvas. And then, there were the dark shadows of her eyelashes against her high cheekbones. His hand went out to the babe, an involuntary reaction. "You will be my family."

He pulled back, embarrassed that again he had given his innermost thoughts voice. When would he learn discretion? When would he learn the cool manners of his brother, Louis, the tact that should be the bulwark of the remaining St. Laurent? He could only stand and stare, the cloak and nails and stone grasped in his hands, as he marveled at this woman.

Move, fool, before she wakes and you frighten her yet again.

As quietly as he could he positioned the ladder. He gathered the stone and nails into his hands and climbed the great height. He banged the nail with short thwacks, hoping not to wake her as he impaled the dark cloth through the nails into holes that were already in the stone wall. Someone had hung curtains over this window before. Thanks be to God.

With one side up, and a glance at the sleeping woman, he moved the ladder to the other side of the window.

Another few, short whacks of the stone and he had the other side up and in place. The cloaks hung together perfectly. A perfect fit.

Christophé stood back and admired their handiwork. The room was back to the dim light and shadows of the guttering candles. With a glance toward Scarlett, he blew out each candle in the room. Next he poked at the dying embers of the fire, sending sparks flying up the chimney, until there was only the dull red glow of ash.

Now for the hole. It was her idea. He was loathe to do it alone. Christophé went over to her and stared for a long moment at her loveliness. He whispered her name, leaning in to touch her rounded cheek.

Instead of turning away as he expected, she reached for him in her sleep, grasping hold of his arm.

"Daniel." She said the name as though she'd been dreaming of him.

He reared back, his heart torn, the pain so sudden, like a sword thrust, that it shocked him.

Her eyes fluttered open. He stared down at her until he saw the realization of what she'd done in her eyes.

Those huge eyes filled with regret. "I'm sorry."

Christophé knew he didn't have any right to an apology. She was a widow. A pregnant widow. Why wouldn't she love the husband lost to her? If anyone could understand that, he should. He shook his head. "No, I'm sorry. I was only trying to wake you." He smiled what he hoped was a gentle smile. "Come and see what we've done."

Scarlett turned in her chair and then rose with a delighted cry. "You've done it!"

"Well. Not yet."

He led her over to the window, then went back and took up a sharp knife. With the point he lifted the bottom part of the curtain and held it out. With one hand on the outside and one on the inside he reached up and poked the knife through, turning it and twisting it into a neat hole. A tiny shaft of light filtered into the room. "Get the prism."

Scarlett went to the table for the triangular cut glass. She came back and held it out to him.

Christophé let the curtain fall back toward the window. He took his time, found the beam of dawn's light, and traced it through the air with one finger. Then he took a few steps away.

They both paused, their gazes meeting, then Christophé smiled. "To my new friend and assistant," he whispered. He held the prism up and up until it caught the light.

They both held their breath and then let it out in a simultaneous rush as the prism caught, held, and then split the light.

The colors of the rainbow arched around the stone room and them.

Red. Yellow. Green. Blue. Indigo and Violet. Six colors.

He tilted the prism this way and that so that the colors danced around them.

Scarlett let out a peal of delighted laughter.

His heart soared.

Rainbow had always been his favorite color.

And now he knew his favorite sound.

A SUDDEN SOUND of a clock striking interrupted their world. Scarlett turned to him, the panic in her wide eyes sending his heart pounding. "What time is it?"

He hadn't paid attention to the time for days, weeks even, and fumbled for an answer. "It must be six or seven in the morning." They listened as the great bell in the town cathedral rang seven times.

Scarlett sprang up from her chair. "I must return. They won't know what to think."

Christophé moved from his place by the laboratory table and grasped her arm. "But you have no cloak."

Scarlett looked down at her nightgown and then back into his face. "I *have* to go."

"Of course. We'll take down the cloaks."

"But you need them for your experiment. And I don't have time to take out the thread."

Christophé walked over to the ladder, quickly climbed up and dislodged the cloaks. Folding the material in half, he was able to wrap the heavy fabric around Scarlett. She reached up and tied it around her neck. "I will bring it back." She looked down and laughed at herself. "And next time, I will be dressed."

Christophé flashed a grin at her. "I like you in your nightgown."

Scarlett sputtered, a red flush filling her cheeks. "My mother will be furious when she sees that I've gone out in public like this again. I still don't know how I will explain being gone so long."

Christophé took her hand. "Tell them you were extending a dinner invitation . . . to a mad scientist who lives in the crumbling castle, whom you met at the market." He smiled down into her eyes. "Tell them you felt sorry for me."

A little chuckle escaped Scarlett's chest. "I do have a soft spot for the downtrodden, that they well know." She looked up into his eyes and he felt the immediate melting that always seemed to happen with her. "It might work."

In the distance they heard a distant rumble of thunder. Scarlett pulled the cloak closer and turned to go. "I must hurry. It sounds like rain."

He glanced down at the baby. "Don't run. Be careful."

Her look was mischievous as she answered, "I am always careful." But they both knew that wasn't true. She never would have spoken to him had she been careful.

Christophé was glad she was a bit of an adventuress instead.

He walked her to the door and watched her leave. Just as she was out of sight, it began to pour down rain. His teeth were chattering by the time he made it to the laboratory and the last embers of the fire. He stripped off his clothes, worrying that Scarlett would be soaked and chilled. He hung his breeches on the back of a chair, close to the fire to dry. Then he wrapped his only blanket around his shivering body and sat in front of the fire, staring into the ash.

Why, Lord? He closed his eyes against the weariness and sorrow seeking to overpower him. *Why now?*

He trusted God's goodness. His promises. But as Christophé sat there, chilled to the bone as much by his thoughts as the rain, he couldn't help but question.

Why did You let me meet my Eve now . . . when I'm not whole enough to give her anything?

Chapter Nine

Scarlett, soaked to the skin, her nightgown and the cloaks clinging to her, crept back into the house. Sleep. That was all she needed. Maybe she could feign illness. It would be easy enough in her condition.

She crept up the stairs, the loose, sodden hem of her nightgown nearly tripping her.

"Scarlett, is that you?"

Her mother's voice sounded from the bottom of the stairs. She turned, grasping hold of the handrail. "It's me—"

"Good heavens, what happened to you?" Her mother raced up the stairs and grasped hold of her. "You must stop this nonsense. Visiting his grave when so pregnant, even in the middle of such a storm!" She grabbed her daughter's waist and helped her up the stairs. "You must stop, Scarlett. He wouldn't want you to risk your health and the child's."

Tears stung her eyes, and Scarlett looked away. What *was* she doing? How could she be so irresponsible? She was a mother now; she should act like one. She should tell the truth. "You are right. It won't happen again. It's just that, I met someone and I was delayed, and then it started pouring rain."

Her mother's brows rose and her lips thinned. "Met someone? Who could you meet at the graveyard?"

Scarlett ignored the fact that her mother thought she'd been
visiting Daniel's grave and plunged in, but her teeth started chattering as she blurted it out. "His name is Christophé, and I—I
in–invited him to dinner."

"To dinner? A stranger to dinner! What could you be thinking?" Her mother reached for her arm and braced her up. "You
are shivering!" Her mother sounded frantic. "Hurry, we must get
you into some dry clothes and into bed. We will discuss this man
later."

Weakness coursing through her, all Scarlett could do was
allow her mother to take charge. She let her mother pull her
through Stacia's room, not even caring that her mother didn't
bother to be quiet. She bustled about Scarlett's bedchamber,
stoking up the fire, then came to pull the nightgown up and over
Scarlett's wet hair—thankfully not noticing the ragged hem—
and handed her a towel. As soon as Scarlett was dressed, her
mother led her to her bed, clucking at her and tucking her in. In
moments Scarlett's eyes dropped shut and she drifted in the first
deep sleep she had had in months.

A FEW HOURS later Stacia crept into the room with hot chocolate and scones. She rattled the tray enough to make Scarlett turn,
sleepy-headed against her pillows.

"Mother sent me to check on you. Can you eat a little?"

Her sister's concerned face made Scarlett's heart skip a beat
as the fact that they would be gone soon slammed into her.

Dear Father, I am going to miss them so. She would live the last month of this pregnancy and the birth without them. Tears stung again, but she lowered her head and reached for the tray. "Thank you."

"You are crying!" Stacia planted the tray on the side table and reached for Scarlett's hands. "Tell me."

Scarlett shook her head and leaned back into the pillows. She tried to stop the sadness racing down her cheeks in wet streams.

Stacia gave her a moment—she was so wise for her years—simply picking up and stirring the chocolate in the cup and handing it to Scarlett. "Is it that we must go? I cannot imagine being left alone at a time like this. You are so brave."

Scarlett took a long swallow of the warm sweetness. She reached for Stacia's hand and squeezed. "You will have to be braver than I. Mother will be a mess in Paris. You will have to navigate the politics, the horrid uprisings, and constant watching eyes. You will have to find the man who can save this family and one that you can love."

Stacia tossed back a lock of dark hair and smiled at her. "I have been waiting for this. My turn. Let me carry us this time."

Scarlett shook her head. "You are so young. I can't bear it. Robespierre can't be trusted. You must trust no one."

Stacia had tears in her eyes too, but her steel-blue depths held the passions and certainty of youth. "I will pray."

Scarlett drained the cup, holding on to its comfort. "Yes. As will I. Every day."

Stacia took the empty cup and passed Scarlett a delicate plate of light, flaky scones. "You didn't go to the grave this morning, did you?"

Scarlett's eyes grew round. "How did you know?"

"That man, in the street at the market. You have met him before."

"Yes." She wouldn't say more.

"Who is he?"

Scarlett took a giant bite and chewed slowly, assessing her sister. "He is a secret."

Stacia grinned. "I love secrets. Tell me."

Scarlett chuckled and downed another fluffy roll, her mouth so full she could only smile around it.

"Tell me!"

She swallowed. "You won't tell Mother? Not anyone?"

Stacia reared back in mock offense. "As if you couldn't trust me!"

"All right. All I will say is that his name is Christophé and he is in hiding . . . living in the old castle."

"Who is he? Why would he live there? It could come crumbling down upon his head while he sleeps! Is he a beggar?"

"Of course not!" Though she wasn't sure if that was true. "He is . . . he is . . . I don't exactly know what he is except that he is a . . . scientist."

Stacia's eyes grew round as she clapped a hand over her mouth and laughed. Then, seeing her sister's serious face she stopped suddenly and gasped. "You love him!"

"No!"

"You do! I see it in your eyes. Even more than Daniel."

Scarlett let the words sink in. She stared at the third scone in her fingers, then put it slowly back down on the plate, which sat precariously on her belly. "I don't know. I loved Daniel. But this is different. I feel . . . I feel I *know* him." She looked up at her sister's pretty face and grimaced. "But I really don't know him at all." She paused. "I think of him all the time. I want to see him

. . . and when I'm with him, it is as if—" she shook her head at her sister, tears rising up again—"I feel I've come home."

"Oh, Scarlett." Her sister gathered her into her arms. "Have a care. Have a care, my dear sister. From the sound of things, he could be anyone."

❧

CHRISTOPHÉ FELL INTO a deep sleep beside his parchment. His head lay on his arms, the fire flickered out, and the room grew cold. But he dreamed of wide, luminous eyes and alabaster skin. Then he saw his sister, crying out to save him. And Scarlett, with her red lips, mouthing forgiveness to him . . . and then he saw them together, riding into Paris where Émilie cried out from another graveyard. Her voice was so strong. It cried out to them both—

He awoke, sat up suddenly, chanting his sanity verse: *"Thy kingdom come. Thy will be done."* He broke into a sob, half-awake and half-asleep. Her face was so clear—it seemed so real. He slid off the chair and onto the cold stone floor. "Help me, Lord. Please, please, help."

❧

AFTER HER SISTER left, Scarlett fell back into the pillows, her stomach full and contented. She thought of Christophé. Of that kiss. It had been little more than a touch of his lips to hers, but it had made her feel more than any intimacy she'd shared with Daniel. She thought back on the days after her wedding. They'd only had four months of marriage before he left for the battlefield in Nantes. Four months of confusion, sometimes hurt, sometimes anger.

It was during that time she learned how the hand's movement on the clock could seem interminable. There were days when she lifted her head at every carriage sound below her window in hopes that Daniel would walk through the door. But even when that finally happened, even when she tried to say something sweet enough or witty enough that he would come out of his world and *notice* her, it was as though she wasn't even there.

Daniel was passionate, but only about his street speeches to fire the citizens' blood-thirst for revenge. The Révolution was his mistress, and Scarlett was beginning to hate it. In that world, there was no room for her at all. The clandestine meetings in her parlor, which she wasn't allowed to attend. The speeches he sat up late at night to write while she blinked, alone, in the darkness of their bedroom. The faraway look in his eyes when she spoke of everyday things.

It hadn't taken more than a few weeks for her to fade into the background of his life.

She tried one night to speak with Daniel, have him reassure her.

He was turned on his side, away from her. He hadn't touched her in weeks, but he wasn't asleep and she felt brave enough that night to reach out and stroke the suppleness of the muscles of his arm with a light touch.

He sighed. "I'm sorry, my dear. But this body is tired."

"Do you still love me?" She wished she could take the words back the moment they left her lips, but she waited to hear his answer.

He turned over, took her hand, and brought it to his lips. "Of course." He looked over at her, their gazes locking. "How can

I make you understand?" He looked up at the ceiling. "I don't belong to myself now. I belong to the Republic."

"You certainly don't belong to me."

He looked back at her, his eyes bright with the passion of his beliefs. "Neither of us can belong to the other until this battle is fought and won. We must deny what we want for the greater good. Do you understand?"

She'd nodded, but didn't really. How was this liberty? What face wore the name freedom? But she agreed outwardly, determined to be better, demand less . . . let go of the man she'd only just won and begun to know.

It was a bitter pill indeed. She'd met her prince. Married him within a fortnight of that meeting. But she grew up little by little, and in the process faced a sad realization:

The world around her—and, more to the point, *her* world . . . her marriage—was nothing like she hoped it would be.

Chapter Ten

The household was in an uproar. They had two more weeks to prepare for the trip to Paris, and Scarlett had decided to have a dinner party.

"Tell me again, Scarlett, why are we having this man to dinner?" Her mother turned from the stove, wiped curling tendrils of dark brown hair out her face and stared at Scarlett.

Scarlett turned from lighting the candles on the elegantly set table. "Mother. I've explained it. He is a scientist. I met him in the graveyard where he walks every morning to—oh, I don't know, to clear his head. He's brilliant and so, so smart. And I like him. I think he could be a friend. And he has no family and barely eats."

"Probably can't cook a carrot." Her mother's smile softened the complaint.

Scarlett laughed. "Exactly. That's why I have asked him to come here and have a good home-cooked meal." Scarlett moved into the kitchen and took up a steaming bowl of leeks and greens and lentils savored with caraway seeds and butter. She leaned toward her mother as she passed by her and gave her a quick kiss on the cheek. "He will be in raptures upon tasting your good cooking."

Her mother pressed her lips together, but more to suppress a smile than scold. "I suppose it will be good for us to extend some charity. He has no family? How did he come here?"

Scarlett placed the heavy bowl on the table, one hand to her low back, which had been aching more and more of late, and sighed. "I don't know all of his secrets yet, but—" she turned and smiled at her pretty mother—"I trust you will wrest them from him."

Her mother pulled steaming hot loaves of golden bread, made from their personal hoard of flour, from the oven. "You can depend on it, my dear."

They shared a glance, each knowing what the other was thinking. This man was something more to Scarlett than mere charity.

A loud knock on the door had all three women pausing and shrieking. He was early! Stacia curtsied to her mother and sister, then smiled her cat's smile. "Allow me."

She took off her apron on the way to the door, hanging it on a hook by the front door, smoothed back her straight dark hair and swung the door wide. Scarlett hurried behind her.

He stood there, tall and darkly dressed in clothes that Scarlett could hardly credit to the meager belongings she'd seen thus far. He was dressed as a gentleman, as the Count he claimed to be, in dark blue satin from head to toe with a snow-white shirt complete with lacy, belled sleeves and an intricately tied cravat. He stepped inside, took off his hat with a flourish and brought, from behind his back, a delicate bouquet of cherry red poppies. He held them a bit awkwardly to his chest and then thrust them toward Scarlett's mother. "I heard you liked the color."

She gasped, fluttered her eyelashes in a way that Scarlett had not seen in years, and reached for the flowers.

"Welcome, to our humble home." Scarlett's mother waved him in, then turned and walked into the kitchen, holding the flowers like a prize from the fair. Over her shoulder she chattered, "Such lovely blooms! Wherever did you find them this time of year? Why, I thought poppies were all spent out, but they are one of my favorites."

Christophé placed his hat on a low side table and walked further into the room, his gaze never leaving Scarlett's. "Why, good madam, I found fortune is all. I could not arrive empty handed."

Her mother started to say something, and then stopped and dug in the cupboards for a vase to place her prize in.

Scarlett took advantage of the silence. "Christophé, this is my sister, Stacia. And my mother is Suzanne Bonham."

Christophé took up Stacia's hand in his, leaned over it for a brush of a kiss and said, in such a gallant manner that Scarlett nearly threw back her head to laugh, "Stacia. So good to meet you." He looked over her hand into her eyes, and Stacia giggled, looking toward Scarlett with a knowing twinkle.

"How kind you are, sir, to grace us with your presence. Scarlett has talked of little else."

Christophé's brows rose as he looked into Scarlett's eyes. "Has she, now?"

"Why, yes. We hear that you are a scientist and have a laboratory in the old Cité. Is it safe, do you think?" Stacia's eyes were wicked with suppressed laughter.

"I think your sister can answer that question, mademoiselle. She has, of late, been an assistant of sorts."

Scarlett glared at Christophé. "Dinner is ready. I hope you've brought your appetite along with your wit." As she passed him to fetch more glasses she grasped his hand and squeezed it in warning.

Christophé's deep chuckle filled the room. The women all paused to hear the sound, for it had been too long since a man was about the place.

They sat down to the laden table. Stacia reached out for the hands on either side of her and bowed her head. They all followed suit.

"Dearest Lord," Stacia began. "Thank You for Your bountiful goodness in this food and this company. Thank You for new friends and for loved ones that we will not forget. Thank You for Your provision as we travel to Paris and to meet our . . ." She paused, and Scarlett heard the emotion clogging her sister's throat. "Our destiny. Thank You for Your care and love and fortitude in all our wanderings. Thank You for Christophé—I don't know his surname Lord, but we thank You for Christophé. Amen."

There were boiled eels and quail in a lemon sauce, vegetables, hard to find this time of year, and fresh-baked bread still steaming as Suzanne took away the cloth and passed the basket. Then they brought out dumplings swimming in chicken broth with bits of chicken. There was so much. It was like a Christmas feast really, and Scarlett didn't know how they had done it. There wasn't that much in the cupboards; it had all just come together.

After dinner they gathered in the sitting room.

Scarlett's mother inclined her head to Christophé as they settled into their chairs. "I am sorry we haven't a bottle of sherry or anything to offer. I'm afraid the times have affected us as well."

"No need to apologize, madam. I am thankful for such a wonderful meal. It has been a long time since I've had such a good time among friends."

His deep voice was filled with a sadness that struck Scarlett's heart. She wanted more than anything to reach out to him, but knew she couldn't. Instead she lowered her gaze to her lap. "For us too."

Stacia, bright as always, stood suddenly and gasped. "Music! That is what we need."

They all looked at her, and she waved her hands and hurried up the stairs.

"Whatever can she be about?"

Scarlett could tell from her mother's tone that, though she smiled, she was a bit embarrassed. "If I know Stacia, she has something in mind." Scarlett smiled at Christophé.

"Resourceful, is she?"

"Oh. That's the least of it," Scarlett assured.

They laughed and sipped their coffee until Stacia descended the stairs, a porcelain box in her hands. Scarlett smiled at her sister. It was a grand idea!

On the bottom stair, though, Stacia tripped. In trying to regain her balance, the music box flew from her hands and landed in the middle of them. It bounced, broke, and then landed at Christophé's feet. He slowly lifted the pieces into his cupped hands.

"Oh!" Stacia's face was white. "Father gave that to me."

She looked ready to burst into tears. Scarlett rose, a slow and awkward movement in her hurry. "We will fix it."

She looked to Christophé, whose eyes told her all she needed to know.

He would keep her promise to her sister.

Christophé studied the box. The workings of soldered metal fell out of the broken porcelain into his hands. He worked the gears and the key to test it, made sure that the mechanics were sound, and then set the metal piece back into the base of creamy white. With a few more maneuvers with his fingers, he had the thing put back together. Only the porcelain was cracked. He turned the key a time or two with a neat twist of his wrist, then held the box out in his palms.

Tinkling music filled the air. The three women around him breathed a collective sigh of relief. He couldn't help his grin. "The box can be fixed. The rest of the piece is sound."

They didn't speak. Just gazed at him as though he were their savior. Then they all rested back into their chairs and let the tinkling of the song fill the room.

After the last notes fell away, Stacia said with a gleam in her eyes, "Did you know, sir, that my sister is a wonderful dancer?"

Scarlett huffed and put her hands to her round stomach. "Not now! Stacia, stop!"

Christophé grinned at the little sister. She was a firebrand, that was certain. But he preferred Scarlett's gentle strength and wary love. He turned to her. "What say you, madam? Would you do me the great honor?"

Scarlett's mother let out a delighted laugh. They were all so sweet, so feminine, so missed. Christophé rose and held out his hand toward Scarlett.

"I will be clumsy." She spoke as if they were the only two in the room.

"As will I." Christophé let his smile assure her. "Have always had two left feet on the dance floor. Maybe now I will have a slight advantage."

Stacia took the music box and wound it as far as it would go, grinning. "Dance, Scarlett. Go ahead and dance."

Christophé took her right hand in his. Scarlett placed her left hand on his shoulder. Christophé grasped what little was left of her waist and swung her into a four step, the only step he knew.

She glided in his arms, so smooth it seemed they were underwater. She must not know how slight she was, even with the babe. How quick she felt . . . how her softness in his arms made him light-headed. Holding her like this, moving with her to the tinkling music . . . it made him feel alive for the first time in a very long time.

There in front of her family, he gazed down at her upturned face and allowed the music to overcome their bodies. He had heard concerts from some of the greatest musicians in the known world. He had attended the opera and musical soirée's in the finest salons in Paris; he had attended symphonies written for the king. But he had never felt so happy while hearing a simple music box.

For it was listening to this music that he discovered heaven in his arms.

∞

WHEN THE MUSIC died away, when his feet and Scarlett's finally stilled, they stood there, silent. Scarlett's mother and sister sat transfixed, gazing at them. The air was too intense, too infused with something beyond them all. The mother's and sister's expressions showed they felt it too—and both looked away. It was like the sun—too intense and bright to be seen by the naked eye. Christophé's gaze returned to his beautiful partner . . . and he suddenly remembered. His surprise! He broke the spell on the room with a deep laugh.

"Ladies, it has been a delightful evening, and I would take my leave except for one thing." When they just stared at him somewhat in alarm, he quickly added with a smile, "Would you like to see the surprise I've brought?"

They looked at him like they weren't quite sure, but they were all smiling now.

"Come. Get your wraps. I have something to show you." Christophé went out the front door while the ladies were putting on their cloaks and picked up the leather tube he'd hidden in the bushes outside the front door.

When he came back in, he held it out to them and smiled while they guessed what it was.

"Is it an umbrella case?" Stacia asked.

"No, it holds parchment and writing utensils," Scarlett asserted.

"What if it's a knife and he means to kill us in our own backyard?" Stacia said in excited glee.

Scarlett just gave her a frown.

"Good heavens, what is it?" Suzanne demanded, wide-eyed.

Christophé motioned them to the back door where they could step out into the yard and be less likely to attract any night patrols watching the streets.

"I think there is a painting rolled up in there," Stacia announced with a light elbow jab into Scarlett's arm.

"But why would we view a painting in the dark?"

"Hush, girls. He's about to show us."

Christophé soaked in the chatter, their anticipation pure delight to his heart. He waited until they came beside him in the middle of the yard, then held up the leather case with flourish.

They watched as Christophé pulled off the leather cap, tilted the tube, and pulled out the long, mahogany cylinder with brass ends.

"It is a telescope!" Scarlett laughed. "I looked through one once, in Paris. It was marvelous."

"Can we see the moon?" Stacia gazed upward.

They all looked up at the velvety sky. Christophé smiled. Even the heavens were cooperating tonight. "It is a clear night, and the moon is nearly full. I believe, Stacia, that you will be able to see many craters on the moon."

The women drew closer, excitement emanating from them while Christophé stretched out the collapsing telescope to its full twenty-nine inches. He turned toward the moon, opened the protective shutter, then placed the eyepiece to his eye. It was just as he thought. The perfect night for stargazing. He lowered the telescope and grinned at them.

"Madame Bonham, would you like to be first?"

Suzanne stepped up, her hands at her cheeks. Christophé showed her where to hold the telescope and watched as she lifted it to her eye. "Just here—" he instructed while he raised it toward the moon.

"Oh my!" She gasped. "It's so big and bright."

"Do you see the dark spots?"

"Yes, yes I do."

"Those are craters."

"But what exactly is a crater, dear?"

Scarlett and Stacia exchanged amused glances.

"A crater is like a deep hole, in the shape of a bowl. There are big ones and little ones, and an enormous one on the moon."

"My turn! Oh, do hurry, Mama!" Stacia had her hands squeezed together, clearly trying to rein in her excitement. And clearly failing.

Suzanne looked through the lens for several more minutes, ignoring her youngest. When she lowered the scope, she had a look of wonder on her face. "Thank you, sir. I had not thought to ever look through one of those in my lifetime. It makes the world seem smaller somehow."

Christophé knew exactly what she meant. "Someday, I believe, we will be able to see planets and stars that are millions of miles away."

Stacia stepped up to Christophé and held out her hand. "May I see stars now? Through this?"

"Yes, but they still look like dim lights. This telescope is one of the best made today. But someday, as they keep improving, we will really be able to study the galaxies of the universe."

Stacia spent several minutes oohhing and ahhing over the moon and then tried to find as many stars as she could. Christophé turned to smile at Scarlett, then paused. She was tiring. She had one hand to her low back and distress rested on her features. Christophé was suddenly grateful her mother returned to the house a few moments earlier, saying it was chilly. Without her here, he felt free to walk over and place an arm around Scarlett's shoulders, pulling her to his side so that she could lean against him. He leaned close to her ear. "Are you feeling badly?"

She looked up at him and shook her head. "Not really. Just tired all over."

"Come, you will see the moon, and then I will leave so that you can find your bed." He turned to Stacia. "Miss Stacia, your sister is tired. Let's give her a turn and then you can have it back if you like."

"Oh, sorry, Scarlett." Stacia immediately thrust the instrument into her sister's hands. "I always forget your condition and how you might be feeling. Here. I'm finished." Turning to Christophé, she dimpled. "Thank you, sir, I can't remember when I had such a lovely night. I hope the men in Paris are as kind as you."

"In Paris?"

"Didn't Scarlett tell you? I am off to Paris to find a husband." She grinned and held her arms out wide into the night air. "To save the family."

She looked entirely delighted in her mission, but Christophé couldn't help the tight feeling in his chest. "Paris is dangerous." He looked toward Scarlett. "Are you sure?"

Scarlett looked down and nodded. When she looked back up at him, she cupped her stomach and her words came out a low whisper. "We have little choice."

Stacia laughed and patted Christophé on the arm as she left. "Don't worry, dear sir. I am looking forward to it."

Christophé had the sudden image of Jean Paul—how perfect this woman would have been for him—and was struck anew at the tragedy that his brother would never have a wife nor children nor . . . anything. His throat tightened, and he could only nod his farewell to the young woman in front of him.

After Stacia left them alone, Christophé stared at Scarlett. This was what life was—a woman to love, children, the day-to-day living that so many took for granted. He was filled with gratitude that he had this night, this moment with her.

He moved behind Scarlett and handed her the telescope. As she raised it toward the moon, he gently tugged her back to rest against his chest. His arms, not knowing what else to do and wanting to support her, wrapped around the sides of her baby. A rush of protectiveness overwhelmed him as she allowed herself to melt back into his chest.

"Do you see it?" His voice sounded deep and low, even to himself.

"Why, yes. This must be a very good telescope as I can see so much more than the time before."

"There are mountains and valleys and craters on the moon's surface too."

"How can you tell which is which?"

"Craters are the easiest to find. Mountains look more like . . . dark lines."

"Oh, yes! I do see the dark lines. And in between each mountain there must be a valley?"

"Exactly. So the moon is not the smooth surface that we once thought. In the last fifty years or so, the moon has been mapped, showing all the stages from crescent to full. We can see what the surface looks like in each stage."

"And stars? Have stars been mapped?"

"Ah. Stars." Christophé lowered his head so that they were cheek to cheek, his eye next to hers. He put his hand to hers on the telescope and slowly moved the piece toward the largest star in the sky. "Here, can you see that?"

"I see a light. It is blurry and fades out on the edges."

"A very good observation. The fading out on the edges is the refraction of the light. Now—" he moved the telescope slightly— "do you see one close by?"

"Yes, it's slightly pink. Are stars colored?"

"Could be, depending on the refraction of the light and how it enters our eye. Some telescopes try to block out those light rays. The stars you are looking at now are in the constellation Orion."

"The hunter? I never could find constellations." Scarlett lowered the telescope and stared at the sky. "Can you show it to me?"

Christophé took her hand in his and raised it up, pointing with her finger. "Here and here is his body. They connect in squares, do you see?"

"Hmm, sort of."

Christophé chuckled. "Now this one connects with this one up here to form the arrow, and these little ones going up and down make the bow."

"Oh. I do see that!"

"And over here, to the other side of the man, behind him, is his shield." Christophé took her finger and connected the four stars that made up Orion's narrow shield.

Scarlett turned and stared at him. "How do you know all of this?"

Christophé shrugged and looked down, smiling. He was unused to so much feminine adoration and didn't quite know what to say.

Scarlett pressed a hand on his chest and smiled up at him. She took a sudden breath, opened her red lips and quoted:

> Snatch me to heaven; thy rolling wonders there,
> World beyond world, in infinite extent
> Profusely scattered o'er the blue immense,
> Show me; their motions, periods, and their laws
> Give me to scan; through the disclosing deep
> Light my blind way.

Christophé stared down at her, undone. "Yes. That is exactly it."

Scarlett rose up on tiptoe to kiss him on the cheek. They walked hand in hand back to the house, a slow stroll in the moonlight.

Chapter Eleven

1794—Carcassonne, France

Christophé pushed the image of Scarlett from his mind with determination as he rose from his bed. Ever since the night he spent with her and her family, she had stopped coming to visit the grave. She hadn't been to visit him either. He didn't know what might have gone wrong; he only knew that she must not want to see him again.

Not seeing her had only heightened his longing for her. He'd dreamed of her again this night. Every night for the past seven days he awoke with vivid, sometimes heated dreams of her. He stood in the chilly room, teeth clenched tight, jaws throbbing. What had he done to scare her off? It had seemed the perfect night.

Turning toward his bed, he knelt down on the hard stone floor, clasped his hands, and bowed his head. "Lord, forgive me my sins. Take this from me, God. I have nothing to offer her and yet, I can think of little else than being with her. Cure me of this torment!" He clinched his eyes tight, his body shaking from the cold and the loneliness that seemed to overwhelm him at the thought of never seeing her again.

Rising from the cot, he threw on his clothes. Work was the only thing that could block all other thought from his mind. He sat at his makeshift desk—two narrow boards stretched over stacks of stone on either side for legs—and reached for the bit of bread from last night's dinner. He would have to go out for food today, he realized as he chewed his last morsel and swallowed. Bending his head over the calculations that had kept him up until almost dawn a few hours ago, he soon forgot the need for bread. Or a woman.

Something wasn't right. In his attempt to measure the wavelengths of light, he had shot a beam of candlelight through slits of paper and studied the properties and behavior of the wave from different distances. After some basic calculations, he changed the experiment to focus on the wavelengths of different colors, but the calculations were all wrong. Flipping open a book at his elbow he studied Newton's calculations. Newton had used geometry and algebra to describe light as waves, which puzzled most scientists. Newton was one of the first to invent calculus, and the new math was so much more elegant, but Christophé couldn't attain the same results with the calculus and he knew that he must. He would never have the courage to write a paper for the Academié de Sciences in Paris without the irrefutable proof of the elegant equation.

An hour turned into three, and then four, when Christophé noticed his hand was shaking so that he couldn't read his own writing. He stood back from the table and berated himself. He would make himself sick, like the time at college when he'd forgotten to eat or sleep for three days. He had lost valuable time recovering and had promised himself never to let that happen again.

Taking his cloak from a peg on the wall, he threw it on, picked up his pouch with its dwindling coins, and rushed into the cold, dreary day.

He made his way to the market keeping the hood pulled low over his eyes. There were many booths selling food. If he kept to the far end, he should be able to avoid the three lovely ladies who sold bread. His heart raced at the thought of seeing Scarlett, but he forced his head down, not looking to the left or the right. He stopped at a fish booth, buying three baked fish pies, then crossed to another meat vendor for some sausages and a hunk of veal roast, well wrapped in salt. At a vegetable booth he bought turnips, then a small melon from a fruit vendor. Satisfied that he would be well provisioned for several days, he turned to go—

Then stopped cold at the animated voices from a booth nearby.

"Oui, merciful God, *c'est vrai.* They were robbed of all the flour and one was injured trying to wrest the bag from the thief's hand!"

Christophé turned toward the pair and listened, his face deep in his hood, his eyes on the cobbled street.

"Mon Dieu! What does the world come to? Poor madame, and so *enceinte* too!" The woman's response only added to Christophé's fear.

He didn't wait to hear more. He ran the length of the market, looking for the Bonham's stall, seeing that, indeed, it was not there as usual. Now only a grassy space opened, like a blank page in a book. Stuffing the purchased food into his bag, he flung it onto his shoulder and rushed through the throng toward Scarlett's street.

The house looked quiet and dark. Without thinking what he was doing he ran to the door and banged on it with all his might.

Stacia answered, opening it a crack to peer out. "Oh, Christophé, it is you. Thank heaven." She opened the door wider and motioned him in.

"I just heard. How is she?"

Stacia smiled a knowing smile at him. "She is fine. Just a sprained wrist where the scoundrel jerked the flour bag from her hand. Would you like to see her?"

Christophé could only nod, his heart still pounding, his throat feeling closed.

Stacia took his cloak and led him up the stairs, chatting away. "Mother went to market to try and trade something for us to eat this week! What with the flour gone, we don't know what we'll eat! We always barter our bread for each week's supply. And those horrible men that broke in . . . why—" she paused, leading him through her bedchamber and turning the knob on Scarlett's door, quieting her voice—"I'll let Scarlett tell you about that."

She peeked into the room. "Scarlett. Are you awake?"

"Yes. Who are you talking to? Is Mother back?"

"No. I was talking to your visitor. Are you dressed, dear?"

"Visitor?" Her voice sounded panicked as they both heard the rustle of covers. "Who is it?"

Stacia flung wide the door and motioned Christophé in with a sweep of her arm. "Why, our very good friend, Christophé!" This she announced with a wide smile and a wicked sparkle in her eyes.

Scarlett held the covers up to her chest and stared. "Christophé . . ."

He rushed to her side, dropping the bag of food onto the floor. "I heard what happened in the market. Are you injured?"

Scarlett pulled her arms from beneath the covers and patted the edge of the mattress. "I am fine, really." She lifted a bandaged wrist. "Just a sore wrist. The doctor says it is wrenched, but should be fine in a week or so. Mother is making me stay in bed." She shook her head and lowered her voice. "I am hoping to convince her that I can get out of it tomorrow." She smiled at him. "Thank you for coming. I—I had not seen or heard from you. I didn't know . . ." She bit her lip, as though loathe to continue.

Christophé sank down beside her; his heart had yet to stop its wild beating. She looked so lovely in a lace-edged gown of midnight blue, with her dark hair spilling over the pillow. "I am relieved to hear it. I thought . . ." He paused and looked down at her small hands. "You haven't been to visit Daniel's grave." He looked up into her eyes. "I didn't know either."

Their gazes locked and she pressed her lips together.

"After the last time, when I nearly caught my death in the storm, my mother convinced me of my foolishness. I will not visit that grave again until the baby is born and old enough to hear about his father."

Christophé felt the world right itself. Of course. She shouldn't be traipsing about the countryside! But he hated to come out of his hiding place, even for her.

"Tell me what happened. I came as soon as I heard."

"Well, the scoundrels did make way with a week's worth of flour."

Stacia, who shouldered her way in with a loaded tea tray, huffed as she sat the tray down, which made a loud clatter on the bedside table. "I wish I had gotten a good look at the scoundrels." Turning to Christophé she shrugged. "I'm sorry there is no bread or cakes to go with the tea. I'm afraid we'll be having boiled beets for dinner." She made a comical face and then plopped herself on a chair nearby.

Christophé picked up his bag and the food he'd just purchased from the market. He handed it over to Stacia. "There are some meat pies and such. Please, let me provide your supper, at least."

"No. We'll not take your food," Scarlett interjected, but Stacia grasped the bag and curtseyed from the room. "Thank you, Christophé. You will stay and dine with us." She smiled broadly as she shut the door behind her.

Christophé took up Scarlett's good hand. "I will go after them. Tell me everything."

෴

THE FEEL OF Christophé's hand around hers was both comforting and disturbing. Scarlett focused on his words instead.

"Certainly not. I'll not have you endanger yourself for a little flour." She didn't tell him that there would be no more. That her mother and sister were postponing the trip to Paris until Scarlett's wrist was healed, as they feared for her safety.

Christophé ignored her protest. "Tell me what happened."

Too weary to resist, Scarlett gave in, waving her bandaged arm in the air. "We were all awakened by a loud crash. I rushed downstairs thinking that Mother had dropped something and as I rounded the corner to the kitchen, I saw three large men, their faces half-covered with scarves, bags of flour in their hands. I was too shocked to be afraid. Shocked and angry. I rushed toward one, grabbed the flour sack in his hands, and tried to wrest it from him. He was much stronger, of course, gave me a good shake and then tugged the sack from my hands. Within seconds they had fled out the back door. Mother and Stacia came to find me sprawled on the floor."

"What were you thinking? You could have been killed!" He glanced at her stomach, a giant mound under the covers. "And the babe. Is it well?"

Scarlett grasped his hand and moved it to lie atop the mound, then smiled when the babe gave an immediate kick. "Oh, I think he is fine. He keeps me awake at night moving about in there."

Christophé raised her hand to his lips and looked deep into her eyes. "How did they get in?"

"Busted through the back door. That must have been the crash that woke me."

"We must fortify the locks."

Scarlett turned serious. "Yes. I've been thinking about how to do that. The wood is broken, the handle and lock useless now."

"I'll repair it. Do you have tools? A hammer and some nails?"

Scarlett nodded. "I believe so. Thank you. We don't notice the lack of a man about the place so keenly as when something like this happens."

"I shall try to be useful." He frowned and glanced around. "Maybe I should stay here for a few days. Make the repairs and see that you all are safe."

Scarlett could not stop a shy smile from lifting her lips. "I think I would like that."

Liar! Her heart accused. *No thinking to it. You* know *you would!*

CHRISTOPHÉ PASSED A sleeve over his sweating brow and wondered for the hundredth time what had possessed him to offer such a thing as to stay at Scarlett's house. Just this morning he'd prayed to be released from a torment he'd never before known— nor did he understand it. Staying in her home meant he would be engrossed with her face and voice and movements and silent looks for the ensuing days. What had he done?

He turned from the kitchen door, having replaced three long planks of wood, and couldn't deny he enjoyed the female chatter as the women cooked and set the table. Perhaps his offer was not the wisest action, but as he listened, he had to admit he was glad he'd done it. Glad he'd offered. Glad they'd accepted.

Suzanne, Christophé noticed, kept a close eye on Scarlett, giving her the easiest chores. When she stopped Scarlett from carrying a bowl loaded with gleaming round potatoes to the table, Scarlett looked at Christophé and rolled her eyes.

He ducked his head to hide the laughter in his throat and turned back to his project. He had spent the afternoon shopping for wood and nails, well hidden in his cloak despite feeling exposed outside his routine. But the Bonham women had only come up with a hammer, and they were depending on him to fix things. That knowledge gave him the courage to approach a local carpenter to cut the wood into the length of boards that he wanted. All he'd had to do was tell the man the Bonham name. The story of the break-in, it seemed, was well known to the townsfolk, and Christophé wasn't the only person wanting to help the three ladies and find the thieves. The carpenter's wife even gave him a cake to take back to the women with the message that if they needed anything to send word.

Coming back, feeling as if he'd conquered something, he'd taken off the busted boards, the frame thankfully sound, and nailed on the fresh ones, making the room smell of fresh-cut wood. Now for a sturdy lock. The blacksmith suggested a long, flat bar of metal nailed horizontally from the middle of the door, with a simple latch piece that connected to another piece attached to the doorframe. The latch could be easily locked by a long metal clasp pushed through the hole in the center of it.

Scarlett came over and peered around his shoulder. He glanced up at her from his crouched position with a grin. "Shall we test it?" She nodded, and Christophé showed her how to secure the lock and then stepped outside. "Bar the door, and I'll try it from the outside to test the strength."

Scarlett closed the door. He waited out in the cool night air, feeling better than he had in days. There was something about making something, repairing something, doing a man's work that could give such a sense of satisfaction. He'd forgotten that.

"Ready," her voice called through the wood, sending a rush of delight through him.

Christophé pressed the thumb latch and gave it a good push. When the door didn't budge, he put his shoulder to it and pushed harder. It seemed sound.

He knocked then. "It seems to be holding!"

He heard her laugh and then pull out the clasp. The door swung wide on her smiling face. "It's wonderful!"

He wanted nothing more than to take her in his arms and kiss her, but stopped himself, only allowing his gaze to rove over her face.

"Come." She held out her hand. "You look famished."

He realized that he *was* hungry. Hungrier than he'd felt in weeks. Must be the physical labor—and the wonderful aromas coming from the kitchen.

For dinner they added some potatoes Mrs. Bonham found in the garden to Christophé's veal roast, along with turnips and fruit. The table was set with pretty dishes and a brace of candles. The women directed him to sit at the head, with Scarlett at his right, Stacia at his left, and Mrs. Bonham at the foot.

"Christophé, we can't thank you enough." Madam. Bonham beamed at him. "Would you say the prayer?"

The rote mealtime prayer from school rose up to his lips but he stopped it from escaping. His other prayers, those spilt-out pleas that kept him sane since the death of his family were also inappropriate. He found himself unsure and embarrassed, not having anything suitable to say. They sat in silence waiting, and then he felt Scarlett's hand reach out across the table and grasp his. The minute her fingers intertwined with his, peace flooded him. He was among friends. Fear had no place at this table.

"Father," he began, clearing his throat, *"please accept our thanksgiving for this bountiful food. We are like children and . . . need You, Your care and Your provision. And please, Almighty God, keep this household safe from evil. Thank You. Amen."*

When he looked up he found tears glistening in each woman's eyes. There was a soft-hearted sweetness about them that overwhelmed him. He had never quite known how it felt to be so needed and admired. Except for Émilie. She had given him a glimpse of this. Thinking of her, it was all he could do to reach for his fork and knife, feeling clumsy and observed as he sliced through the thick roast.

Stacia broke the spell by laughing and pressing her napkin against her mouth. "Wouldn't you like to stay, sir? Mother could adopt you!"

He looked at Scarlett, who looked genuinely appalled at the thought. Stacia laughed again, and her mother tried to speak before the youngest at the table said something truly shocking. Before Mrs. Bonham could get out more than a word to pass the potatoes, Stacia blurted out: "Or you could marry Scarlett. That might be more to both your liking, I think."

Scarlett gasped. *"Stacia!"*

But Christophé only smiled, finding that he couldn't stop the flood of joy Stacia's words brought to his chest. Maybe he could marry Scarlett. Maybe it didn't matter that he had nothing but a crumbling castle and a name to keep hidden. Maybe he could just stay and make a simple living here, with them.

The meal progressed without further event. The women talked of spring cleaning. Christophé assured them he would replace the latch on the front door tomorrow, along with any other household repairs they might be able to find for him. There was a leak in the roof over Madam Bonham's bedchamber, a broken window frame that would no longer open, a rusty pump handle over the well, and a number of small jobs that could keep him busy for days.

After dinner Madam Bonham insisted that Stacia would help her clean up while Scarlett entertained Christophé in the parlor.

"How is your wrist feeling?" Christophé took his place on a wooden chair.

Scarlett sat across from him on the settee. She looked down at her wrist and then slowly unwound the bandage. "The swelling is down. It is still sore, but not the constant throb it was two days ago."

Christophé came over to sit beside her. "Let me see it." He took the slim arm in his hands and traced the delicate bone of her wrist with a finger. "Does that hurt?"

She shook her head, but pain skittered across her eyes. She looked up into Christophé's eyes, and they both paused.

Christophé leaned forward, his eyes on her lips. One hand cradled Scarlett's injured hand between them, while the other reached around and gently cupped the side of her face. "Scarlett," he heard his throat murmur.

She made a sound, and he didn't know if it was in distress or anticipation or something in between. But she didn't pull away.

"Scarlett." He said it again as his lips touched hers. They were as warm and sweet as cherries. He wanted nothing more than to gather her up into his arms, but he was conscious of her injury and held a safe distance between them.

She didn't seem to feel the same way though. She pulled her arm free and held it loosely around his back, pulling him closer. She deepened the kiss and he suddenly realized, she was the more experienced. He had some experience, some encounters that he really didn't even want to remember, but Scarlett had known married love, where nothing, he imagined, was held back. She was the expert now, but that didn't seem to matter.

Within moments they were both lost to the sensation of each other.

❧

THE NEXT MORNING Christophé found Scarlett up and alone, cooking eggs and the leftover potatoes in a skillet.

"You are up early." He came up behind her and reached for her waist. She shied away, giving him a stern look. "We mustn't. You mustn't. I shouldn't set a bad example for Stacia." She finished as if she had been rehearsing the lines all night.

Christophé moved a little away. "Of course. I'm sorry."

"Oh. Don't be sorry! It was . . . it was lovely. But I, well, I can't believe you could have any interest in me now."

What was this about? He frowned. "Now? What does that mean?"

Scarlett gestured toward her giant stomach. "I'm about to have another man's child. And I look . . . so . . . immense." She turned away, stirring the potatoes around and around.

Christophé shot a glance toward the rest of the house, assured himself that they were truly alone, and then went to stand at her back. He didn't touch her. Merely leaned in and whispered into her ear. "I've studied the stars and the moon as close as any man. I have watched white light split into the colors of the rainbow. I have written mathematical equations so elegant that they took my breath away. But you . . ." His voice deepened, grew husky. "You are a wonder I didn't know existed. You *are* beauty."

She inhaled suddenly and looked over her shoulder at him, eyes wide. "Oh."

"I can hardly force myself to stand here so close to you and not touch you."

"Oh . . ."

He backed away then, relishing her look of confused disquiet. He walked over to the table and sat down, enjoying the feeling of knowing how best to handle her despite his lack of experience. For some reason he couldn't fathom, with this woman everything came easy.

She brought over the breakfast, careful to avoid his eyes. He tried not to look at her, not knowing what he might do. Instead he talked of things like broken doors and latches and hard, cold metal. How could she think she was unappealing just because she was having a baby? It was unfathomable.

The rest of the day, and the days after that, took on a comforting routine. Scarlett was always up early to cook for him. He worked at the projects, occasionally leaving for supplies and watching his coins dwindle to next to nothing, but not caring. Sometimes he went back to the castle for clothes or tools or some item that he'd scavenged from the wreckage of the place that might prove useful.

He'd found something here. Happiness. At being among them—these women, this family. And he was secretly glad that Scarlett had stopped visiting Daniel's grave.

❧

THAT EVENING, AFTER dinner, he was in the parlor alone, looking through their small collection of books, when he noticed a nail sticking up from a floorboard. It wouldn't do for Scarlett to trip over such a thing, and so he rose to fix it. It was just under a small round table. He bumped the table as he crawled underneath it, sending a small stack of papers fluttering to the floor. He rose, thinking to put the papers back, when a name leapt off the one on top: *Robespierre.*

Christophé froze. Everything in him shifted, slowed, then stopped. His hand began to shake. He shouldn't read it, but he knew he must. He had to know what link this household—this now-beloved household—had to his sworn enemy. Hurriedly, he flipped the page open and read.

> *Dear Madames and Mademoiselle de Carcassonne,*
>
> *I deeply regret the news I must bestow upon you, dear ladies. The flour stores here in Paris are being hoarded, locked down from any persons except by the full vote of the Committee. They have agreed that any surplus flour outside the immediate needs of the city will be exported and traded to help fund our glorious cause. You will receive three more shipments, another month. That is all I can promise.*
>
> *I realize this will put a great imposition upon your household, but alas, my hands are tied. In knowing your glowing hearts for the Révolution, I feel you will understand. Have you thought of taking up weaving? I am greatly encouraged that the south of France is contributing to our meager funds through the sale and export of cloth. The city is becoming famous for it! I hope that such an endeavor will meet with your full satisfaction.*
>
> *Scarlett, please write when the child is born. I should like to celebrate such an event with you . . . an increase for the Robespierre name! I foresee great things from my grandnephew (should we be blessed with a boy) and another hand and mind and heart for our glorious Republic.*
>
> *Ever in your service,*
> *Maximilian Robespierre*

Christophé gasped for air. The baby—a grandnephew? That meant—

He heard Scarlett coming from the kitchen. Placing the paper back onto the table he looked around the room as if searching for a mooring place.

He saw his dark cloak, reached for it, lifted the newly installed latch, and fled into the night.

Chapter Twelve

Scarlett heard the front door close and lifted her head. As she walked into the sitting room she paused while a trickle of unease snaked down her back.

Where had he gone?

Her steps took her to the front door. She opened it, swung it wide, and peered outside. A memory of her childhood assailed her—opening the door for her father as he came home from work, boots mud-caked, shirt sweat-soaked. She'd looked up and up until she saw his face, his splitting grin and then felt the safety of home as he swung her into his arms and held her close. She remembered the feel of his whiskers pressed against her cheek and the way her smile was so big that it hurt. He would carry her through the door and stand her on a chair so that she could be nearly as tall as he was.

"What did you do today, *mon cher?*"

And with that question, she would tell him everything. How she'd gone to school and faded in with the other uniformed girls. How she'd helped her mother in the kitchen after school and loved the arranging of flowers for the dinner table. How she'd helped Stacia copy her letters or figure a math equation that was just a little beyond her sister's grasp.

Scarlett remembered how he would hug her to him and tell her how proud he was of his big girl. Then, he would turn and cuddle Stacia, and finally her mother. Some nights he would catch her mother up in his arms and lead her in a dance. There wasn't any music, but Stacia and Scarlett would watch, round eyed, as they twirled together, laughing, their mother's head thrown back in suppressed glee, as their father showed them the magic of the world. How had it ended so abruptly?

Shaking herself free from the past, Scarlett opened the door further and looked around. There was no one there. No sign of Christophé. She looked down at her shoes and let out a great exhale. Something had gone wrong, she was certain of it. But what? How was she to fix this?

Her face lifted to the night sky. She saw all that Christophé had shown her—Orion's belt, the face of the moon and . . . so much more. He had brought the magic back into her world. Now . . .

Would he leave her too?

❧

CHRISTOPHÉ RAN LIKE the hordes of hell were dogging his heels. He ran, feeling a familiar breath on his neck. He ran as if the nightmare had come to life.

"*God!*" The cry escaped as he reached the castle and ran through it room by dark, crumbling room. He stumbled to every window and looked out at the night sky. He took one look and then ran to the next glassless hole, wanting some other image, hoping for a miracle. "It can't be." Another window. Another look into eternity's endlessness. "Not *her* too. I can't bear it."

Robespierre took everything from him. His home. His family. Life as he'd known it. He left Christophé with nothing. And now . . .

The woman he loved, the light in the midst of his darkness, belonged to the man he must hate. And her babe, that mound of life and hope within her, was his enemy's as well. Tainted with the poisonous blood of a calculating murderer.

Christophé had looked on the coming birth with such anticipation. A family to love again. Innocence would once again enter his life, bringing them all joy. Now . . .

All he knew was pain. Anger.

Betrayal.

The Lord's Prayer sprung to his mind. It was the one thing that he had clung to in all the madness—Émilie's death, Jasper's help, the sudden flight here. But he couldn't say it. He no longer wanted God's will to be done.

"No. Your will hurts too much." It was more a whisper than words as he slid down the wall to the floor and grasped hold of the stones beneath him, clawing at them. "Not Your will. Not anymore."

There was only one thing he wanted.

Revenge.

❦

HE DIDN'T KNOW how long he sat there, but after countless heart-pounding moments where senseless thoughts ran through his mind, a plan formed. Christophé jumped up and ran down the steep, sloping curve of the stairs to his room. He took up a sharp razor, then a bowl—which he filled with water from a barrel in his laboratory—and a ragged piece of cloth. He brought the supplies to the only mirror he had, a broken piece in which he could barely see half his face. Laying his supplies on the old, scarred table, he propped the mirror against a jar, positioned it just so, and then began shearing his hair off with the razor.

It fell in piles on the table—dark, silky strands held together by static electricity, which made him think of Benjamin Franklin and his famous experiment with storm clouds, lightning, and a kite. But he turned his thoughts from science. That would not help him now.

Once the length of his hair had been cut off, he took up the soap, lathered it into his hands, and rubbed his scalp with the bubbles. Taking up the straight-edge razor, he proceeded to shave his head. His scalp surprised him, how like the moon it was. Not a completely smooth surface as one might think. No, there were bone and indentions and skin so white, attesting to the fact that it had never seen the light of the sun. He left the hair on his face, a few days growth. Then he pulled the red cap of freedom—ha!—over his head. They called it a Phrygian cap. He didn't care what they called it as long as he didn't look like who he was: an aristocrat, a blue blood, a bloody count awaiting the guillotine's blade.

He studied his reflection in the mirror, and allowed a grim smile. They wouldn't recognize him now. They would not know.

He pulled out a sack and stuffed it with all the food he had, filling his mouth as he worked, chewing and swallowing without tasting, knowing he would have to run far this night—on foot.

A long loaf of bread was grasped in his hand. He paused, looked at it, knowing where it had come from. Scarlett. Scarlett's bread.

He laid it on the table, looked at it for a long moment, and then went to the fireplace and grasped the long handle of a shovel. His arms bulged and he began to sweat as he shoveled out great heaps of burning embers. He heaved them to the table . . . onto the bread. Leaning over, he blew onto them until a small flame caught the bread. He watched as it burned, turned black, and then caught the wood of the table. Smoke filled the room.

With a groaning yell, he wiped his experiments to the floor, saw the glass shatter and the chemicals quickly turn black and smolder in the lack of air in the room. He saved one glass—the one full of turpentine, an accelerant for fire. He grasped it in one hand, paused, and then blocked all thought. His arm heaved back and then he threw it toward the fire. The room burst into flames.

He backed away, shielding his face and his eyes. He grasped the bag, his last possessions in the world—clothes, some food, a little money, and his own family heirloom, the Trencavel goblet—then turned to run from the castle.

He blocked out all voices and words, except one.

Revenge.

Without looking back, Christophé ran into the night.

SCARLETT WATCHED AS her sister stuffed her belongings into a trunk. She had day dresses, frilly bonnets, gloves, hats, and a few precious evening gowns. She borrowed the best jewelry and hair accessories her mother and Scarlett had accumulated over the years. And she had so many shoes—low-heeled slippers of every color and high-heeled shoes with bows and baubles and lace adorning them. Her foot was a little smaller than Scarlett's, but she assured her sister that she could shove some wadded paper into the toe and make do. Most particularly with a delicate blue satin pair that boasted a glass jewel of the same color on the top and a silver-hued fabric heel. Stacia would not be going to Paris without those in her arsenal.

Scarlett couldn't help her grin. Then she laughed out loud. "You are worse than I was!"

Stacia slanted her a coy look and demure smile. "I'm not as pretty as you, so I shall need the added confidence."

Scarlett nearly howled at that. "You will take Paris by storm, my dear. You have no idea."

"Are the ladies so ugly there?"

Scarlett laughed. "Of course not. Well, a few, I suppose, when compared with you."

Stacia twirled around in her simple dark green satin traveling dress. She took up a tall hat from the bed, a hat a little outdated with its huge peacock plumes dipping to one side, and placed it on her head at an angle. Going over to Scarlett, she dipped into a low curtsey, her eyes moving from the floor to Scarlett's eyes with a small smile. "I am so pleased to meet you, monsieur. I, uh . . . What a lovely coat you have."

Scarlett's eyes grew round and she clapped her hand over her mouth. "Don't say *that!*"

"Well! What should I say?"

"Ask him about himself, what he does, where he goes, what is important to him."

Stacia frowned, her eyebrows knitting together. "That sounds horrible."

"It is."

They fell onto the bed together, laughing hysterically.

After their giggles had died down, Stacia grasped Scarlett's hand in hers and they both lay quiet . . . looking up at the ceiling for a long time.

"It will all be all right, won't it, Scarlett?"

Scarlett stared at the ceiling. She thought of their father and her husband and now the disappearance of Christophé and felt anger fill her. How could he leave with no explanation? How could he hold her one minute and then abandon her the next? She had gone over and over every detail of the days he'd stayed with them but could find no explanation for his disappearance. Still, she didn't want Stacia to worry, so she squeezed her sister's hand and whispered, "Yes. Everything will be all right."

Stacia leaned up and grinned. "I have to admit I am excited! I will find the best man. Someone upright and faithful and true. Someone I can admire." She giggled and placed a quick hand on Scarlett's mound. "And I will not start having babies for a very long time!"

Scarlett grimaced as she tried to rise from the bed. "Help me up, will you? Your very fat sister cannot rise from this bed!"

Stacia was obviously trying to suppress her laughter as she heaved Scarlett from the bed. Scarlett stood, her hands unconsciously going to the center of her low back. "If you won't have babies, you will have to invent some reason not to sleep in the same bed as your husband, my dear."

Stacia shoved another pair of shoes into the bulging trunk. "Is it awful? Did you hate it?"

Scarlett shifted her weight from one foot to the other and contemplated how much to tell her sister. "What do you know . . . of the marriage bed?"

Stacia shrugged. "I know what happens." She turned, a mischievous glint in her eyes. "But I don't know how it feels. Does it hurt?"

Scarlett smoothed her hand over her stomach, thinking. Their mother had always been mum on this subject, so if she didn't tell Stacia anything, she would have to discover it for herself—just like she had. Was there anything she wished she had known beforehand? "It's not unpleasant. The first time can be painful, but, after that, well, it can be rather pleasant." She felt the heat rise to her cheeks.

Stacia giggled. "You liked it!"

"Well . . ."

"You did! You liked it! I always thought it was just something I would have to endure."

"It will be difficult to turn away a newly married husband. I can tell you that much." Scarlett giggled. "I am afraid, dear sister, that marriage means babies in most cases. So enjoy your slender figure while you can."

"Oh, I don't like the sound of that!" Stacia looked into the trunk of beautiful, tiny-waisted dresses. "I don't want to get fat!"

Scarlett shrugged. "I hope to regain my figure soon after the birth. As will you if you have babies. It is only for a time. And Stacia. Can you imagine? A little human . . . a baby . . . with some mix of his face and mine. You will change your mind once you've found love."

"Did you love him so much?"

"Yes. I thought I did."

"You're not sure?" Stacia looked as surprised as Scarlett had been the first time she admitted it to herself.

Scarlett looked down, not knowing how to answer. "I thought I was sure."

"And what of Christophé, do you love him? Is it different?"

Yes, it was different. It was completely, wholly different. But how could she put into words the finding of her other half? And it didn't matter anyway. "Christophé is gone." Scarlett tossed a delicately beaded bag onto the bed. She shook her head, then stared back up at Stacia. "Christophé is gone."

Suddenly a long, low cramp seized her stomach. Scarlett bent over. Stacia ran to her side. "Are you all right?"

Scarlett straightened, bracing herself against the tall bedpost. "I'm fine. This has been happening of late. It will come and go but I don't think it is the true thing yet."

"Should I call Mother?" Stacia wrung her hands together.

Scarlett shook her head. "No. Mother is to know nothing of this. She can barely leave as it is, and you have to go. You both have to. We don't have any choices left to us. You and mother will leave in the morning as planned. I will be fine. It is just getting near the time, that's all."

"But I don't want to leave you like this."

Scarlett took a few steps closer to her sister's lovely face. She gripped it between her palms. She looked deep into Stacia's light brown eyes. "Listen to me. We don't have much time. The flour is gone. The food stores are small." She grinned. "We can't knit or spin or sew and you know it. There is only you—our beautiful prized—" she sputtered a laugh—"pig."

"Pig!"

"Well, at the fair. The best our family can produce. You know what I mean."

"If you weren't pregnant and having a cramp right now, you know that I would jab you for that." Stacia glared at her, chest puffed out, chin up.

"Sorry," Scarlett said with too straight a face. "I will be fine. You can jab me if you like."

They both looked at each other and laughed.

Stacia grew suddenly serious. "I don't want to leave you."

"Women have babies every day, and I am not due to have this one for a month yet. There is a good doctor here in Carcassonne. I like him. I've spoken with him. He will be here as soon as I need him."

"But you will be all alone! Who will go for the doctor?"

"I will go to the neighbors; they will get the doctor if I am unable. Don't worry about me."

"I wish you could come with us. I will need your advice!" Stacia nearly wailed the plea.

"My only advice is to pray like I've heard you do, and trust no one, not even Robespierre. Follow your heart. Look for a man of worth. And hopefully"—Scarlett smiled—"he will have a little money too."

Chapter Thirteen

They went to bed early in preparation for the departure to Paris. Scarlett tossed and turned. Her bed was soft. There were pillows at her back and one in between her legs, and she was ensconced in coverlets. But she couldn't sleep. What had happened to Christophé? Something was terribly wrong. She didn't know what, but she knew that something did not add up, even to a scientist's mind.

After an hour of being unable to sleep, rearranging the pillows and trying to ignore the constant ache in her back, she rose to pace the room. Her nightgown billowed out around her feet as she walked back and forth, a candle her only light. Finally she threw on her clothes and tiptoed through Stacia's room.

"Scarlett? What's wrong?"

"Go back to sleep."

"What is it?"

"This babe makes me have many outings to the necessary room, is all."

Stacia rose up on an elbow, her hair falling in a dark pool onto the white sheet where the full moon cast a glow on her bed.

Scarlett could see her furrowed brow. "And you get fully dressed for that trip."

The sarcastic tone in her sister's voice couldn't be missed. Scarlett sighed, walked over, and sank down on the feather mattress next to her sister. "I'm going to see Christophé."

"I'm coming with you."

"No!"

"Yes! I'll not have you out roaming the city alone at this hour."

Scarlett sighed, realizing she was glad for the support. "All right. But you must let me speak to him in private."

"Of course." Stacia grinned. "I'll just watch and learn."

Scarlett jabbed her in the shoulder. "Hurry then. Get dressed." Stacia changed as quietly as possible and then they tiptoed from the room while Scarlett pointed out the creaky stair as they made their way down to the front door.

"Oh. Now I understand!" Stacia exclaimed when they heard the front door click shut behind them and walked out into the night sky. She turned around and around, her head up, taking in all the bright stars. "No wonder you come out at night."

"It's lovely, isn't it? I find it peaceful."

Stacia turned to Scarlett and grasped hold of her hand. "It is beautiful."

Scarlett took firm hold of her sister's hand and led her into the street. "Yes, but with an element of danger. We must be quiet. Cling to the shadows."

"Are the patrols out, do you think?"

"The patrols are out more and more. Looking for anything that doesn't look normal. And two women wandering about after dark, unless they are fallen women, will be greatly suspect."

"What could they suspect us of? We are known as bakers, nothing more."

"In this time, dear one, we could be anyone."

"Like Christophé? They are looking for someone like him?"

"Exactly."

They were quiet and solemn as they traversed the bridge to the other side of Carcassonne. They were careful as they slipped passed the twin walls and entered the old castle. Then they stopped.

"This way to Christophé's laboratory. Come. Quiet though." Scarlett grasped her sister's hand in hers. A flock of dark birds took sudden flight, up and then out of the broken roof, frightening them both. Stacia pressed her hand against her mouth, eyes wide with mirth and fright.

"Come," Scarlett directed.

They padded across the stones of the once-great hall of a medieval castle, made their way down a narrow passage . . . then Scarlett stopped.

Smoke. Fire. The smell was strong and undeniable. She swung open the door, and they both put their sleeves to their faces as a charred room came into view. The stones were coated with black. There was shattered glass on the floor, and all around they saw devastation.

"What happened?" Stacia questioned around her forearm.

Scarlett looked around the room. Saw the charred remains of the table she knew was Christophé's work table on the floor. "I don't know."

She turned and hurried to the room where Christophé used to sleep. Flinging open the door, she rushed in. The bed was

rumpled, but nothing else was there. All his clothes, his belongings were gone. She walked further in and turned around, finally
seeing her sister in the doorway.

"What happened to him?" Stacia asked.

Such a simple question.

But she had no simple answer.

Except: "He is gone."

"Gone?"

"Yes." She knew it as deep as she knew the babe inside her.
Christophé was gone.

LATER THAT MORNING Scarlett announced her plan.

"I'm coming with you."

She'd spent the hours after returning home packing her
trunk. If there was one place Christophé would go, it was back
to Paris. She wasn't going to stay behind while her sister found a
husband . . . and Christophé deserted her without even a word of
explanation. He had to be in Paris.

Her mother stared at her, aghast. "But Scarlett! You cannot
travel so far! The child is coming soon!"

"The babe is not due for another month, and I feel fit. I do
not want to be left alone here. And you will need me to speak
with Robespierre, to convince him of his duty to help us."

Her mother looked unconvinced, so Stacia intervened.
"Mother, she will be fine. We need her. You know we will do
nothing but worry about her the whole time we are gone. Just
think. She will have the baby in Paris—with us to help her."

Scarlett's mother looked at her daughters, and both Scarlett and Stacia knew they had won. "Very well. If you think you can travel such a distance."

Scarlett laughed and gave her mother a hug. "I've already packed."

⁓

THE WOMEN ROSE early the next morning and carried their trunks to the front door where they set them down. They had arranged for a neighbor to tote them by cart to the inn where they would meet the morning stage.

Their mother looked around the house one last time, making sure the fire in the kitchen was completely extinguished, and reached for a basket of food. She bustled into the parlor, out of breath, her cheeks flushed pink. Looking at Scarlett, she stopped. "My dear. Are you certain?"

Scarlett crossed her arm over her chest. "I am." She wasn't, though. She wasn't sure of anything anymore.

Her mother shook her head and gestured with a hand. "I can hardly bear leaving you behind and was glad of your decision, but now. It will be taxing. You might fall into labor on the way and then what will we do?"

Scarlett let out a laugh. "I truly hope not. But if it occurs, we can only pray a doctor will be traveling with us that day."

Stacia grasped Scarlett's arm. "Come, worrying will do us no good."

There was a knock on the door. Stacia tied the ribbons of her hat under her chin as she walked to the door and opened it. "Oh, Pierre. Thank you for taking the trunks. We wouldn't get very far if we had to carry them ourselves." She smiled at him prettily, which had the man nodding and stammering.

"It's nothing, mademoiselle. Just sad to see you ladies leaving for Paris."

Stacia dimpled at him. "It will only be for a little while. You will watch over the house? See that ruffians don't move in?"

"Of course."

Stacia lifted the lightest trunk and followed Pierre out to his horse and cart. Scarlett and her mother walked beside the slow-moving animal.

The inn was bustling with activity when they arrived, in the early light of morning. Scarlett pulled the brooch from her pocket and held it out, staring at the simple flower design that was so elegant, the stones flashing in the light. Her heart leapt in her chest as she remembered Daniel giving it to her on their wedding day. His brown eyes had held her gaze for a long moment, with such a look of happiness in them. The recollection brought sudden tears. "Oh, Daniel . . ."

Gathering her resolve, she took the jewelry to the innkeeper. "Might I buy passage to Paris with this?"

The man took the brooch between meaty fingers and turned it this way and that. He grinned at her revealing crooked, yellow teeth. His gaze taking in her rounded form. "Looks like a fine enough piece, madame, but you sure you want to travel all that way in your condition?"

Scarlett pressed her lips together, looking down at the brooch in the man's hands. "Yes, I must get to Paris."

"Well, you bought yourself a ticket then."

Stacia leaned forward and gasped. "Not your brooch, Scarlett!"

Scarlett turned and led her away from the counter. "I have no choice. We were struggling to come up with the funds to send you and Mother. I had to do it."

"Oh, it's so unfair."

"Yes, dear sister. Sometimes it is."

As the carriage clattered over the cobblestone road they saw the old pigeon towers, the place where their ancestors had trained the birds to fly with messages of news of the world. They now stood empty, like church spires, some round or square, tall, reaching into the blue of the sky, and roofed with slate or tiles. Their thick, old stones knew stories that Scarlett could only imagine.

It wasn't too long before they began to pass through the towns and villages of southern France. At the larger towns they would stop where the passengers could purchase food or drink, take care of necessities, and walk the kinks from their legs. The horses were watered or changed out for a fresh set, and then off they went again.

About eighty miles southeast of Paris they stopped in Orléans. It was an ancient city, the city of the famed Joan of Arc, built on the bank of the Loire River. They stopped at the Hotel Groslot as Scarlett had heard that it was being turned into a town hall for the Révolution. The use of Robespierre's name easily bought them a quiet room in the back, complete with a comfortable bed, firewood for the fireplace, and a decent meal.

"How did you know about this place?" Stacia fell back on the bed with a contented smile.

Scarlett shrugged. She didn't really know. Some lost memory of a conversation had surfaced as soon as they'd arrived in the river town. "The Révolution has arms stretching all over France. I remembered the name being discussed."

Stacia propped her hand against her cheek. "Scarlett, what do you really think of this Révolution?"

Scarlett turned from the full-length mirror where she was removing her hat and the pins from her hair. As the long, heavy length fell against her back she brushed it back with her fingers and looked at her sister. She paused, not sure how to answer. She saw her mother looking silently between her daughters.

Scarlett finally shrugged, her hand curving around her rounded stomach almost unconsciously. "When I heard Daniel speak of it, I thought them so noble. I thought he was so good. And that what he said about freeing the poor people from the excesses of the aristocrats was so true. Now——" she shook her head——"I don't know. They are doing such horrible things in the name of freedom. When I think of the senseless deaths . . . I think there must be another way. It can't be right."

Stacia nodded, accepting Scarlett's words. Then she grinned. "Well, at least for tonight we have a comfortable place to sleep." She spread her arms out on the bed and sighed with contentment. "I'm glad you came, Scarlett," she said with a smile directed at the ceiling. "Mother and I would be sleeping on the ground or some hard floor without you."

Their mother shook her head. "You girls need to sleep. We have another two or three hours of travel to Paris tomorrow, and I want you both feeling your best."

Chapter Fourteen

The carriage clattered over the Pont-au-Change, an enormous stone bridge that connects the Right Bank to the Île de la Cité, the island in the middle of the Seine. Stacia hung her head out of the open window and gasped at the sights. "Scarlett, is that Notre Dame?"

Scarlett leaned around her sister's shoulder the best she could. "Yes. Isn't it grand?"

Stacia looked all around. "It is so huge! And the city is amazing! Look at all the houses and shops. I cannot believe you lived here for nearly a year." She turned her head to look at Scarlett. "It must have been like a dream."

"Yes—" Scarlett sighed—"it was."

They turned west on Rue de Rivoli, passed the Tuileries Gardens with its round pools, ornate shrubbery and statues, then came into an octagon-shaped square. Summer had come early, and the lilacs and flowers were in full bloom, making a glorious sight.

A little further down, Scarlett gasped. "They've torn down the King Louis statue." In its place sat an enormous scaffold—and the guillotine. Looking at the blood-stained monstrosity, a shiver ran down Scarlett's back.

Stacia wrinkled her delicate nose. "What is this place?"

"It is called *Place Louis XV.* People often gathered here and in the gardens."

An older gentleman seated across from them spoke up. "Don't let anyone hear you call it that now, citizen. It has been renamed *Place de la Révolution* and is the place where the king was guillotined along with anyone they find supporting him." He paused and Scarlett fought a shiver as his gaze traveled the three of them. "Be very careful what you say, even to each other. There are eyes and ears everywhere in Paris and soldiers just waiting to arrest and imprison their next victim."

Stacia stared, wide-eyed, at the man and then at Scarlett.

"My thanks." Scarlett's mother nodded to the man. "I have not been to Paris in many, many years. So much has changed."

The man blinked several times at her, then crossed his arms over his chest and pressed his lips together as if fearing to say more.

They drove north through the square and Scarlett pointed to one of the buildings. "There, the Duplays' house. I hope that is where Robespierre is still staying."

The carriage pulled up, and Scarlett and her family disembarked. She had never known such nervousness as she did walking up the steps to the door. What if he turned them away? No. She was family, which made her mother and Stacia family by association. He would have to help them.

The door was opened by a pretty young woman with dark hair and intelligent eyes. "Yes?"

"I am Scarlett Robespierre, here to see Maximilian, my uncle."

"Citizen Robespierre is not in at present." Her eyes dropped to Scarlett's protruding stomach. "He usually returns at the dinner hour."

"Might we wait for him?"

The woman looked appalled at such an idea, so Scarlett quickly added. "We have traveled so far, all the way from Carcassonne. Please. He would appreciate your care of his relatives, I am certain."

The woman looked torn, obviously not wanting to displease Robespierre. She muttered something under her breath and looked about to break out in a sweat. "I will send a note to his office. Until then you are welcome to take refreshment in the salon."

Scarlett inclined her head in agreement. It was as good an offer as she was going to get.

The women settled in to wait, Stacia exclaiming, albeit quietly, about the grandeur of the city while they took tea and delicate, petite cakes and pastries. When the serving girl had departed, Stacia leaned over and whispered to Scarlett. "That was brilliant."

Scarlett reached for another cake, not remembering when anything had ever tasted so good. "What?"

"The part about 'taking care of his relatives.' I think she would have kicked mother and me out immediately. I'm so glad that you came."

Her mother agreed. "Yes, dear me, Scarlett. I am so glad you are here."

Scarlett smiled, grateful to have overcome the first obstacle—but painfully aware the greatest one was yet to come.

Over two hours later, Robespierre finally made an appearance. He looked worse than she remembered—his pockmarked face the pallor of souring milk, his thin lips compressed. He wore the powdered wig of the old Regime, and his neck and shoulders twitched, causing his head to move about in an odd, grotesque way.

Scarlett swallowed the giant lump of nerves in her throat and rallied. She rose as he strode into the room, held out her hands toward him, and saw him recoil as if a serpent reached for him. He made an abrupt move with his head and then turned away from her toward a settee. "Citizen Scarlett," he exclaimed as he sat across from them, "whatever are you doing here? I find it shocking that you are traveling in your . . ." He couldn't seem to finish the statement. His gaze darted toward Scarlett's rounded stomach and then quickly back up at her face. But not once did the man look into her eyes.

"Maximilian," Scarlett reseated herself and clasped her hands together. "It is so good to see you again. Are you well?" She delivered the question with a slight tone of correction and offense.

He seemed momentarily at a loss for words. "Yes, merci. And this must be your mother and sister."

Stacia bowed her head and gave him that graceful, sweet smile. "So good to finally meet the man who has taken such good care of us all these months. We are indebted to you, Deputy Robespierre."

Their mother joined in a little too brightly. "Indebted, indeed, Deputy Robespierre."

Apparently feminine praise did not sit well on the man's shoulders. He fidgeted. "Well, yes. Just doing my duty. But, why have you come?"

Scarlett gained his attention with a delicate clearing of her throat. "Dear uncle, what choice did we have? With the flour depleted, we have no way to carry on. As my only surviving male relative, we were hoping we could further depend upon your good will."

"You should have stayed, my dear. Paris is no place for you to be. The Révolution commands all of my energies. I have little time to see to your welfare."

Scarlett chuckled. "We have little need of your time, uncle. Only a roof over our heads and the basic sustenance deserving of any relative. We have come to find Stacia a husband and as such, add to our resources."

Robespierre's gaze swung to the young woman. "Ah." But he looked even more disturbed. "The moral character of the nation should be every citizen's chief concern, not domestic happiness."

"Of course," Scarlett replied in a low voice. "I suppose living on your charity is nobler than a future husband for Stacia."

Before Robespierre had time to respond to Scarlett's impertinence, she plunged on, intent and determined. Her smile never wavering, looking him directly in the face for a silent second, she waited for his gaze to reach hers. When it finally did she asked softly, "How is Daniel's aunt? Your dear sister, Charlotte?"

Robespierre rose, the nervous moving of his neck and shoulders worsening. He made for the door with a mumbled excuse. "Haven't seen her. Pressing business. Must get to my writing."

As he opened the door to leave them, Scarlett called out to him. "Uncle, shall we stay here?"

He paused as if remembering the reason they had come and his responsibility of finding them lodging for the night. He turned his head toward them, then back around, and then toward them again as if he didn't know which way to go. "For now."

As the door closed, Scarlett's mother's mouth fell open. "Good heavens!"

It was the only thing any of them could think to say.

⌒♾⌒

THE CHATEAU WAS boarded up, pitch dark and as still as the death it had witnessed. Christophé closed the door through which he and Émilie had escaped that night so long ago and leaned against it for a moment, getting his bearings. He felt his way along the wall to the back stairs of the mansion and mounted them. A feeling of unreality assailed him as he groped through the dark toward the main quarters. The air in the place was stale and damp; he couldn't quite breathe deeply enough, and panic grew in his stomach.

He found the library though, made his way to a long window, and drew back the curtain. Moonlight spilled into the room with such a cold light that it only added to his unease. He turned from it, needing a candle. The room had been gutted of anything of value. Even the rugs had been ripped from where they'd lain, soft and pliant under their feet for so many decades. Christophé limped toward the desk, the injury from his journey flaring up. He cursed the ill luck of buying a horse with the last of his stash of coins only to have it slip on the muddied road and fall, landing on his leg. But at least it had been he who was injured and not the horse. As unmanageable as the mare had been, she'd had the strength and stamina to get Christophé to Paris in a little over a week.

A search of the desk proved that whoever had looted their home had been thorough. There wasn't even a dust mote to be found.

Giving up, Christophé made his way slowly to his bed-chamber. As he did so, something nagged at him. A memory long buried . . . The room was completely dark and he was forced to go by touch alone. There. There it was. He pulled a deep box from a space behind the bed. He was surprised they had missed it.

Opening the box he felt through the contents like a blind man, looking straight ahead in the dark, noticing how his sense of touch was becoming more alive as he turned the objects over and over in his hands. Then, there it was. A long candle that he'd used to light gunpowder for some long-ago boyish prank he could barely remember. He smiled as his fingers wrapped around the flint and tinder.

He stuck the candle firmly between his clasped thighs but found he was out of practice. It took several tries to get the thing to light. Once it did, he felt a small measure of success. He studied the welcome flame, as bright and cheery as Scarlett's lips—

No! He pushed her name from his mind. Enemies of circumstance—that's all they were now.

Holding the lit candle high, Christophé wandered through every room in the chateau. He searched every nook and cranny, every secret place he could remember. He found little—an old blanket to cover himself, a broken chair that he might be able to fix, and half-stale loaf of bread. He sank down on the floor and ate it until it was gone. Finally, he lay on the floor, pulled the thin blanket to his chin, used his curled arm beneath his head for a pillow, and fell into a deep sleep.

For the first time in a long time, he slept the sleep of the dead in the room where he had grown up.

⌒⌒

THE WOMEN TOOK a collective breath and stared at one another.

Stacia had her hand clamped over her mouth, her eyes wide. "Oh, Scarlett. You were so brave and . . . and well spoken. I was terrified. He was the most revolting little man I've ever seen."

Scarlett shushed her with a strong look and a little shake of her head.

"Well," their mother remarked, ever innocent of the dangers around her. "I can't say that I am encouraged. It seems we've landed in a hornet's nest." She took a sip of her tea and stared across the room.

A girl came in to clear away the dishes, stopping further discussion. Scarlett watched the slight girl thinking she must be sixteen or seventeen years old. Her blonde hair came to her shoulders, but her face looked somehow familiar.

The girl kept her head down, seeming shy.

"What is your name, dear?" Scarlett asked as she passed her plate into the girl's hands.

She glanced up into Scarlett's eyes, her face frozen and terrified.

Scarlett gave her a kind smile. "Don't be afraid. I am no one to fear."

But the girl only stared, wide-eyed, for a moment and then bolted from the room.

Chapter Fifteen

ind Robespierre.

Find Robespierre.

Find the beginning of the horror and end it. It was the only way to go on.

Christophé woke to the chanting demand, got up and limped to the box where his childhood items lay scattered across the floor. He reached in, took up the knife that he'd hidden away because he knew its glistening sharpness would cause his brothers to take it, his mother to forbid it, and his father . . . well, he didn't know what his father would have done should he discover it. He had never really known his father very well at all.

Christophé studied the knife in the gleam of dawn's light. He turned it this way and that, the deadly sharpness stirring something tight and strong in his chest. He imagined thrusting it into Robespierre's chest, hearing the ribs crack. He closed his eyes and imagined the man's last breath . . . then fought the wave of nausea at the images in his mind.

The prayer lifted to his consciousness. *"Thy will be done."* Then Scripture, the one that assured *"'vengeance is mine,' saith the Lord."*

Christophé gritted his teeth against the truths he'd embraced for so long. Crushed the words pushing into his mind. Vengeance. It was what Robespierre deserved. He couldn't wait until the judgment of God.

Taking up his cloak he swung it around his thin frame and quit the room with more energy than his body should have. He'd lost weight on the journey from Carcassonne, so much so that he had to tie a slender rope around his breeches to keep them up. Not eating to finish his experiments had given way to not eating for the simple reason of lack of funds. He had turned from Count's son to roadside beggar in the space of a few years.

Once out onto the streets of Paris he kept his head down, his boots clipping across the stones, the leg feeling better after a good night's rest. The breeze was gentle as he looked out at the quarter where he grew up. He heard the familiar sounds—birds chirping in the distance, the wheels of a carriage over the cobbled street, people passing by . . . but now he sensed an underlying fear. Heard the hushed tones of those afraid.

Anger rose up to his chest. What had the Révolution done to this city? They were all enemies now, or possible enemies. His eyes narrowed as he looked up, catching the eye of a lady in an expensive dress. She shied away, afraid.

He was glad.

A dark laugh escaped him. He reveled in the power of his mission. He balanced on an arc of time. Something was about to happen, something that would change the course of history.

Something he would cause.

It was a heady feeling.

His steps quickened and it wasn't long before he stood in front of the Duplays' house, where Robespierre lodged. All

Christophé needed was a quiet moment. A darkly lit hall. Robespierre's private sitting room. Just a few stolen minutes.

One perfect moment.

He knocked at the front door. A young woman answered it.

She took in the red cap Christophé wore and smiled. "Yes, citizen? May I help you?"

"I'm here to see Maximilien Robespierre. I have a message for him."

The woman shook her head. "I am afraid he is not to be disturbed just now. Might I give him the message?"

"No." Christophé tried to ignore the impatience burning through him. "It is a verbal message and I must give it to him personally. Do you know when I might come back and find him available?"

The woman glanced around the steps and surrounding area outside the door. In a low voice she said, "He usually leaves for the Jacobin Club at 8:55. You might walk with him?" She pointed down the street toward the club's building.

Christophé pulled out his pocket watch and looked at the time. It was already 8:35. He nodded toward the woman. "Merci. I will wait here."

The woman backed away, shutting the door behind her. Christophé stood in the tiny alcove and considered his options. He did not want to confront Robespierre in the middle of the street, where he would be seen. It had to be somewhere private. With a quick decision he pressed his thin frame against the wall next to the door and hid behind a large plant.

The irony of it struck him. Robespierre had waited in the St. Laurent hall for hours for Émilie and him to come out of hiding. Now he would be the hunter.

A noise sent the blood rushing through his veins. He had a cloth ready in one hand, soaked with a chemical that would render the man senseless should he need it, and the knife ready in the other.

Everything in him stopped. Stopped thinking. Stopped listening to the insistent voice that said, *"Don't do this!"*

The chatter of voices sounded from inside the house and then the door opened. Would Robespierre be alone?

The man came out the door, accompanied by four women. Christophé's heart felt caught in his throat. No. It wasn't possible! He was hallucinating. Hunger had driven him mad . . .

And yet, she was there. Scarlett. It was her rounded form coming down the stairs.

He pushed back into the wall, shock upon shock as he recognized Suzanne and Stacia, followed by what must be a servant girl—

Wait. The girl. Those golden braids tight against her scalp.

His eyes narrowed, and he took in the slim shoulders. He started shaking as he realized those shoulders still had the same taut boniness he had grasped against his chest for hours in their hiding place in the family chateau . . .

Turn around! His heartbeat was fast in his chest and making too much noise. It couldn't be! He had watched Émilie mount the steps to the guillotine. Émilie would *never* be with Robespierre.

He shook uncontrollably now, making a sound that reverberated around him. He pressed further into the wall. *Please . . . please . . . let none of them hear me.*

Just as he thought it, Scarlett jerked back and turned. Her eyes met his and she inhaled.

Christophé shook his head slowly back and forth, pleading. Stacia grasped her sister's arm. "Scarlett, what is it? The babe?"

Scarlett turned quickly back around and yelped, leaning over her stomach. It had the desired effect of immediately capturing her younger sister's attention, of rushing them down the steps. "Just a small pain. I'm sorry to have frightened you."

They followed her. They did not look behind.

Christophé slid to the ground. His hand grasped at the stones, needing the anchor.

He'd seen her at the guillotine. He witnessed her familiar blue dress and erect carriage mount the stairs. He watched as they locked her body into place. He heard her thin cry. Now it appeared that Robespierre had the power to further torture him with a serving girl that looked like his sister.

Just one more reason to make sure the man never drew another breath . . .

"Émilie . . ." Her name gasped out. He clutched his chest, feeling his heart ready to burst within the cage of his ribs. "I miss you."

◈

SCARLETT'S SUDDEN ANIMATION held them all captive as they walked to the market. She chatted inanely about the city and all the places there were to visit.

Robespierre took little notice. He seemed deep in thought and troubled. At a cross street, he bid the women good-bye and turned toward the offices where the Convention held their meetings, but not before he had passed coins into Scarlett's hand. "Buy whatever you need. I will see you at dinner."

Robespierre had given the serving girl a list of items that he wanted, which she handed to Scarlett without complaint. She was such a quiet girl, Scarlett thought as she gazed at the top of her mop cap. And had such responsibility in Robespierre's household. It was puzzling.

"Will you tell us your name, dear?" Scarlett touched her shoulder, covered by the light gray servant's dress.

The girl looked up, met Scarlett's eyes with innocent blinking, but didn't speak.

Scarlett's paused, studied the girl's face. It came to her in a rush. In the light of day, with the rays of the morning sun shining upon her young face . . . *she looked like Christophé.*

Their gazes held, and Scarlett saw a blank stare that chilled her. Then the girl looked down at the street, her hands clasped tightly together in front of her.

Scarlett blinked rapidly, her heart pounding in her chest. The babe moved, sudden and strong, and she inhaled, grasping her stomach. *Oh, please God! Not here!*

Scarlett stopped and gripped her stomach, which brought her mother and Stacia rushing to her side. But the pain passed quickly and she brushed off their concern. Taking the girl's hand, Scarlett kept her attention on the silent girl as she led the women through Les Halles, the central market in Paris. She never spoke aloud, but she did point out the best stalls to buy meat and fish and homegrown produce when asked.

Scarlett managed to guide her over to a fruit stand by taking a gentle grip on her elbow. She allowed her mother and sister to forge ahead with their packages, then pulled the girl into an uncrowded aisle. She gently took hold of the pointed chin and lifted the girl's head. Their eyes locked, and Scarlett saw panic in them.

"I know who you are." She spoke in a soft, soothing voice. Christophé had refused to speak of his sister. What had happened? "Your surname. It is St. Laurent, is it not?"

The girl gasped and pulled away, but not before Scarlett saw the sudden burst of tears in her eyes. She started to run away. Scarlett reached for her, tried to run after her, but soon realized she couldn't catch up. So encumbered by the babe and her rounded body, she was soon gasping for air. She leaned over, her head tilted up, watching the fleeing heels of one Émilie St. Laurent.

⚬

"DISAPPEARED?" ROBESPIERRE THUNDERED at Scarlett, causing her to rear back. The last few hours the women had looked for the girl all over the marketplace, all the while Scarlett's pains increased in intensity and frequency. She didn't tell anyone. She tried her best to push through each one by walking fast with her sister and mother, searching and calling, not knowing what would happen to the girl in the unpredictable streets of Paris. Scarlett even ignored the sudden bursting feeling and the trickle of liquid running down her leg.

But now, Robespierre wanted an accounting. "She was *mine!*"

"She was a servant," Scarlett reminded him softly—so softly that he lifted his head and glared at her with slitted eyes.

Scarlett shrugged, remembering the games of society. "Surely, Uncle, you would not desire to keep such an unreliable person in your employ." She paused and allowed a note of suspicion to lace her next words. "She was so young to hold such a position in your household."

He looked ready to impale her. A sudden pain gripped her whole stomach, but she stilled her mind to one focus and blocked it from her mind. This moment meant everything.

Everything.

153

She touched his sleeve. "I will find you a better servant. I can see that you need a woman here to help you run things. You are too busy with the more important work of the Council to be worrying about runaway servants." She paused, all compassion and innocence. "Unless she was more? A distant relative perhaps?"

Robespierre jerked away from her touch and searching gaze, taking a deep swallow from his glass. "Of course not." His clipped speech dripped with anger.

"Good." Scarlett laughed, a carefree, tinkling sound that chimed around the room. "We shall put your household to such rights that you shall not have a worry of how anything is managed as your head rests on your pillow. Trust me, Uncle. We are so very grateful for your care. Let us take good care of you—as you have of us."

He turned and stared at her as a shiver followed by another deep spasm racked her womb. He nodded once, quick and hard. "Merci." With that, he left the room.

Scarlett sank into a nearby chair and gripped her stomach, her brow breaking into an immediate sweat.

Her mother spoke from her seated position in the salon. "Whatever are you up to, Scarlett?"

Stacia gave her a small smile. "You are better at this game than I realized. I am learning much watching you."

Scarlett started to smile, but the pains took over. Without someone to rescue, her whole being concentrated on the task of giving birth. She curled inward and groaned.

"Scarlett!"

They rushed to her side.

Scarlett turned her head against the pale blue silk of the Louis XIV chair. "Don't tell Robespierre. Tell him nothing. Not yet."

Chapter Sixteen

hristophé stumbled down the street into the white light of a city square. He gazed up at the scaffolding and then the guillotine itself. It was just a short distance from Robespierre's door. How convenient, he thought in a distracted way. His gaze left the guillotine and rose to the blue sky.

"I never thought You to be cruel." He knew it was a sin, blaming God. He thought of Job and how he had wrestled with his life crashing down around him when he had been so good, so upright. He thought of Job's understanding of God . . . so now Christophé wrestled. Why would God allow him such a pitiless moment of heart-stopping hope?

He took the knife from its hidden place within his cloak and stared at it, seeing how paltry it was, how small he was. *Go home*, he told himself. Never mind that he didn't have one.

He weaved down the walkway and street, like a man who has too frequently imbibed, heading back toward the chateau. Passersby avoided his staggering steps and vacant stare, clearly afraid of the knife that hung loose in his hand. He was sweating profusely as he rounded the stone edges of the mansion and slipped through the back door. Without care or caution, he stumbled up the servants' stairs, images of Émilie mounting the platform, of her strapped to a wooden board, of the sound of the thick blade as it swooshed through the air, and then the cheers of the crowd. It replayed in his mind in vivid detail and sickened him so much that he had to cling to the handrail on the stairs and stop. With effort from deep in his belly he clenched his teeth, forcing his mind away from the ghastly memory and on something more stable, more solidifying to his legs—revenge. He began to climb the stairs again, imagining how he would do it.

Robespierre. Whenever he'd seen the man, Robespierre had always given the room a chill, as if a dark presence was among them. Even the most precocious child would shy away from this vile being. His too-pointed chin, the powdered and curled wig, and those ever-moving wide-set eyes . . .

Christophé had seen the man before he brought destruction on his family and home. He recalled those times now, how Robespierre often stood in the darkest corner of a room, observing, slowly sipping from his wine. Then he would blurt something out. And it was either brilliant or inane. As if his mind and heart were never in tune. One moment clumsy and even reckless, then next he had an air about him that had everyone on pins and needles. Waiting and not a little frightened of what he might do next.

Christophé pushed open his bedchamber door. It creaked loud in the stillness. He stepped over the threshold looking toward his bed. "How will he die?" The whispered words flowed into the quiet.

A shadow moved. Too quick. He hadn't even thought. The knife came up but slipped into the elements of air, gravity taking it slowly down as a blow crashed down on his arm. He watched the knife, as it turned and twisted to land, point first, into the wooden floor. Something hard cracked against his skull. Time slowed. He tottered and turned—and saw him.

In the last second of consciousness a voice sprung to mind that wasn't his own. A cackling voice that asked with pleasure: *How will he die, indeed?*

Christophé slid to the floor, a black haze overtaking him.

⤜∽⤛

SCARLETT GASPED WITH the pain. No one had told her. Why had no one told her? No one had warned her of these inside-out twisting spasms that seemed neverending. Her head was pressed back into the pillow and her fingers clawed at the thin sheet beneath her heavy body.

She shook her head, a sound coming from her throat that she didn't recognize. Wimpering. For the first time in her life, she was truly afraid.

Stacia sat at her right side, reaching for her hand, murmuring words Scarlett couldn't bear to hear. How strong she was. How good she was doing. How the midwife had been sent for. How Robespierre had disappeared and they knew not where he had gone.

All Scarlett could bear to focus her thoughts on was a face. It rose into her mind's eye when the pain was too much for her to bear. It took hold of her as strong as the heaving of her womb. Her lifeline. Her hope. She turned toward Stacia during one of her resting moments and spoke quickly, knowing it wouldn't last long.

"Christophé. You must find him."

Stacia patted her arm like a mother with a two-year-old. "Dearest, Christophé disappeared, remember? We don't know where he is."

Scarlett shook her head against the pillow, her body tensed like a bow string, sweating through her clothes and the bedclothes. "He is here. In Paris." She just managed the words before another wave of spasms racked her.

"Ohhh." She bit down on her lip, feeling the delicate skin split, tasting of her own blood and curling inward as her body demanded her full attention. She clenched her eyes closed and blew air like a stallion tied to a rope and seeing the fencing-in of his future for the first time. She clutched her mound with arms full of strength, wishing she could push on her belly and force this scene to its close.

The pain ended abruptly, but Scarlett knew it would not be the last. She fell back panting, reaching for Stacia's hand. "St. Laurent. Find the place where they lived. He will be there." She sighed out the last, all the strength leaving her. "I know it."

Fear tinged Stacia's features as she stared into Scarlett's eyes, as though Scarlett was talking out of her mind. Scarlett glared at her sister with an intensity that she never allowed herself to use. She'd always been gentle, loving with the girl that was her best friend. But this wasn't the time for anything but sure demands. "Go. Christophé St. Laurent. His father was the Count of St. Laurent. Ask questions, quietly, carefully, to only those you think you can trust. You have an intuition like no one I've ever known. You can do this. Find him. Or . . ." The pains started again. Scarlett reared up and bellowed, a guttural sound, making Stacia look even more afraid by her ferocity. "Or we are all lost!"

"Lost? How can we be lost without him? We will be in more danger if we admit knowledge of him." Stacia smoothed back Scarlett's sweat-pasted hair.

There was a noise from outside the door. People were coming. Scarlett lifted up, grasped tight hold of Stacia's hand. "The serving girl. The one who disappeared."

Stacia stared into Scarlett's eyes, her face an intense picture of concentration.

"She is Christophé's sister. I don't know what Robespierre has planned, but he cannot be trusted. We have to find Christophé and warn him."

Their mother rushed into the room, an unknown woman on her heels. The woman looked to be aged beneath a hat that appeared even more ancient. Too old for such work, certainly, but her eyes glowed with intelligence and took in the scene with immediate clarity.

Stacia squeezed Scarlett's hand. "I'll do it." She leaned in and kissed Scarlett's cheek. Her words were a whisper in her ear. "I will find him."

As another wracking pain bent Scarlett's body, no one noticed as Stacia slipped silently from the room.

∽

STACIA GRASPED A long, blue scarf and flung it around her neck and over one shoulder. She dashed to the bureau where she had seen Scarlett hide the coins they hadn't needed at the market today. Scarlett was a smart one, she marveled, scooping them up into her palm and hearing them clink against her palm. Smarter than she'd realized. The way she'd handled Robespierre today. The way she'd bargained at the stalls to save some of her uncle's precious money for them. Stacia pulled on elegant walking shoes, hooking the eyes as quickly as she could, and allowed herself a small smile. She was learning much from her sister in how to navigate these treacherous waters, but she also knew that Scarlett had complete faith in her for this task to come. The thought gave her strength as she let herself out of the house and turned toward unknown streets.

Stacia made her way quietly down the darkening streets toward the place where they had been shopping. There had been a woman at the market who was selling bread. The Bonham women had struck up a conversation about the business. She was the type of woman who, upon first meeting, would tell her whole life story. She was gleeful, almost, for an audience and a fount of information about the area. She lived only blocks from Porte Berger. She had been kind. And she had invited them to visit her.

Stacia rapped on the arch-shaped door, hoping she had the right address. She waited, her heart speeding up as the sound of metal clattered against the latch. The door swung wide. An older man, plump and round, with a frown on his face, met her.

"What do you want?"

Stacia stuck her chin up and decided to brazen it out. "Your wife. Madame Latrice. I need to speak with her."

"At this hour!" The man howled at her and reached for her arm, dragging her into the room. "With the patrols out! Mon Dieu! You will have all our heads!"

"But she invited me to visit."

Then he turned and shouted into the house. "Suri, *qu'as tu fais?* Foolish woman. Your tongue is like a viper, ready to strike us dead!"

The man left with heavy-footed steps, still shouting in a tirade of French expletives.

Stacia pressed her lips together and waited.

A few moments later, the woman rushed into the room, her cap askew as if she'd just pinned it on. "Citizen Bonham." She reached for Stacia's hands and clasped them hard. "Ah. From the market. What are you doing here?"

Now was the time to come up with a really good story. Stacia squeezed tight the woman's hands. "Please pardon my unexpected visit. It's just that I was . . . hopeful today. Remember I told you that my mother and sister and I were bakers in Carcassonne? And then, quite suddenly, the flour gave out. We've come to Paris to make a fresh start and I thought"—she smiled up to the woman—"that you might help us find a supply so that we could bake again." At the woman's distressed look she quickly continued. "We have some money." She patted her nearly empty pocket. "I thought, perhaps, we could pay you to supply us and thus increase your profits too."

A gleam came into the woman's brown eyes. "Well, I don't know. It is so dangerous. Anything we do can be so scrutinized." She looked to be warming to the subject though. "You shouldn't be out this time of night, mademoiselle! Oh! I should not even be calling you that. We are all citizens now. No more titles of any kind! I forget!" She raised her arms in the air in distress. "Mon Dieu, these times we live in!"

Stacia ignored the woman's distress and continued in an even voice. "Of course. I am so sorry to bring you any distress. We are new to town and it is not so confining in Carcassonne. I am ignorant. But, please, won't you help us?"

The woman seemed torn but couldn't seem to help the occasional glance toward Stacia's pocket. "I will see what I can do. There is a supply, if one has the coin to pay."

"Merci." Stacia reached into her pocket and brought out a few of the precious coins and then started to turn away. She turned back suddenly with a frown between her eyes. "Might I trouble you with one more question before I leave?"

The woman looked about the room and then leaned in. "Yes?"

"Old friends." Stacia lowered her voice to a whisper, then said the next in quick staccato. "The Count of St. Laurent. Have you heard what became of him and his family?"

The woman looked ready to swoon, but eager too. She pulled Stacia close. "All killed. At the guillotine some years ago." She paused and then grew even quieter so that Stacia had to lean in to hear the next words. "But it is rumored that the youngest son escaped. No one knows what happened to him."

Stacia reared back. "Oh. My goodness!" She leaned in herself. "If I wanted to pay my respects, just quietly within myself, with no one to know, where would I find their house?"

The woman gasped. "You must not go there, dear. Patrols are everywhere, but most especially where the nobility lived."

"I can be careful, just to pass by and say . . . adieu. Please. There are no churches to visit. I can hardly believe how they've been looted and turned into storage houses. I am sure there are no graves to visit. I do not know how else to pay my respects."

"If you are caught paying your respects to the nobility you will be thought a traitor and turned over to the Convention. No one shows respect for anything except the beliefs of the Révolution."

"I will be careful. No one will know anything except that I passed by. I will not even pause in my steps."

The woman sighed in mock resignation. "The chateau is on Rue St. Honoré." She waved her arm in a direction. "Close to here. Go that way, then left on Rue de Louvre, toward the river, you will see Rue St. Honoré. Take that road a little ways. A grand chateau. You will know it."

"Merci." Stacia gripped her hand, the rush of accomplishment soaring through her. "You are a good friend."

Chapter Seventeen

There were few people on the street now. Dusk was turning into night, the time when the patrols were out looking for anyone breaking the strictly enforced curfew. Stacia's heart beat within her but she was only a little afraid.

Mostly she was filled with the excitement of a secret mission.

Her skirts swished around her ankles as she broke into a near run. Only three blocks more. The city passed by in a blur. And then, there it was. She looked up and up at the huge stone edifice, with its sharply slanted roof and spires on each corner giving it the look of a cathedral. It was nothing short of palatial. She ran up the wide steps and reached for the ornate door handle. She pressed her shoulder and her weight into the door. It wouldn't open. It was, of course, securely bolted. She heard a noise behind her, a jangling of reins and the heavy beat of horses' hoofs. Two mounts with stern-looking men riding them were coming up the street just a few feet away. She dove for cover behind some shrubbery near the door. Sure enough, the men wore upon their uniformed lapels the cockade of the Republic—red then white then blue then white again. For purity, they said.

Stacia held her breath as they passed by, saw them looking to the left and the right and then laughing at some comment she couldn't quite make out.

She waited for several long minutes after they had gone and then, hugging the walls of the building, skirted around to the back, looking for windows that might open. She even climbed up onto a raised terrace to push against two double doors. Everything was locked.

Of course the chateau would be secured! *Scarlett! Why did you send me on such a fool's errand?*

At the back of the building was the servant's entrance. Stacia crept to what seemed a small door. Actually it was normal size, just small compared with the other. She tried it, expecting nothing. The latch clicked and gave way! She eased the door open, peered into the dark stairway—then slipped inside.

The air was close and dank as she crept up the shadowy stairs. Fear assailed her—along with the sense that everything was not as it appeared.

She smelled something pungent . . . unpleasant. She mounted the next level of stone steps. They were wide and grand, strictly for a servant's use, signifying the wealth of the family. As she climbed, she realized what the terrible smell was.

Blood.

Her footsteps soundless, she glanced about for some sort of weapon. Reaching the main landing, she groped around until her fingers closed on a familiar item. A poker near a fireplace. She grasped it firmly in hand, and then headed up to the second story, the stairs now very grand and curving. She pictured the balls and soireés, the social events they might have had here. Lovely women in ornate dresses. Men in tailcoats and intricately knotted cravats, enchanted by the St. Laurents and what must have been a picture-perfect family. Stacia felt a stab of sadness imagining the place in all its glory. Now it seemed little more than a huge, echoing tomb.

She reached the second story and crept across the grand foyer, then down a wide hall. Rounding a corner she saw a flickering light. Someone was inside that room.

There was no sound, just the pale light and the feeling that whoever was in that room, it was not Christophé. Her mind screamed at her to turn and run or wilt to the floor in fear, but she had to know. What if it was Christophé? She took a tentative step forward. And then another and another, until she was at the open door. She pressed herself against the wall, craned her neck, and peered in. A noise sounded from the room, and she reared back against the wall, her heart pounding so loud she was sure she would be discovered. She heard a voice that sounded recent and familiar.

"I have you now. The last of the St. Laurents." The man grunted, and the sound of a body being dragged across a rug sent chills down Stacia's arms. Booted feet swung into her line of vision and she gasped, then clamped her hand over her mouth, terrified that she might have been heard. She held her shaking body very still as the man continued. "You thought I killed her, didn't you?" Dark laughter sent tremors through Stacia's spine. "She was too sweet. Too innocent. I couldn't do it. I could not send that child to the guillotine." Another laugh, but this time it sounded hollow, like it was coming from a man whose mind was broken. "So I made her my servant. And a fine servant she is."

The man's words . . . the sound of his voice . . . suddenly all the pieces came together, and Stacia bit down on her lip to keep another gasp from escaping. The servant—Émilie. The voice . . .

Robespierre. He was here.

Oh, gracious Father in heaven! *Christophé*. It had to be.

What was she to do? Everything within her wanted to charge the room and demand something . . . some justice. But she had only a poker and little strength to use it. Instead she crept to the door's very edge and waited.

She heard a deep sigh of utter exhaustion. She heard the bed creak and covers being pulled up. Within minutes, she heard the snores of someone who must be certain that the man on the floor was dead.

She waited a long while, her head leaning against the ornate paneling of the hall. She lectured herself silently. *You must go in. You must discover the identities of these men. You must find Christophé.*

As soon as the snores grew more even, Stacia crept into the room. There was a small fire lit in the fireplace which, thankfully, gave a little light. And there was the man on the floor, his face turned away from her . . . and blood. Blood on the floor next to his head.

Her stomach turned as she averted her gaze.

Then she remembered her mission—Scarlett's sure words echoed across her mind: *If we don't find Christophé, we will all be lost.* She looked back at the man on the floor, then crept closer to his still form.

It was he. Stacia's hand went to her mouth to keep herself quiet. He looked to be dead. Before she could think, she reached out and took firm grasp of his wrists, then—as quickly and quietly as possible—drug the body from the room.

She refused to look at him, but knew in some deep part of her that a bloody swath was following them from the room and down the hall. She pulled the body to the stairs and then paused to catch her breath. At the top of the stairs, she took a firmer hold on his wrists and pulled him down, step by slow step. Praise be to God that Robespierre's snoring still sounded in the distance.

Finally she reached the back door. Now what? She couldn't drag his body all the way to Scarlett's side. Never mind the patrols. She didn't have the strength. She looked down and gasped. His skin was very pale.

"Christophé," she whispered. "Wake up." She reached out and touched his cheek. It was cold.

There was no hope. He was dead. Her sister's second chance. Stacia felt anger fill her. It was unfair!

"No. No." She knelt down beside him and placed her ear on his chest. Yes, there it was—a heartbeat. She shook him harder, hissing in a loud whisper. "Christophé, you have to wake up!"

Christophé swallowed.

Stacia sat back a little, relief flooding through her. He was coming around. She shook him harder and whisper-screamed into his ear. "Christophé, Scarlett needs you. Remember Scarlett? Wake up for her."

He roused and turned his head toward her, eyes still closed. She grasped tight hold of his arms. "Scarlett needs you and we have to get out of here . . . now!"

Christophé blinked and gasped. So much so that Stacia shushed him. "We must escape. Robespierre sleeps upstairs. He thinks you are dead. We have to get out of here, now."

He nodded and sat up, his hand going to his head.

Stacia took off her scarf and wrapped its length around and around his head, tying it in the back. The bleeding didn't seem so bad now. "Do you understand what I'm telling you?"

"Yes. Yes." He sat against the bottom stair blinking and looking more and more himself.

"Come then." She stood and helped him up, then led him, stumbling and half-supporting him, from the chateau. They tottered together down the empty, windswept street. Whenever Stacia heard a noise, she led them into the cover of a bush or around the corner of a house where they would cower for long minutes. Christophé leaned heavily against her, silent, determination etched on his set features.

After what seemed hours later, they inched into the street where Robespierre lived. "Come. Just a little further."

Christophé shielded his eyes as if he was looking directly into the sun.

Stacia urged him up the steps to the front door, tried it, and gave a little prayer of thanks that it wasn't locked. She pulled Christophé into the suite of rooms that belonged to Robespierre.

A tiny laugh escaped her chest as they cleared the threshold. They'd made it. And more . . . it was the last place on earth Robespierre would look for his enemy.

Scarlett's screams were evident the moment they entered Robespierre's sitting room. Christophé looked down into Stacia's face, his features intense, but the color had returned to his face and Stacia thought he had gained some of his strength back. "Take me to her."

"I wouldn't consider anything else." Stacia assured him, then leaned in and whispered. "But first I must rid the room of the other women. We must keep you a secret."

"Who is with her?"

"My mother and the midwife. She has been laboring to have the babe for a long time." Stacia motioned him to follow her. "You will be seen if you stay here. Follow me."

Stacia took him to Robespierre's bedchamber. When she started to lead him to the bed, Christophé shook his head. "I'll just sit down over here."

Stacia nodded. "I won't be long. Rest for a few minutes."

Her mother and the midwife looked up as she opened the door to the bedchamber that Scarlett, her mother, and she shared.

"Stacia." Her mother motioned her over. "I can't believe you have slept through the last hours."

Stacia shrugged, feigning nonchalance. "Let me talk to her. I want to be alone with her for a few moments."

The two other women looked at her askance. "The birth is at any minute. We cannot leave her."

"Leave me!" Scarlett shouted with more vehemence than any of them had ever heard come from her red lips. "Leave me with my sister."

The midwife frowned at her mother. Their mother's face paled as she looked back and forth between Stacia and Scarlett.

"Mother, please. I will fetch you if Scarlett needs you."

Her mother pressed her lips together, worry lines framing her mouth. "For a few moments only, Scarlett. The child is coming very soon." She threw up her hands as she left the room, saying to the midwife, "She has no idea. No earthly idea what's to come."

As soon as the door closed, Stacia rushed to Scarlett's side and grasped her quivering hand in a tight grip. "I found him. He's injured . . . a rather nasty gash on his head. But he walked here . . . for you, Scarlett. He walked here on the strength of knowing that you need him."

"Where is he?"

"In Robespierre's bedchamber. It was the only place."

Scarlett looked ready to cry and shake Stacia at the same time. "Are you insane? He could come back at any moment and find him. We have to move him!"

"Don't worry about Robespierre. I don't think he will return any time soon."

Scarlett could only stare at her as if she'd gone mad while panting through the next contraction.

"I will bring him. He is waiting to see you. But the women will come back at any moment. Oh, I have so much to tell you! Robespierre . . . he was there. In the chateau with Christophé. I think he thought he had killed him. You were right. We have to escape. All of us. And we must help Émilie get away from him!"

Scarlett reared up suddenly and curled around the mound, grasping her upraised knees. She gasped out. "Bring . . . Christophé . . . to . . . me."

Stacia ran to Robespierre's bedchamber, then grabbed and pulled on Christophé's arm. "Come. *Now.*"

❧

CHRISTOPHÉ STRUGGLED AGAINST the sudden dizziness as he stood. His head was still sore, but he at least had most of his strength back. Stacia grasped his hand and led him through the dark rooms to Scarlett's bedside.

"It's coming. The baby is coming," Scarlett gasped out as they entered the room.

"I'll go and get mother and the midwife."

"No. Wait!" Scarlett no sooner got the words out before she bore down again.

Christophé dropped to the foot of the bed. He lifted the sheet covering Scarlett's body. The babe's head was crowning. "Let it come."

She heaved up and curled over the ball of her stomach as her hand reached out for Stacia's. Christophé sensed everything within her body focusing on the push as she took a great gulp of air. Her face turned as red as her lips, her breathing suspended. He held his as well, knowing he was witnessing a miracle.

Then Scarlett groaned and pushed with all her might, Christophé came alive. He could feel the life-flow rush back through his veins and into his heart, sending it pounding so he thought it might burst through his chest. He watched, shivers slipping up and down his spine as the baby's skull ruptured through membrane and flesh and blood.

Serendipitous laughter broke from his chest as the head broke free. He stared at the closed slits of the eyes, the tiny bluish lips, the soft cheeks.

He looked up and saw Scarlett, this women who had become such a part of him, gasp. Their gazes locked as she took a giant gulp of air and then bore down against gravity and space and mass and any calculations he had ever imagined. She became everything in creation at that moment.

She became the giver of life.

He gasped, a profound shiver traveling up and down his frame, as the babe's shoulders broke free, slick and alive and moving. His throat tightened as the rest of the body slipped as silent as time into his hands.

Thy kingdom come. Thy kingdom come. He knew the words like an ancient chant and in them found peace. He looked down at the child whose veins carried the blood of Robespierre—and then saw himself and knew. Fool. Utter fool. That's what he'd been. So focused on destruction and revenge. On death. When what mattered was here.

Love. Life. Renewal.

Thy will be done.

He would not kill Robespierre. He would not seek revenge. For as he gazed into the tiny infant's face, he knew the power of life . . . sensed the sure presence of the Giver of life . . . and it changed everything.

As the infant's wails filled the room, two women, one Scarlett's mother and another he didn't know, burst through the door.

"Christophé!" Mrs. Bonham's hand rose to her throat.

He turned, her grandson cradled in his hands. *"Ma mère."* The words he hadn't been able to say for so long broke free from his heart. From now on this woman would be his mother. *"Grandmère* . . . it is a son."

Chapter Eighteen

*S*carlett fell back against the pillows. She closed her eyes briefly as a small smile played on her lips. She heard the midwife come forward to cut the cord and opened her eyes to watch her mother take up the baby and wrap him in a soft blanket. A few moments later the afterbirth was delivered, and then the midwife, quick and efficient, cleaned Scarlett and placed fresh sheets underneath her.

Stacia reached for and squeezed Scarlett's hand. "You were right, Scarlett. A boy."

Christophé clung to the bed as he made his way toward her and sat on the edge next to her.

Scarlett's heart panged in her chest as she saw how thin and tired he looked. His hair had been shaved and was now tiny bristles; there was dried blood on his head and on his cheek. "You are hurt. You need a physician."

"No." He looked over toward the babe who was being cleaned with a cloth and warm water. "I just need to rest." He looked back at Scarlett and gave her that half-grin that made her stomach flip. "He's wonderful, Scarlett. You did well."

Scarlett felt tears spring to her eyes. She looked up as her mother brought over her son and settled him into her arms. "Meet your son, my dear."

As she brought the tiny baby into her chest and felt Christophé at her side, staring down at both of them, she was filled with love for both.

"What will you name him?" Stacia studied the tiny babe, eyes wide.

"André." Scarlett traced his rounded cheek. "André Robespierre."

"Brave." Christophé leaned in to look at the child. "André means *brave.*"

Scarlett gazed into Christophé's eyes. "He will need to be brave in such a world as we now live. It is a good name."

Christophé reached toward her, his fingers making a light caress against her cheek. "Yes."

Scarlett looked to her mother. "Please look at Christophé's wound." She turned back toward the man she loved—the man for whom she had many questions. But they could wait. His wound couldn't.

The midwife came around the bed, felt Christophé's forehead, and studied the wound on his scalp. "The cut is deep. We'd best fetch the surgeon to stitch it up."

Christophé roused, shook his head. "No. Find Jasper. The apothecary on Rue de Laine. He will know what to do."

The midwife angled a look at him. "Jasper Montpelier? I know of him. I have bought remedies of his over the years." She tapped her fingers against her folded arms. "He was arrested some time ago, I think. But if I recall, they let him go." She looked at Scarlett's mother. "I will show you where it is, but then I must leave. I have another patient to see today."

Christophé's head had jerked toward the midwife. "Was Jasper imprisoned?"

"For a short time, I believe. But I have been to his shop since and he seemed the same as he has always been. Irascible creature." The midwife looked over at her mother. "Come along, Mrs. Bonham. It's not far."

Her mother fluttered her hands in the air and sputtered. "I can't leave Scarlett. What if something happens? I need to be here with her. You never know what might go wrong with a newborn. I need to watch over them."

Stacia spoke up. "Mother, go. I will take care of Scarlett and the baby."

When she still looked torn, Stacia continued. "I will better deal with Robespierre if he comes home. We must keep Christophé hidden from the man. No one must know he is still alive and in Paris. Do you understand, Mother? You must not speak of him. Robespierre cannot know that we have ever met him."

Their mother looked ready to burst into tears. "You are keeping secrets from me, and I can't bear it. Why is Christophé's past so mysterious? Does he know your uncle, Scarlett? Scarlett?"

Scarlett looked long at her mother and decided she must tell her. "Christophé is Christophé St. Laurent. A count's son. He was hiding in Carcassonne."

Immediate understanding showed on her mother's features. "The castle."

"Yes. He has been there for a long time." Scarlett's voice lowered. "I don't know why he returned to Paris." She looked at Christophé, but he remained silent.

"Well, it sounds as if he has trouble enough on his own, dear. Don't expect men to tell you everything. They never do."

Scarlett exchanged a frustrated glance with Stacia.

Determination filled her with renewed strength. "Mother, please. Go and fetch his friend, Jasper. Tell him what has occurred. If Christophé is asking for him, I'm sure he can be trusted. If Robespierre returns we can say that Jasper is my physician."

Scarlett scooted to one side of the bed, André in her arms. She touched Christophé's arm. "Lie down here and rest until they return." Turning to Stacia she said, "Get him some water, please. And a cloth. At least we can wash some of that blood away."

Scarlett settled back into the pillows and closed her eyes, exhaustion overwhelming her. She could only hope that when she awoke, Christophé would tell her why he ran from Carcassonne . . .

And if he was running away from her.

⁓

RAP. RAP. RAP. Jasper heard the sound somewhere in his consciousness, but couldn't place it. He bent back over his experiment. Could this chemical really dissipate into a vapor that was more effective when inhaled? What if, when compounded, it was injected? That would make it penetrate the systems more quickly and effectively . . .

Rap. Rap. Rap. The sound came louder now. Stroking his chin, he stood and cocked his head. Ah. The door. Someone was knocking.

He hated to leave his experiment at half mast, but he had visitors at this hour so rarely he reasoned it must be of some import. Wiping his hands on the long, stiff apron he wore to protect his clothing he pushed his spectacles up upon his balding brow and headed to the door.

Rap. Rap. Rap! Whoever it was, they were of a persistent nature. He pulled the heavy door open and stared at the two women on his threshold. One was older, impatience pinching her face. The other woman was, well, rounded in a way that he recognized in some distant part of his brain as pleasing. And her face . . . well . . . he couldn't quite explain the impact of that finely sculpted face. So he stood there, dumbfounded.

Clearly they were waiting for him to speak. "Yes?" It was the best he could manage.

The sour woman exchanged glances with the other woman. "That's him." With that, she turned to go. Jasper watched her retreating back, confusion mounting, then turned toward the pleasant one.

"Yes?"

The woman looked as confused as he. Like she'd been led to his door on a lark and now didn't know what to do about it.

"Would you like to come in?" Jasper ventured, trying to help them both. "My shop is closed for the night, but if there is something you need? Something I can help you with?"

The woman rushed inside nodding, a gushing of sentences coming from her mouth. "Oh, sir. Are you Jasper? I don't recall your surname, so I do apologize. Christophé . . . he just sent me here and well, I-I'm not very sure what I'm here for except for that nasty gash on his head." She was looking about the place as she spoke and then spun toward him, voicing her perplexity. "You have no wife?"

Jasper didn't know quite what to make of the tumble of words, or the question. Was something wrong with his shop? Normally, he wouldn't care what someone thought of it. But this time . . .

He didn't want her to leave.

That had never happened to him before with a woman, but he turned his thoughts from that to the one thing he recognized as sense. "Christophé, did you say? Do you know him?"

"Oh, my, yes. Well, we've met on occasion. I don't know much about him, not very much at all really, but he is . . . well . . . courting my eldest daughter, Scarlett, and she just had a baby. Oh, that doesn't make any sense does it? Scarlett is a widow. We have recently come to Paris from Carcassonne. But Scarlett was here before, a few years ago, and married. He died. Well, of course he did, as I said Scarlett is a widow. And she met this man who claims to be a scientist named Christophé. Charming man—showed me the stars through his telescope. May the Lord be merciful! I've never seen anything like it before in my life! Well—"

Jasper interrupted her tirade. "Is Christophé here? In Paris?"

"Well, yes, of course he is in town. He is in Robespierre's bedchamber! Which is very inconvenient as the man might come back at any moment and discover him." She smiled up at him, satisfied. Clearly she felt she had explained everything.

Jasper choked back a chuckle even though her story sent shafts of panic through him. She was truly deranged and just so . . . lovely. He found it hard to concentrate on anything but the idea of taking down her silver threaded brown hair and seeing what it would look like framing such rosy, rounded cheeks.

"Madame, please, follow me and let me provide what meager refreshment I can." He led her through the shop and then up the stairs to his private apartments. She followed him into the salon, while he glanced about the room. Now that he'd invited her, did he even have anything to offer? When was the last time he went shopping? He honestly couldn't remember. Brushing those thoughts aside, he poured her a cup of cold tea and pressed it into her hand, directing her to an over-stuffed chair he had found from a refuse heap many years ago.

He blinked, as though seeing it for the first time. The piece looked like it belonged back there. He turned to hide his embarrassment, and after a moment of searching he found another cup. Pouring his own tea he sat across from her, brows drawn together so tight he could feel the tension line in between. "Let's start at the beginning, shall we? Your name, madame?"

"Oh, you mustn't call me madame, sir. Haven't you heard? We are all called citizens now."

Jasper brushed away her concern. "I am too old and stubborn to change my form of address to a lady. So, your name?"

"Suzanne Bonham. From Carcassonne, as I said. I am here in Paris to help my youngest daughter, Stacia. She's quite beautiful and so smart, and it is our hope she will find a husband." She leaned in and spoke in a conspirator's voice, shaking her head. "I can tell you, it is not going very well. Why, with this Révolution taking up everyone's attention and things so . . . so unrecognizable. What are we poor women to do? We did bake bread for a time, keeping to ourselves, supporting ourselves, but then Robespierre wrote that he couldn't send more flour, and what were we to do but come to Paris and make Stacia a match? Scarlett said it was the only thing left to us."

Jasper started. "Did you say Robespierre?"

"Yes, yes. Scarlett's uncle by marriage. She is a widow now, as I said, but Robespierre is the only male relative we have left and with the flour gone, we really had no choice."

"And Christophé? Did he come with you?"

"Oh, good heavens, no. Christophé had disappeared from Carcassonne, breaking my poor daughter's heart, though she didn't show it, but *I* knew. I had little hope of ever seeing him again." She took a quick sip of her tea and then wrinkled her nose and sat the cup back on the tea tray. "He was living in that ancient castle. Why, it's a wonder the whole monstrous roof didn't cave in on his head. Scarlett said he was doing—" she lowered her voice to a whisper—"some sort of experiments there. I don't know what that is about, but after we arrived in Paris, Stacia somehow found Christophé." She clasped her hands in her lap, the trail of words coming to an abrupt end, and then, "He is hurt. Badly hurt. He sent me here to you. To *Jasper*."

He found to his amazement that he understood this lovely lady's tale as well as any intricately hidden apothecary recipe. "So Christophé is in Robespierre's house?"

"Yes. We said we should send for the physician, that nasty gash in his head, you know, and he said 'no' we should find Jasper. The midwife—" she motioned to the door and the disappeared woman—"brought me here. You . . ." Her eyes widened, and he saw sudden horror in their depths. "You are Jasper, are you not?"

Jasper couldn't help his smile. "Yes. I am Jasper. Please, madame. Allow me to gather up some tonics, bandages, and such, and then we will be on our way."

Suzanne become quiet, looked down at her clasped hands in her lap. As Jasper went to find what he needed, he heard her murmur, "Such a day, it's been such a day."

Jasper turned from his steps toward his laboratory. "Is Robespierre there? In the house?"

Suzanne shook her head, a ringlet bouncing against her full bosom. "Oh, goodness no. But if we happen upon him, we're to say that you are Scarlett's physician. As she has just had the babe, you see. André, she's named him. Christophé says that means he is brave. And, well, no one would question a doctor in the house at such a time."

So the women were hiding Christophé. Jasper heartily hoped he did not meet up with the man called Robespierre. Robespierre might recognize him from the interrogation he'd undergone after Christophé had escaped. It was still hard to believe he'd convinced them that he had no idea a man was in his spare bedchamber. The busted window frame, the one Christophé must have broken when he fled, had helped, making it look like someone had broken into Jasper's house to hide. Maybe there was a God after all.

His hand paused as he reached for the medicines. Thoughts buzzed through his mind, and he allowed a small smile. Better pack some poison with the medicines for his friend.

One never knew what opportunities might present themselves.

Chapter Nineteen

*S*uzanne told Jasper everything he could ever want to know about the three Bonham women as they walked back to Robespierre's lodgings. He could scarcely believe Christophé was being hidden beneath his enemy's nose. It didn't sit well, and there was nothing he wanted more than to spirit the young man away to the safety of his own home.

The only thing Suzanne hadn't mentioned was her own marital state, except that she'd said Robespierre was their only living male relative, so she must be without a husband. He kept reassuring himself with that thought.

Turning his head toward her, he studied her profile. She was just middle-aged, probably ten or so years younger than his fifty-five years. She walked at a brisk pace without growing very winded. Heaven knew she could talk and walk at the same time—both at a breakneck speed. He was surprised—no, shocked—that the constant chatter didn't grate on his nerves. He'd always prized his solitude and quiet.

"My dear," he spoke into a brief lull. "Have you been a widow long?" He wouldn't ordinarily ask a new acquaintance such a personal question, but who knew when, if ever, he would see her again.

"Oh, yes. Let's see . . ." She concentrated, counting on her pudgy fingers. "Just under nine years. That's right. Almost nine years ago my dear Frederic died in an accident."

"What kind of accident? If you don't mind that I ask."

"Oh, no. Not at all. Frederic was a jack-of-all-trades. We never really knew what kind of job he would take next. They always ran out, you know. When the things were built, or the field was—" she waved her hand, apparently looking for the right word—"harvested, or whatever he was currently about. He always worked himself out of jobs. One job, his last, was to help repair the roof for Cathédrale Saint-Nazaire-et-Saint-Celse, a very grand cathedral in Carcassonne. It was a long job, should have taken months. But one day—" she looked over at Jasper and shook her head, her voice filled with dramatic sadness—"he slipped off the roof at an enormous height. They said he died immediately."

Jasper touched her arm. "And you with two young girls. What did you do?"

Suzanne compressed her lips together and then let out a little laugh. "I suppose we became jacks-of-all-trades too." She laughed again. "I've never really looked back on it to think about what we did, but we had many odd jobs, from taking in sewing and laundry to selling garden vegetables. Why, Scarlett even learned masonry and was helping to build garden terraces and walkways for a time." She smiled over at Jasper. "God has taken care of us."

"Then Scarlett married?"

Suzanne looked up into Jasper's eyes. "Daniel Robespierre. A very grand young man, or so Scarlett tells me. I never had the chance to meet him. Scarlett sent us an allowance then and Stacia and I scraped by."

"Daniel Robespierre . . ." Jasper mused. "I believe I have heard of him." He didn't tell Suzanne that the man had been famous as a young hothead, stirring up debates and tempers with a natural orator's command of his audience. "How did Daniel die?"

Suzanne grew quiet. She looked up and pointed. "Look. We're nearly there. Do you see the house?"

Jasper knew the place. It was near the new headquarters for many members of the Convention. He personally tried to stay as far away from politics as he could, but now . . . in this new world where everything was turning upside down and inside out, no one could escape its vortex.

Jasper thought he had pressed the dear lady enough for now and let his next question fall away. "Let us hope Robespierre is not at home," he said instead. He didn't tell Suzanne how truly worried he was if they happened to come face-to-face. Not only had they met once before, he recognized that Robespierre may have heard of him as he was something of a renowned person in the city for the healing arts. His potions, the concoctions that he studied and perfected over the years, the herbal remedies for anything from a sneeze to the plague, had made him something of a magician in the city of Paris.

He could only hope his face was not as recognizable as his potions.

⚮

ROBESPIERRE WOKE TO an empty feeling. Like a giant, gaping gulf that was black and unfathomably deep. He heard cries coming from somewhere and then realized the source, this blackness. His mind, not quite fully awake, replayed the death signatures he had signed. In the light of day, in the righteous strength of the Révolution, he hadn't batted an eye. But at night, he saw them. Saw their hands grasping up at him from this hellish hole, saw their heads on the point of a spike, demanding justice. Heard them cry out for the freedom he claimed he stood for.

He turned on the unfamiliar bed and, for a moment, felt the void open wider, deeper.

He was six and waking in a bedchamber with his siblings. There was always that single, shattering moment where everything went from dreamy sleepiness to terrible truth. Where a new day to run the hills in his home in Arras was snatched away with smothering despair, the sudden sitting up in bed and clutching the covers to his thin, six-year-old chest as the knowledge that their father had left them struck him.

His mother too. Dead in the childbirth bed birthing his youngest sister. After that, his father had packed the four of them off to his maternal grandfather's house and simply . . . disappeared. The aunts and his grandfather had raised them.

Both parents lost to a bloody birth.

Blood. Red blood. Thick and never-ending . . . *blood.*

And now it spilled all over France.

Would it haunt him forever?

He couldn't go back to the Duplays' until Scarlett had birthed the babe. He knew she was close, he could tell she was hiding the signs, although why he couldn't fathom. All he knew was that he would stay here until he learned that the deed was done. He closed his eyes and allowed the memories to wash over him.

He'd taught himself to read and write, and by the age of eight was sent to the college of Arras. He'd thrived there, holding fast to the accolades from his teachers for his ability to read fluently, grasp the higher levels of mathematics, and memorize any fact they gave him. And he'd begun to notice that he had a strong voice, a voice filled with conviction, when he spoke. His grandfather and father had been lawyers, and it appeared he had inherited their gift for public speaking and debate.

The bishop of Arras noticed his early brilliance. Maximilien could still remember his heart rising to his throat when he learned of the bishop's recommendation to the school that was every scholar's dream: the Lycée Louis-le-Grand in Paris. There he studied the Roman Republic and their democratic ideals. The rhetoric of Cicero, Cato, and Rousseau. The brilliance of Voltaire. They said man could be free. *All* men. Not just the nobility that kept him firmly from reaching his potential. They said he could be everything he believed he could be.

It was then that he'd decided in some deep, semiconscious part of himself, that *he* would be the champion of such freedom. But he was afraid. Many times, when in a social context where he knew he didn't belong, he would have to command his legs to stop shaking and his palms to cease their sweating. He would remind himself of his worth . . . no matter the cost.

He clenched his eyes shut, remembering the day he had been appointed the one out of over five hundred pupils to give the address of welcome to the king on behalf of the entire college. Louis XVI and his bride, none other than the famed Marie Antoinette, were rumored to be stopping by the college on their way to Versailles.

He remembered it like it was yesterday. The crisp air that left fogs of breath close to their faces. The falling rain. And he, with his heart bursting so hard it felt outside his rib cage. They waited for hours in that rain, watching for the swaying black roof of a carriage, longing to hear the mud spattering against the wheels as it came, headlong and full of wonder, toward their huddled little group.

The king was coming. The king was coming to them! Maximilien clutched his paper, where he'd painstakingly written and rewritten out his speech, against his sodden pants. The king was coming to hear him. He prayed it was so with everything in him.

Four hours and twenty minutes later, the carriage with its outriders, wearing uniforms in royal blue and gold, the colors of the king, finally rounded the turn in the road and came into view. The coach itself was so grand and gleaming black as it swayed back and forth, growing bigger as it came up the drive that Maximilien accidentally wadded the speech in his fist against his leg as he watched their progress. Was it really *him*?

When Maximilien saw the emblazoned coat of arms of the king of France, he nearly choked. Looking behind him, he saw awe on the faces of the other students reminding him of his place of honor and importance. He locked his heels together, straightened his shoulders, and took a deep breath. Excitement spread throughout his body as the wheels, rimmed with gold, turned and turned and then came to a stop directly in front of him, splashing mud and water onto his spit-shined, best-day shoes.

He waited for a long minute for the door to open so that he could begin. The paper with his speech was a shaking, crumpled, sweaty ball in his hand, but he didn't need it. He had memorized every line of that speech days before. He was the chosen one. He was to give a speech to the king.

The King of France.

But it wasn't to be. King Louis only waved from behind the blurry glass and then sunk back into the plush cushions that were his life. Maximilien heard laughter coming from within the coach. Confused, his body strained forward, trying to see past the glass that separated him from royalty. It hadn't yet occurred to him that they might not open the door. He stood poised, turned out in his best coat and standing in the rain . . . waiting for hours for this honor.

Finally his professor nodded for him to begin.

Was he really to start? To deliver the address to nothing but a prettily painted wood box on wheels?

Tears sprang to his eyes, a further embarrassment. He could feel the impatience of the king's men, hear the stomping of the horses' hooves in the mud-clogged street, and saw the glare of the coachman. It finally dawned on him.

They were all waiting for him to begin.

The rain dripped down his neck, and he felt the cold for the first time as he stuttered out the words. He heard a laugh or two, quickly smothered. Then something took hold of him. Of his gut and his soul. He near shouted the rest of the speech, hoping with everything within him that this lethargic king would hear him. That he would be honored by the words, yes, but even more by the cadence and conviction of this young man's voice.

Nothing. There was nothing.

The king condescended to sit up and wave . . . a brief gesture that wasn't worth remembering. That was, in fact, more of a slap. A kick. A turned head, as if Maximilien was no more than a fly to be shooed away.

And then they were gone.

All the grandeur of court rode away on wind and melted before his eyes in the mist of the drizzle and the tears that he couldn't manage to hold back.

And so the message his parents' abandonment gave him was confirmed, by no less than the king himself.

Maximilien meant little. He was small. He was nothing. No one.

His heart turned hard that day. Hard and glowing with purpose. He *would* mean something to the world. If it took his last breath to accomplish it . . . he would mean something strong and powerful enough to bring them all to their knees.

And now, he did.

Robespierre blinked, letting his eyes open and become accustomed to the dim light in the room. His had been *the* voice in this mighty Révolution. The king's own neck severed at his gentle suggestion. He smiled and inhaled the victory of it, remembering the stricken queen's face, how she, too, mounted the bloody steps.

Oh, revenge, how sweet your taste.

Oh, recompense, how you fill me with joy.

Oh, redemption and the mighty hand of righteousness, how fitting you are upon my shoulders.

Robespierre smiled.

Freedom has such a beautiful name, he mused.

And its name is Death.

He rose in the bed of his enemy and looked at his hands. They were coated with the blood of innocents. He held them up to his face and stared, breathing hard through his mouth.

No!

Yes!

But their blood cried out to him, demanding to be heard. *"No!"*

He rose from the bed, still staring at his hands. "I will not hear you! Do you hear me? I will not listen!" He wiped his hands against his breeches as he took a step toward the low-burning fire he had lit hours ago when he plotted the demise of the final St. Laurent.

Well . . . not quite the final . . .

Émilie's sweet, innocent face rose up into his mind's eye. "Pure. The only thing pure." He lifted his face to heaven. "I spared her for you."

There was no peace in that prayer. Turning from the fireplace, he looked toward the floor where his enemy lay conquered.

No one was there.

Chapter Twenty

Thin, wailing cries woke her. Her head was full of dreams, which faded away as the cries grew loud in her ear. What were they? Who made them? Finally, she remembered, and then reared up. André. He'd been born. He was here, right here next to her.

She winced at the slow, creeping ache in her pelvis and turned with care toward the small, moving bundle. "*Mon cher. Mon cher,*" she crooned, curling toward the waving arms and increasingly unhappy cry. "What? What is it?"

She drew him close against her body, her lips brushing his rounded scalp where dark hair grew in tufts. "Come. Come to me." Her hand reached for his long, slender fingers, and he grasped quick hold. He turned his head toward her, his eyes the slits of a newborn, rooting with his rosebud mouth.

She smiled, wonder resonating through her chest like an expanding light, as his arms and legs waved, his wail growing truly distressed now. "Are you hungry? Is that it?" She worried so that she didn't know, would never really know, all he needed. "Here."

She unbuttoned her gown and offered him his breakfast. Had Daniel been alive she might have had a wet nurse, but she was glad not to. She wanted to be the only one who was her son's whole world, at least for this little while.

A movement from across the room made her turn. Christophé was sitting in the room's only chair against a far wall.

"You shouldn't be in here. Robespierre could be home by now. He will want to see the baby."

Christophé stood, wobbled a little, and then straightened. "Never felt so weak and dizzy before. Not accustomed to it. Forgive me." He walked toward the bed. "I won't stay long. They have put me in a maid's room, but I couldn't sleep. I had to see you."

Scarlett looked down at her son, who had drifted back into a contented sleep. She paused, working up the courage to ask the only question she needed answered. "Why did you leave? I thought . . . I thought you cared about me." She couldn't look at him, so instead moved André to her side, turned away, and fixed her gown.

"Of course I do." His voice was strong and sure behind her.

"Then why?" There was anger and hurt in her voice, but she couldn't help it. "And without even a word. You just . . ." She turned back toward him, not caring that he would see her tears.

"It won't make sense to you."

"Tell me."

He walked over and sat on the bed next to her. She could see the shadow of his beard and more—the shadows in his eyes. Finally he spoke. "Robespierre."

"My uncle?"

"My enemy."

Scarlett thought through his words. Christophé was an aristocrat. The Count of St. Laurent, as there was none of his family left living. Was Robespierre responsible? She stared into his haunted eyes and knew. Of course he was. Why hadn't she put it together before?

"How did you know?"

"That Robespierre was your uncle?"

"Yes."

"I found a letter in your house. Something about flour. That he could send no more."

"Oh . . ."

That night after dinner when he had disappeared. He'd found the letter and the name of his adversary scratched at the bottom. She felt stupid. She should have guessed.

With careful moves so as not to wake her son, she scooted into the center of the bed and gently touched Christophé's head, her fingers feeling the bristling shortness of his hair.

"You cut your hair."

"I needed a disguise for Paris."

"What were you planning to do?"

"Kill him." He said it quickly—so quickly that it took a moment for her to feel the shock of the words.

"That's why you came to this house that day? You were going to kill him?"

"Yes."

"I saw you and at first I wasn't sure it *was* you. But then I knew. I tried to distract them."

Christophé grasped hold of her hand. "You did more than distract them. You saved my life."

"You can't still mean to go through with it."

Christophé took a long, deep breath. "No, not now." He leaned close to her and brought her fingers to his lips, brushing them with a kiss. "He took my family. I thought he took you away from me too. How could I love you knowing who you were? But God has shown me the truth. I won't forget again."

All Scarlett's misgivings dissolved. "There is one more thing God has given you."

Christophé kissed her hand again. "What is that?"

"The day you came to this house for Robespierre, do you remember seeing a servant girl with us?" She fought to keep the emotion from her tone, but failed.

He blinked, such pain in the depths of those stunning blue eyes. "Yes, I remember her."

"When I asked her name, she wouldn't answer. At the market, just a little while after I saw you that day, I asked her if her name was St. Laurent. *Émilie* St. Laurent."

"Don't." Christophé slid from the bed and stood beside it, balling his hands into fists. "Don't do this, Scarlett." His face was tight and drawn, turning pale. "It is impossible. She is dead. She was guillotined. I . . . I witnessed it."

"No." Scarlett shook her head. "When I asked her name, I saw terror in her face. It was her. Your sister. But . . ." She looked down at the bed. "She turned and ran away."

"I *saw* her. I saw her mount the steps. I saw them strap her to the board and slide it beneath the blade. I heard it. The blade. I *heard* it." He shook one of his fists. "I saw her head in the basket."

Scarlett pounded her fist on the bed, forgetting to care that she might wake the babe. "What if it wasn't her? What if it was someone else?"

"I can't believe it unless I see her face."

How she wanted him to believe! To take hold of this hope. *Please, God, let him hear me.* "I told you, she ran away. I don't know where she could have gone. But, believe me. *Believe* me when I tell you."

He turned to stare at her, and Scarlett put all her heart into her words.

"Your sister is alive."

🙞

A SOB ROSE to Christophé's throat, his hand reached into the air as his body collapsed into a chair. Scarlett's words slammed into him like a second blow to the head.

He was dizzy, not sure of the emotions flooding him. A sound escaped his throat—a sound unlike any he'd ever made before.

Scarlett climbed from the bed and came to sit next to him on the wide seat of the chair. He leaned his face into her neck, felt her arms encircle him, and then he heard himself say her name over and over.

Was that haunted, pleading voice really his? It was. And it seemed his heart was breaking. "I can't bear it . . . if I believe it and it's not."

Scarlett's arms tightened around him. "Trust me."

Christophé looked up into Scarlett's sure face. "We have to find her. Before he does." He was starting to hope.

"When you are recovered. We will find her then."

"I can't wait. What if Robespierre finds her first?"

Scarlett shook her head. "She can't have gone far. Think. Where would she go?"

He looked at the floor, seeing the thick carpet in swirls of reds and blues. Seeing the colors. "I told her to find the red door. I told her to go to Jasper's." He looked up at her. "But she didn't find it." The image of the door rose in his mind. It was a faded red, maybe hard to see in the dark. Maybe she had mistaken it for another color. Or . . . Thoughts exploded in his mind. What if to Émilie red looked another hue?

He felt a heaving take place in his chest as he gave way to hope. "I think I might know."

"Where? I'll ask Mother and Stacia to look."

Christophé stared at Scarlett with fire in his eyes. "No. It's too dangerous." He stood and paced the room, then turned back to her, feeling, for the first time in a very long time, the fire of a new dawn burning in his chest. "Jasper. We have to find Jasper."

Chapter Twenty-One

No sooner had he uttered the plea than the door to the room burst open.

Christophé spun, fearing the worst. Instead, he found himself facing Scarlett's mother and a sprightly looking, white-haired gentleman.

"How is the baby?" Suzanne came around the bed to gather the sleeping infant into her arms. "Oh, I missed you," she crooned to him.

Christophé moved forward, legs a little unsteady. *Thank You, God. Thank You.* "Jasper."

Jasper quickly closed the gap, not saying anything, just holding him up and assessing his person. Finally the older man spoke. "What happened?"

Christophé shook his head. The women were in the room. "Not here. Come." Christophé led his good friend to the sitting room, praying Robespierre would not come back and find them there. Sinking down onto a chair, he rubbed his prickly head and then winced in pain, remembering the injury.

"Robespierre. He came to the chateau. I didn't know he was there. I . . . wasn't thinking." Frustration leaked out in every word.

"He was waiting in my bedchamber. Tried to kill me. Nearly succeeded."

"Why didn't you come to me? If he thought you were back in Paris, you knew the first place he would look would be the chateau."

"I couldn't put you in danger again." Before Jasper could argue with him, Christophé leaned forward, letting elation fill his voice. "Émilie might be alive."

Jasper sat down on another chair as if his legs had been swept out from beneath him. "It cannot be. We saw her—the guillotine."

"She was here. In this house. She was . . . his servant." The last word dripped with bitterness. He looked up into Jasper's shocked face. "I am afraid to fathom his reasons for keeping her alive and in his household." Tears rose up to blind him. "But I am so *glad*."

"Where is she?"

Christophé gritted his teeth against the impotence creeping through him. "I don't know. Scarlett says she ran away from Les Halles. No one knows where she has gone."

"Alone in the city? That doesn't bode well."

"We have to find her."

Jasper took his spectacles off and polished them with a shirt tail as he always did when in deep thought. "Extraordinary. Émilie alive. And you, monsieur, are not in good enough shape to go looking for her." He paused. "Why did you come back to Paris?"

"To finish the job."

"You should have contacted me."

"I couldn't risk endangering you. From what I've heard, you barely escaped prison and the guillotine the last time I stayed with you. And anyway, this was something I had to do on my own."

Jasper softly cursed. "You were safe in Carcassonne. Why would you risk your neck? You can't stop him, you know."

"I thought I might. And anyway, I'm glad I came back. I would have never known Émilie is alive if I hadn't."

Jasper leaned back in his chair. "Yes, well, there is that, I suppose. We have to get you away from here and soon."

"Yes. And then we must flee France."

"Where will you go?"

"To London. I have friends there. Friends from school. Scientists that I've written to. They will welcome me." Christophé looked at Jasper, letting all the fear that belied those words reach his eyes.

"The Republic dissolved the Académie des Sciences, you know."

Christophé made a harsh sound in his throat. Of course. "This new government has no place for ideals, does it? They will murder anything in their way."

Jasper's jowls wobbled as he shook his head. "Freedom, they call it." He stood, came forward, and motioned for Christophé to sit up. "Let's have a look at that gash."

"You're a physician now?" Christophé complied as best he could.

"The best one you are going to get."

After a few moments of probing Jasper stood back, his bushy, white eyebrows raised. "That must have hurt. It will need to be stitched up. What did he hit you with?"

"Don't really know. Just a blow and then nothing."

"Tell me."

"He was there, in my bedchamber when I came in. My mind was distracted, so I wasn't being careful. He must have been standing just behind the door as I didn't have time to turn. I heard him though. I knew it was him. He clubbed me with something, something hard and metal. I heard the crack, felt a flash of pain and then just . . . fell to the floor. Next thing I remember is being awakened by Stacia, Scarlett's sister. Somehow she dragged me out of the room, down the stairs, and to the back door. She was shaking me and commanding I wake up." He grinned. "And I did. Had little choice in the face of her determination, I suppose. We walked here with her half carrying me all the way."

"Stacia." Jasper's eyes lit up. "The youngest. Suzanne told me about her daughters." He laughed, his face looking younger somehow. "They are good women, are they not?"

Christophé stared at Jasper in astonishment. He'd never seen such a response from the man in any way that wasn't connected to experiments and concoctions. He half-grinned at his old friend. "Why don't you tell me about it while you do your magic on this skull of mine."

Jasper turned a little red, covering his embarrassment by stooping to pick up his bag. He pretended to be busy pulling out various vials and packets of dried herbs. He finally turned toward Christophé, saw his knowing look, and shrugged. "You've caught me, I suppose."

"Do you mean *she* has caught you?"

Jasper threaded the long needle and held it out for Christophé to see. "Be careful, son. I have painful instruments in hand."

Christophé couldn't help the happiness that flooded him. He had always wondered if Jasper was ever lonely. He leaned his head down and waited while Jasper cleaned the wound and then mixed up a poultice. Jasper eased a little of the mixture into the gash in his head and then took up the glinting needle. "Do you love Scarlett, then? Suzanne thought as much until you disappeared." He asked just as the first prick entered the tender, swollen flesh.

"Mon Dieu. Yes. I love her." He rasped out against the pain.

Jasper chuckled. "It's painful? Love?"

"Have you never been in love?" The needle stabbed again, causing a hissing between Christophé's teeth.

"Of course. When I was a young man like you I loved."

"Why did you never marry?"

Jasper took another stab, seeming to enjoy it. "The two women my heart chose—one when I was a young man and the other in my middle years—didn't care to live with the other side of me. I long ago accepted the fact that I could never give a woman what she would need. I am too . . . occupied of thought. Too inside myself."

"I fear I am the same. What do you think it is that women need?" Christophé really wanted to hear the answer.

Jasper shrugged. "I suppose a husband's presence. Not every minute, I am sure. They seem to enjoy flocking together, but often enough that they are not lonely."

"And you couldn't give that, could you?"

"Could you?"

The question loomed as Jasper bit off the thread and tied it. He stood back. "You will heal. You just need a few days' rest."

"I can't stay here. It's too dangerous, and I must find Émilie."

"You mentioned staying in the maid's room. Would Robespierre enter that bedchamber?"

"The women have convinced me that he would not. He is hardly here at all, always about his evil work. They want to hide me until I have recovered."

"Then stay for a few days. Just until you regain some strength. He would never think to look for you in his own house." Jasper chuckled, poured Christophé a glass of water from a pitcher on the side table and pressed it on him. "I think you can trust these women. They want to take care of you."

Christophé leaned back in the chair and took a long, slow sip, letting his tired eyelids fall shut. "You asked what I could give a wife."

Jasper stood in front of him, the look of a loving father on his face.

"Before all this—" Christophé waved his hand around— "I couldn't have given very much. But now . . . I didn't know. The babe. He slipped out into my hands. He opened his eyes and the first living thing he saw was my face; the first sound, my voice. What is science and discovery against that flash of heaven in a newborn's wide eyes?" Christophé grasped his friend's old, thin hand. "I thought I would hate him, this child. Instead I found a miracle pouring from my heart to his."

"A son," Jasper said softly, looking at Christophé, wonder twinkling in those old eyes. "You are as close as I ever got."

Christophé grasped tight to Jasper's hand. "I want Scarlett's son to be my son. I want her as my wife. But before any of that—" he looked into Jasper's eyes—"I have to find my sister."

"You'll not do anything for a few days."

"I'm weak, yes. But how can I wait when I know she is out there all alone?"

"You won't be any good to her if you catch infection. Rest, good food, and more rest." Jasper looked as stern as any father. "I will look for Émilie."

He was too weary to argue. For now. "Three days. Then, if you haven't found her, I will start my search."

❦

AFTER HELPING CHRISTOPHÉ back to the bedchamber and saying good-bye to the women, Jasper stopped outside the door, listening for movement in the household. All was silence, and he found himself inordinately hungry and needing a quiet place to think. He should go home, but instead made his way to the kitchen in the rear of the house. Someone was sure to be about in the kitchen and, as the physician, it would not be amiss to feed him before they sent him on his way.

The smells of roasting meat led him to an open doorway. There was a long table in the center of the room for preparing the food, pots and pans were scattered about and hung on the wall around an enormous fireplace. The place was hot, making his cheeks feel flushed, but the smells were heavenly.

A woman sat at the table across from someone, talking to him. Her eyes were downcast and she had a cast of nervousness on her face.

The man's back was to him. Jasper started. Robespierre? Heart pounding, Jasper turned, as if he were looking for someone and hadn't found him, and started to walk back out the door.

"The quail is delightful." The silky voice came from the man in the shadows.

Jasper's heart began to beat double. *Fool! You should have escaped while you could.* Now what would happen to his promise to Christophé to begin searching for Émilie immediately?

Turning, he allowed his gaze to lock with the man's. "Is it? I am rather hungry." Best to act unafraid. The leaders of the Republic could smell the taint of fear like bloodhounds on a hunt. Jasper walked over to the table and bowed a little. "Are you visiting someone here?" Though smooth as new silk, there was something dark and threatening in Robespierre's voice.

"In a way. I am a physician. I was delivering a baby."

Robespierre's head jerked up. "Scarlett's baby?"

"Yes. She delivered about an hour ago." It was a lie, the baby was several hours old, but Robespierre would not know that.

"Is it . . . are they well?"

"Oh, yes. A fine babe. A boy." Jasper smiled, warming to the subject. "Are you related to her?"

Robespierre's head did a little odd jerk that resembled a nod. He motioned Jasper to sit across from him.

The woman rose and backed away. "I'll fetch him a plate," she said to Robespierre. He smiled at her, more of a stretching of his lips across his teeth than a real smile. "Scarlett is my niece by marriage. Recently arrived from Carcassonne."

"So you are a great-uncle? My congratulations."

Robespierre waved the sentiment away. "Do I know you? You look familiar."

Jasper bowed his head toward the man and shrugged. "Jasper Montpelier, and you sir, must be Maximilien Robespierre. It is an honor." He thought it better not to mention the circumstances of their last meeting.

Robespierre didn't look as if he quite believed him. The plate came, and then Robespierre leaned forward. "Do you have your papers on you? I know I recognize you from somewhere."

Jasper debated whether he should pull out his citizenship paper—revealing his address and how many times he had attended various meetings for the cause, which were exceedingly few—or pretend he'd left it at home. The price for not carrying the paper at all times could be heavy indeed. He might be immediately arrested and questioned. Might even be imprisoned. That thought had the blood draining from his face. He looked down and dug into his waistcoat pocket. "Should have it here somewhere. Always carry it with me."

He pulled the folded paper out and passed it across the table with a benign smile. Robespierre wiped his mouth and hands with a cloth, reached for the paper, and unfolded it.

Jasper watched the man's face as he read it. Robespierre looked up. "Who lives with you?"

"No one. My father passed on several years ago and I now live there alone."

"Wait." Robespierre paused. "I remember now. You are the apothecary. You are no physician."

Jasper kept his focus on his food, and his tone casual. If Robespierre only remembered him as an apothecary, he just might get through this unscathed. It was hard to imagine the many inquisitions the man had been involved in. He might not remember. "The midwife sent for me. Your niece suffered some excessive bleeding. I have herbal remedies for such things, and I often assist midwives and physicians. Many people think of me as both an apothecary and a physician."

Robespierre looked unconvinced, but picked up his fork and began eating again.

Jasper took an inward sigh of relief, digging into his own plate of food.

The meal progressed in silence until Robespierre stood, threw his cloth on the table, and nodded once to Jasper. "I shall leave you now, citizen. I have a new nephew to meet." He walked a few steps and then turned and looked back at Jasper. "I hope Scarlett remembers a physician assisting her." His lips stretched across his teeth again, the smile making him look even more ghoulish. "I know where you live."

Chapter Twenty-Two

Jasper fled, cursing his hungry stomach for getting him into such trouble. What had he been thinking to stay at that house one second longer than necessary?

Once on the busy street he felt a bit safer but couldn't shake the feeling that someone was following him. Every time he looked behind him, he saw the same man in the distance—or at least, he thought he did.

Thinking quickly, he decided to visit his neighbor, Rene Basset, an old physician who long ago retired from his profession. He banged on the door, clutching the lapels of his waistcoat, pretending to appear every inch a man with no cares. When there was no immediate answer he banged again, looking behind his shoulder down the narrow street.

A short, stout man turned down the street, looking in a hurry and winded. It was the same man Jasper had seen since Robespierre's lodgings! He *was* being followed!

Jasper reached for the latch and rushed into the entryway. It wouldn't do to look like he was knocking at his own front door.

Voices sounded from the salon. Marguerite Basset was some thirty years younger than her husband, his third wife, and, as

Rene had admitted to Jasper over a bottle of burgundy, a challenge to his aging nervous system. Jasper had laughed heartily at that and hinted at a man's folly when a beautiful woman was involved.

A folly that was making itself known, if the heated argument he was hearing was any proof. That explained why no one had heard the door.

He cleared his throat and called out, but not before he heard the words, "But Rene. It is Madame Récamier! We must attend! I cannot disappoint her!"

A sudden noise of people moving caught Jasper's ears. His cheeks burned as he fumbled with his hat. Rene came from the room. "Jasper! Has something happened?"

There could be no other explanation for him barging in, and Jasper decided to nod. His shortness of breath was real as he reached out to grasp the man's hand. "Pardon my abrupt entry, my friend. I knocked, but when no one came to the door, I let myself in. I believe I am being followed and didn't want to go home just yet."

Rene looked distressed. "Come in. What has happened?"

Jasper followed Rene into the salon where Marguerite sat with carefully arranged skirts and a pleasant if false smile upon her pink lips.

"Please forgive my intrusion, madame. No one heard my knock and I was in something of a tight spot on the stoop." He allowed the drama of the scene into his voice as he stared at the carpet near the young woman's pretty feet. "I saw Robespierre today, and I believe he was having me followed."

"Oh, my! Do sit down and have some sherry!" The blond woman leapt up to pour for them, bringing him a crystal glass from her own elegantly turned hand. "Robespierre? I have not seen him in an age, so busy he is with our dear cause." Scorn dripped from her tone, but Jasper knew it wasn't directed at him. Robespierre had dug his own grave and climbed inside, waiting for the people who had at first backed him to decide he was going mad with this new power he held. Marguerite circulated with many who secretly discussed the political upheaval of their day, and Jasper would not be one to underestimate her.

"Pray forgive me again, madame, but did I hear you mention Madame Récamier? Such grace! Such beauty! It would be a distinct pleasure to meet the woman some day." He sighed as if he would never get the chance.

Marguerite's smile finally reached her eyes as she looked at Jasper, his fumbling entry forgiven, and then up at her husband with a challenge in her eyes. "You see, Rene? Not everyone is as disinclined toward the pleasures of Madame Récamier's salon." She turned her flashing eyes to impale Jasper, causing him to understand, in that moment, why his dear friend had lost his heart to such a one. It would be hard to resist any request from that heart-shaped, upturned face.

"I have been invited to her salon this Saturday. Jasper, dear, I am sure that you of all people realize the great honor. Please——" she tilted her round cheek toward a shoulder, her lips curving up at him in such a way that made his breath catch in his throat despite himself—"wouldn't you come with us? Why, I do believe Rene would think it great fun if only you would come too."

Jasper looked down, all meek compliance. Out of the frying pan and into the fire. "Of course, madame. Anything to smooth a good friend's time." He allowed his glance to dart toward that friend and saw resignation in his eyes—and a touch of humor.

"But Jasper will need to bring a woman too. To make the party even, you see."

The two men locked gazes, both agreeing they'd been had by the other.

An idea dawned, sending the first real excitement about such an excursion in years coursing through Jasper. "I know just the woman." He laughed at the shocked expression in his friend's eyes. "And she has a lovely daughter looking to enter Parisian society. Do you think Madame Récamier would mind?"

"I'll send her a note in the morning to ask, but her salon is always a crush. I doubt she will mind." Marguerite pressed her lips together in a pretty pout. "Why, Jasper, why haven't you told us you were getting out of that musty smelling laboratory and going about in society? Who are these new acquaintances?"

Jasper shook his head. "Not so, my dear woman. I was called upon by Suzanne Bonham, recently arrived from Carcassonne with her two daughters. The eldest daughter, Scarlett, just delivered a healthy babe and needed my assistance."

Marguerite's eyes widened. The woman was terrified of pregnancy. He knew this because she came to his shop once to ask if he knew of any remedy to keep her from becoming pregnant. "How is she?"

Jasper waved a hand, "She's fine. A widow of the nephew of Robespierre. They are all three lovely women. Her younger sister, Stacia, is, I believe, husband hunting."

Marguerite clasped her hands together in joy. "Oh, how exciting! I shall hint as much to Madame Récamier. She is a veritable matchmaker!"

After another half an hour of catching up, Jasper rose from the settee and shook his friend's hand warmly in his. "Thank you for allowing me such an intrusion. These days—" he shrugged and knew the disquiet in his old friend's eyes was reflected in his own—"we hardly know what will come next."

As he left the room he thought about how thankful he was for old friends. The Révolution was nothing anyone of his generation had expected. Like all things young and impetuous, it had started like a fire, born from great need from the cold knowledge of little food and fire. But this fire spread throughout France with little thought for who or what it destroyed in its roaring path toward so-called freedom. The people no longer knew whether to quench it out or let it burn on. They could only stand back from the intense blaze and hope they survived long enough to know the charred remains of a country.

No king. No queen.

No government they could understand.

They only wanted one thing: enough bread to fill their children's stomachs.

⚬⚬⚬

JASPER WALKED THE short distance back home, looking over his shoulder, thankful there was no sign of the man who had been following him. He let himself into his quiet house, immediately looking for writing instruments to make out an invitation for Suzanne. Finding paper in his desk, he smoothed out the sheet and stared at it. The quill was old and had to be sharpened twice before it was acceptable for such a task.

A few minutes later, Jasper blinked, staring at the small, compact handwriting of his note. Would she agree to accompany him to Madame Récamier's famous salon? Oh, he hoped so! He sent the note off, hiring a lad of about ten to deliver it, and then took a turn, and then another and another, about his sitting room. He sat down and pondered. How best to start the search for Émilie? The people who attended Madame Récamier's events were well connected and informed. Possibly he could find some help there. The only problem would be knowing whom he could and could not trust.

This would not be easy.

The next hour seemed unending as he busied himself in the laboratory, trying to distract his thoughts. That not working, he eventually turned to cleaning the house—a task he didn't remember ever giving him much satisfaction.

Finally a knock sounded at the door. He opened it, anticipation mounting in his chest. Ah, finally! The messenger boy. The lad tipped his hat and held out the folded paper. Jasper offered a few coins and the boy grasped them and ran off down the street. Jasper didn't watch his flying feet. He hurriedly shut the door instead, settled his spectacles over his eyes at the correct angle, and shook open the note.

> *My dearest Jasper,*
>
> *Stacia and I would be honored to attend Madame Récamier's salon tomorrow at one o'clock. You are as a knight in shining armor, come to rescue us and lead us in these treacherous times. I shall persuade Stacia to put upon herself a meek and sweet-natured mien (if possible, dear sir) in the effort of gaining her a husband. Why is it that we women have to pretend to be something we are not to snare a husband, I wonder? It seems so unfair to the men in question. Why, you all must be shocked when, after the service, we prove ourselves with opinions and something of a brain. I have heard though, that Madame Récamier is no fool. I am greatly looking forward to meeting a lady made with such bold opinions and spirit.*

As you said in your letter, it would be foolish to see you again here at the Duplays'. Though I despair that you cannot visit us, I know that sending letters and secret rendezvous are our only recourse. Let us meet at the marketplace as you said, so that we might carry on together to the esteemed lady's salon.

You are in my thoughts,

Suzanne Bonham

For the first time in his life, Jasper's mouth went dry. A knight? He'd never considered himself of such sturdy ilk. He was a scholar, an aging one at that, bent over some experiment or recipe. He wasn't the type to notice much beyond what lay directly in front of him. He could feel the advancing years in his bones each morning. He could hear the creaking in his back as he bent, feel the tension in his neck after hours of having his arms extended to pour and mix and fuel the fire. He didn't deserve to find love at this time in his life . . . not when life everywhere hung in the balance on the next accusation.

But he smoothed the letter against his chest with his bony hands, smoothing and smoothing it, feeling her close to his heart. He chuckled at himself. What foolishness! And yet he couldn't help the lightness in his steps as he finished straightening the room, seeing it for the first time as a woman might . . . as Suzanne must have seen it when she was here. His eyes grew wide.

"Have mercy!"

SUZANNE BRISTLED WITH energy as she stared into the gilt-framed mirror above the washstand in her bedchamber. She patted her chest, seeing that her bosoms were nicely but modestly displayed for a woman her age. Her heart beat against her hand as it rested there. She shook her head at herself, watching the fat curls bounce against her shoulders. Not too much gray yet. Not very much at all. She turned and picked up her hat, a lovely creation that Scarlett had made from the odds and ends of other hats and adornments the three of them collectively owned. Scarlett truly had a flare for piecing something elegant out of outdated fashions. Suzanne sighed. Scarlett had such potential. What was the girl going to do now?

That thought scattered away as she set the new creation on her head, turning her chin this way and that. It was pale pink, round brimmed with a little height, only shorter than a man's would be. From its brim a froth of tiny white flowers and a large white feather cascaded nearly to her right shoulder. Her dress was white, a gentle pattern of white embroidery along the length of the skirt with flowing lace sleeves at her elbows. Her overcoat was dark red, almost black and shining silk. She looked into the mirror and smiled a smile that she hadn't worn in a long time. At this moment, she didn't feel a mother, nor a widow, nor an aging woman. At this moment, she felt as happy and silly as a young woman. There was a wide pink bow beneath her chin that covered her plump flaws quite well. Her white collar rose from behind her neck, giving her height that she didn't really have. She looked down and felt a moment's glee despite herself. On her feet were pointed-toed, dark red slippers. They made her feet look so small and narrow! She couldn't help her chuckle.

She smoothed down her dress, feeling the underskirt rustle against her thighs, a rustle of memories washing over her. It had been so long since she'd felt this way.

She looked back into the glass, sure in the knowledge of what had gone before and excited for what might yet come. Then she thought of Jasper, and the woman staring back at her fairly glowed with happiness. Like the girl she felt, she clapped a hand over her mouth as a laugh escaped her throat.

Maybe it wasn't too late for love after all.

⁂

STACIA MET HER mother in the hall.

"Ma Mère! You look wonderful!"

Suzanne grasped her youngest to her in an embrace. "Merci, my dear. And you look like the most beautiful maiden in Paris. Are you anxious to be going to such a famous salon?"

Stacia was dressed in the height of fashion, in a high-waisted gown of white muslin with black rickrack around the collar, waist, and hem. Her bonnet was white and voluptuous in its ruffles and lace, leaving plenty of room for her wispy fringe to fall, dark and shining, against her forehead. She wore her hair partly up and partly down, with ringlets of russet brown framing her cheeks and forehead and hanging down around her shoulders. She brandished an unopened umbrella with one hand and grasped her mother's wrist. "We must hurry! We can't be late!"

Suzanne looked absently at the hallway pendulum clock. "Let us make haste. Have you said good-bye to Scarlett?"

"Yes. Yes, of course. Now let us go."

They arrived by a hired carriage at the marketplace, where they tumbled out in a froth of skirts. Once there, they scanned the area for Jasper. Suzanne spotted him first. "There he is." They stared in astonishment as they saw the effort he had put into his dress. Black trousers, a white shirt, cravat and waistcoat, trimmed in green and a long green tailcoat. Upon his gray head sat a fine tri-cornered black hat.

Suzanne quickly grasped Stacia's arm and set the tone. Chin up, shoulders back, they walked with all appearance of grace and stateliness toward him. Suzanne reached out to grasp his hands. "Jasper. Are we not late? I do hope we are not late."

Jasper shook his head at them, making Stacia stare at the bald spot on the top of his head as he removed his hat.

"Not at all. You are a vision, my dear." He seemed to have forgotten Stacia was there, for he didn't comment on her appearance at all. "Come, I have a carriage waiting."

Stacia looked quickly down, commanding herself that the corners of her mouth didn't rise. The man only had eyes for her mother.

THE CARRIAGE GLIDED over the cobblestone road, making Stacia think of a ride through the clouds. It stopped abruptly at a tall, brick building on the city's fashionable side of town. As they stepped down from the carriage, Stacia wondered if the visit would go as smoothly as the ride.

A man in Révolutionary dress met them at the door, complete with red stocking cap and one red and white and blue circular cockade attached to his lapel. He wore a red shirt, white pantaloons, and a long, blue coat that touched the white turned-over tops of his dark blue boots. Stacia pressed her lips together as he swept them inside with the words, "Welcome to the salon of the Révolution."

Her mother gave Stacia a worried glance and then plunged into the dimly lit entryway. Her mother leaned close to whisper in Stacia's ear. "It will probably be best to just look pretty and not say too much."

Stacia rolled her eyes. *Yes, as long as they don't rile me.*

As they entered the salon they saw a crowd of about fifteen, most of them dressed in the colors of the new government, though the women had far more freedom in their choice of dress. Jasper grasped Suzanne's arm in his as if he wouldn't soon let go and led her about the room, making the introductions to his neighbors, Rene and Marguerite Basset. They, in turn, introduced the three of them to Madame Récamier.

She was a lovely, younger woman, her eyes twinkling with intelligence and mischief as she hugged Stacia's mother. She kissed Stacia on the cheek and whispered, "Oh good, another pretty bird in the room to distract them." Her effort was friendly as she waved them to the empty chairs next to her.

A man sat down next to Stacia, stretched a large, muscular leg displayed in his tight breeches and stockings out so that his foot nearly touched hers. Stacia slowly sat further back into her chair and moved her feet away.

"Citizen Bonham," the man thundered. "You are new to Paris, yes? I know I would remember you if I had seen you before."

Stacia blushed. Why didn't the silly man quiet his voice? He was gaining the attention of all in the room. She inclined her head and softened her voice to a near whisper. "We have come from Carcassonne."

"And what brings you to the city?"

Stacia glanced at her mother, seeing no help there. She shrugged, "We're come to see my sister's uncle, Robespierre."

The room itself seemed to gasp, and now all eyes and ears truly were on her face.

After the startled expression left the giant man's face, a look of speculation crossed over it. "And what business do you have with Robespierre?"

Stacia's heart was pounding in her chest. Something told her the next words she uttered were very important to the room full of people surrounding her. Something else told her it would be better to charm than rile. She dimpled prettily and shook the curls resting against her bosom. "Why, good sir, Robespierre is a distant relative, and my mother and sister and I heard of all of the excitement happening here and decided we couldn't miss another moment of it."

She leaned forward as if to tell him a great secret, smiling slightly and allowing the feeling of suppressed glee to enter her eyes. "He was rather put off at first. He *can* be so terrifying." She shrugged delicately tilted her head to one side. "But he seems to be coming around." She glanced at her mother, hoping and praying she would understand what Stacia was doing and play along. "He's grown quite used to us by now, hasn't he, Mother?"

Her mother looked alarmingly perplexed, so Stacia plunged forward before she could speak. "Why—" she paused as the whole room waited, clearly in anticipation of further shock— "I do believe he's becoming quite . . . *hen-pecked*." She turned back and let the corners of her mouth rise in a triumphant gesture at the room. "All bark and no bite, that sort of thing." She stared at them, smiling and blinking and waiting.

Finally the man beside her burst into laughter. It seemed a signal of some sort, as the other men and women seemed to allow their tension out in a wave of giggles and laughter. Stacia knew they were laughing at her, not with her, but that had been the goal: to make herself look like a half-wit, a young woman incapable of political intrigue.

She was only too pleased it had worked.

Turning back around her gaze briefly rested on Madame Récamier. The woman smiled with closed lips at Stacia and gave her a little nod. Stacia looked away, but knew there was one woman in the room she had not fooled.

Chapter Twenty-Three

Émilie St. Laurent. Yes, that was her name. Scarlett—the pretty woman who had plunged into her life like a breath of fresh air with open, unafraid eyes and a stomach so large Émilie could hardly tear her gaze from it—had said it. Reminded her who she was.

She wasn't a servant girl. Not that she thought she couldn't be or wouldn't be again. It wasn't that she deserved any other place in the world. She was lucky to be alive. But those words. Those three words had reminded her that she didn't belong in Robespierre's household. Somehow, in the blur of the last few years, she'd forgotten the girl she had once been.

Émilie made her way down the narrow street, the place where her brothers used to play, preferring the bustling life there above their quiet chateau gardens. She'd peered out of the tall, mullioned glass of an upstairs window, sewing her sampler—or pretending to do so, but really wishing, wishing so hard, that she could be allowed out there with them. A boy's freedom. How she'd longed for it.

Christophé had led her down this same street that night. The night they ran from their family ruin. She looked back and forth, still puzzled by his words. Shouldn't there be a red door? Had she heard him wrong?

It was the only place she could think to go now. To the red door down this quaint, familiar street. Since fleeing the marketplace and Scarlett and everything familiar, she'd come back to this place. Since running away from Les Halles she'd waited in the shadows of the gardens of the chateau until dusk, when she could move about without fear of being captured.

But as she searched yet again, she found the same hopeless answer: There was no red door.

At least, none she could see.

As she'd returned to this street over and over, knowing her brother would never have lied to her, memories stirred. It was strange. Color. She had noticed at an early age that people would point to something and say it was red or green . . . but she had always seen blue or gray where they pointed. She'd not thought too much about it until now. But her fruitless search tickled her memory, forcing her to recall that she'd always seen colors in a different way.

A little girl was walking ahead of her. She was playing alone along the path by her home, rolling stones as far as she could across the cobblestones. The girl's mother appeared from around the front door and called to her in a sharp voice.

"Rinslet? Come in, child. It grows dark."

The woman took a long, suspicious glance at Émilie, who waved as if she knew the woman to put her off. Rinslet started to run away, but something in Émilie rose up, some fear of being left alone on this street looking for the door again. With all her strength she pushed air and sound out of her throat, speaking for the first time in years. "Rinslet?"

The girl stopped and turned toward Émilie. "Would you like to play a game?" Her voice sounded raspy from nonuse, but the child nodded eagerly, forgetting her mother's demand.

Émilie bent to the girl's level. "The doors on this street. Are any of them red?"

The girl was about eight and looked up and down the street in concentration. "I don't think so."

"Run quickly up and down and see if you can find a red door."

"What will you give me as a prize if I find it?" The child quirked up her nose at Émilie.

Émilie dug into her pocket and pulled out one of Robespierre's coins. She held it out in her palm, letting it shine in the fading light. "If you run very fast, I will give you this."

The child took hold of the challenge, looking at Émilie with certainty in her young eyes. She did run fast, faster even than Émilie could have run. She ran all the way down the street to the end of the block, looking at every door, then crossed the street and ran, lightning fast, down the other side. She arrived at Émilie's side huffing and puffing, trying to catch her breath. "There it is—" she pointed just down the street on the other side. "It's faded red, but it's a red door." She held out her hand for her prize.

Émilie handed over the coin, emotion clogging her throat. It was just where Christophé had pointed that night so long ago. "Merci."

The child bounded away, as she gained entrance to her house, Émilie heard the complaining of a mother with a dawdling child.

Her heart pounded in her chest as she made her way, step by slow step, toward the pointed-out door. It did look different than the brown doors. A grayish sort of green. And so her suspicions were finally confirmed. She didn't see things as others did. It explained her mother's exasperation at her attempts at needlepoint and sewing of any kind. It explained why she sometimes seemed befuddled by instructions that others found no difficulty following. It explained why they said her father had green eyes but she'd only seen a grayish color.

Father . . .

Thinking of him had the usual effect. She wanted to back up from life, crawl into a hole, and hide forever. He'd always been the one to bend down and whisper sweet words into her ear. He was the one she loved to tilt her head back so as to admire how tall he was, how grand. He was the one to sit in her little chairs and attend her tea parties, pretending as she did that the dolls were real and the tiny cups held enough tea to fill them. He brought flowers each time she invited him. Varying colors that she only now realized must have looked different to him. But he hadn't cared. He wouldn't care now . . . if he were alive. He'd just loved her.

Émilie fought back the tears, demanding of herself some inner strength that she knew she shouldn't need at her age. But she wasn't one to feel sorry for herself. Instead, she walked up to the door, took a deep breath, ignored the pounding of her heart in her ears, and knocked as hard as she could.

There was no answer.

She beat again, looking over each shoulder to see if anyone was coming down the street. She did not want to hide in the bushes of this street in the dark ever again.

Nothing and no one.

She tried the latch and found it firmly locked. Looking side to side, she saw that a low window was cracked open, letting in the evening breeze. Taking courage—and her skirt—in hand, she shimmied around some bushes and pushed the window open. It took a few tries as the casing was rusty and old, but finally it was open enough to allow her slim body to slip through.

Let it be Christophé's friend. Please God. Let it be my brother's friend. It was her only thought as she slipped through the opening and slid to the floor.

The room was a wreck of glass tubes and bottles, stacks of books and notes, barrels of odd-looking plants, some green and alive but most brown and dead looking. The room smelled of a combined strong smell that reminded Émilie of medicine.

Where was she?

There was a very low fire burning in the grate. She went to it, found the poker and a stout piece of wood, which she threw on the flame, igniting it into a blaze. The room turned into shadows and dancing light. Whenever she moved, a great shadow leapt across the ceiling and far wall. She laughed a little, thrusting out the poker like a sword, watching the shadow match her moves. Then she realized how loud the sound must be and quietly put the toy away.

She was in the shop part of the house, she realized as she wandered into the large room. Off to the side was a flight of steps and a long, narrow handrail against the whitewashed wall. She grasped hold of the railing.

The steps creaked a little and she stilled, waiting for any sound from the living quarters. When none came, she crept on. At the top of the stairs was a closed door. Slowly, quietly, she pressed her thumb against the latch. The door creaked open, leading to a short landing and then opening into a hall. She crept down it, step after step, not knowing if she walked into another trap or the haven Christophé spoke of so long ago it seemed a part of some dream.

There was a half-empty glass on a table, a low fire in the grate, as down below, and no one. No sound. She must be alone.

She crept further into the room toward the warm glow, which gave the room a sense of sanctuary. She turned from the fire's brightness and saw a shawl on the settee. It looked strangely familiar. She stepped toward it, reached out and grasped it to her chest, then raised it to her face. She buried her face in the softness and the scent.

It smelled like Scarlett.

How or why that could be, she couldn't fathom, but she felt it was a sign from God. Sinking down on the settee, she felt bone weary. She curled onto the settee, wrapping the scarf's long, colored length around her as she laid her head on a pillow, stared into the yellow flames and felt her whole body go lax. She didn't know why, but for the first time since that terrible night . . . she felt safe.

∽

JASPER WALKED THE short distance from the market to his door with light steps. After their visit in Madame Récamier's salon, he had taken Suzanne and Stacia for an early dinner. The afternoon had had mixed results. On one hand he could hardly believe how well it had gone with Suzanne, though Stacia said she was unimpressed with any of the men she'd met today. But he hadn't any luck finding clues to help him with Émilie's disappearance. He'd dared not bring up the St. Laurent name, but had asked about the Duplays', where Robespierre lodged. The men he'd spoken to seemed bored with the topic, and he'd let it go.

Still, he couldn't help but feel a rising, expanding joy in his chest as he thought of Suzanne. Her presence was a pure delight. How soon could he see her again?

And where could he find a girl hiding in a city as huge as Paris?

He turned the long, old key in the lock and strode into the shop, where he unwound his scarf and hung up his best waistcoat. He fingered the coat . . . thinking he might want to investigate his closet for something appropriate and, well, *dapper* to wear the next time he saw Suzanne. For he surely would see her again.

With that thought bracing his steps, he took lively strides up the stairs toward the sitting room, thinking to get a drink of water before finding his bed. The fire was very nearly down to ash. He started toward it, then a movement caught his eye. He thought, at first, it was his cat, Simone. But no, his pet died many years ago.

Suddenly alert to danger, he shrank back, waiting while the shadows in the room stilled. There was a soft sound, as if someone was breathing. The sound came from his settee.

He crept forward, fearing one of Robespierre's henchmen had come and fallen asleep awaiting his arrival. But no. His gaze took in a girl. She was curled up like a cat, her head resting on a long arm, her legs curled up by her stomach, her lashes long and flickering in the shadow light.

She was a pretty thing.

That was his first thought. His second thought was that she looked just like Christophé when he'd fallen asleep on this very piece of furniture. They'd had a late night discussing the mathematical equations of calculus. He'd only been fourteen at the time, and Jasper remembered how astounded he'd been at the boy's mind.

And how proud he'd been.

How odd that this girl resembled that young Christophé.

"My dear?" He gently shook the thin shoulders.

She didn't at first respond, so deep asleep and at peace she was. He stared at the bright curls against his pillow and something inside him stopped. Those golden curls . . . the same shade as the girl who climbed the guillotine steps . . . her face, so like Christophé's . . .

"Mademoiselle?"

She roused, turned, and then sat up, terror in her wide, staring eyes.

Jasper held out a calming hand. "Please. Do not be afraid."

She clutched the pillow to her chest. "Are you . . . Jasper?"

"Yes." He sought to make her at ease. "I am Jasper. And who might you be?"

She glanced about the room, as though ensuring they were alone. Her voice sounded strange, croaky—as if it had been unused for a long, long time. "I am Émilie."

The words hit him like a blow. His legs failed him, so Jasper knelt down beside her. His movements slow and reverent, he took up the child's hand. "Christophé was right," he whispered in awe.

Her voice quavered. "You are Jasper? My brother's friend? With the red door?"

"Yes. Christophé is one of my very best friends. Did he send you here?"

"Yes." She pulled her hand from his grasp, using it to brush the curls away from her face. "A long time ago. I hope I'm not too late."

"Of course not." He paused, not knowing if he should say the next but then deciding that he should. "We thought you were dead, you know. We watched in a crowd as a girl, who looked just as you do, took the steps of the guillotine."

She looked up into his face and he saw her eyes in the flickering shadows of the firelight. So like Christophé's face, but younger. Still so innocent despite everything. "I don't know why, but Robespierre kept me alive, in his house. I was his servant."

Jasper pretended this news was of no great import, although it ascertained that the man in charge of the Révolution was, indeed, going mad. What kind of man, who held no punishment back from an aristocratic neck, would take this girl into his household to serve him? Jasper was afraid to ask and know what Robespierre might have done to this innocent child. Instead, he focused on the good news. "We are so glad. I've seen him, your brother. He is looking for you."

"Christophé is dead." Her voice was dead, too, as she said it.

"Émilie, listen to me, my dear. Christophé is here. He is alive and searching for you."

She shrank back into the cushions of the settee, distress warring with disbelief on those delicate features. "No." She shook her head, fingers turning white as they clutched the pillow to her like a beloved doll. "He wouldn't have left me."

"He thought you were . . . guillotined. Like the rest of them. We watched it together. We both thought it. But your brother, he came back. He is even now in Paris. He knows you are alive. Scarlett told him that you are alive."

"Scarlett." The name escaped her throat like a plea.

"They want to find you. I am so glad you remembered to come here." He stood up and then sat beside her, taking hold of her hand. "In the morning. We will tell them. We will go to them . . . together. You are not alone anymore."

She shuddered and then reached for him and fell into his old arms. She clung to him as if she had finally found a safe place, a place to release all the tide held back until she was home. "Christophé!" Her tears wet his shoulder. "Thank you, sir. Thank you."

Jasper clutched her thin shoulders as she trembled in his arms. His heart broke anew. "My brother said the man with the red door would help. It just took me a long time to find it."

Chapter Twenty-Four

$\mathcal{S}$carlett woke to a knock on the door.

"Come in," she called out, thinking it was her mother or Stacia.

The door opened, and she sank within to see Robespierre enter, nattily dressed, peering at her from his odd green glasses.

"Scarlett, how are you?" He came further into the room and stood against the door as if uncomfortable. "Might I see him?"

Scarlett motioned him in, though everything within her wanted to send him away. But they were living in his house and there should be no reason for her not to show him his great-nephew. So she pasted a smile on her face and motioned him closer. "Of course. Come and see."

As he neared, she suddenly remembered. Christophé! Where was he? He had been sitting beside her and she must have drifted off to sleep. Had he left while she was still asleep?

Turning her fears aside, she focused on the task at hand. She held the babe, wrapped in a blue blanket her mother had made months ago out of the softest yarn, against her chest. As Robespierre perched gingerly on the edge of the feather ticking, just at her side, she looked up into his eyes and watched the play of emotion cross his face. Robespierre leaned forward, his chin a little at an angle so that he could see down through his glasses.

"Would you like to hold him?" Maybe if she were nice enough to him, he might open up and tell her what she needed to know about Émilie.

He looked startled and then pleased, giving her a barely perceptible smile. Scarlett eased her hand to the back of André's head, supporting it as she passed the bundle into Robespierre's arms. The man looked ill at ease and entirely frightened as he adjusted his hold.

"Just hold his head, like so," Scarlett instructed softly. "His neck is weak yet."

Thinking of his infant neck, the place where the guillotine sliced through, hearing the word spoken in the room, startled them both. Robespierre tried to cover it by nodding quickly, his lips pursed in concentration as he cradled the infant boy. He looked to be holding himself very still as he brought the bundle into his chest, the black waistcoat a stark comparison with the light blue blanket and innocence within.

After a long, silent moment, Robespierre's hand rose and paused. Then, with surprising gentleness, he touched the rounded cheek with the backs of his fingers. He looked up at Scarlett and blinked rapidly, then cleared his throat. "What have you named him?"

"André. André Robespierre."

Robespierre tilted his head toward one side as if considering the name. Scarlett wasn't sure if he approved, but it was her baby, she could name him what she wanted. The room became silent, as if neither of them knew what to say next.

Scarlett recovered first. "Please thank the Duplays for allowing us to stay here. I know we will have to find other lodging soon. We are taking one of the daughter's bedchambers. And now, with a baby that often cries, we are such a disruption to their household."

Robespierre's lips pinched, clearly displeased at being reminded of his responsibility. "I will speak with my sister, Charlotte. She lives alone."

"Thank you, Uncle."

They fell silent again, and Scarlett wished she could snatch André back, but Robespierre just sat there, staring down at the babe. His intensity made her grow more and more uneasy.

"Uncle, I know the monarchy had to be ended. But all the deaths. Tell me, please. What is this Révolution about?"

She knew she risked much in the asking. He could accuse her of treason just for voicing a doubt against the new Republic. But perhaps this moment of new life would be her only chance to discover who this man really was.

His face turned stern and unyielding. Her heart beat as his eyes, suddenly alight and fiery, met hers. "Daniel explained it to you. He explained it with his death. How can you ask such a thing?"

Had she gone too far? Her heart galloped in her chest, but she raised her chin and looked at the baby. "I am a mother now. What lies ahead as the future of France will be his future." She looked up at him letting the fear she felt for the future into her eyes and voice. "I find I care more than I ever did, as my life is no longer my only concern. Sir, look at him. Tell me his future."

Robespierre looked down and his features softened. Scarlett let go of the tight hold she had of the coverlet. She'd said the right thing. He understood. Robespierre bent and brushed his lips against the downy head, his voice a low, terse murmur. "His future will be the new glorious France. Virtue winning over vice." He looked up at Scarlett, the fire and ice back in his eyes. "I am a Révolutionist, Scarlett, an agent of change for the common man. I am feverish with it both day and night. Révolution is the sounding beat of my heart, the flowing of my blood, the heated nature of my skin. I will not breathe without the intention of using that breath to enliven that great cause. Do you understand?"

His voice, his eyes, his tense body, all bore the intensity of his words. His conviction. But there was something more. Something . . . strange. Something frightening burning in his eyes. A desperate, determined passion that seemed so all-consuming that Scarlett wouldn't have been surprised if his eyes had rolled back into his head.

So it was true.

Robespierre was mad.

Inwardly she shrank from him, wanted to snatch her baby back and run away to safety. Outwardly she lifted her brows and her chin in apparent accord with his thoughts. "Well spoken, Uncle. Thank you for reminding me of our cause and all that we strive to achieve. I can only hope and pray that André will grow up as dedicated to our France as his father was and as you, sir, are."

A look of pleasure quickly came and then went across his face, like a sudden happiness that had to be squelched. Looking back down at the baby, he gave him one more touch, his finger tracing the shape of the boy's skull. Scarlett briefly closed her eyes as her stomach rolled within her.

Thankfully Robespierre seemed finished with the visit. He held the child toward her, and Scarlett's arms shot out to gather her babe close.

"I will be gone most of the next few days as there are many tasks ahead of me. You will be all right? I know the doctor came to see you."

Scarlett nodded, a forced brightness in her eyes. "Ah, yes. He left me some medicines." She motioned toward the table where a packet of tea and dried herbs rested. "I am fine now. I don't believe I will need him again."

Robespierre rose from the bed, straightening his waistcoat with short jerks. "I will take my leave then, good *citizen.*" There was a subtle warning in the word. He was going to watch her closely. He looked once more at André. "Daniel would have been very proud. Congratulations, my dear."

"Thank you, Uncle." She managed. Increasing fear filled her as he walked, straight-backed, from the room. As soon as the door closed, she took a long, shaking breath. "Congratulations, indeed," she said on with a weak voice, leaning back onto the pillow, seeing the man's face again as he talked about his only love, his lifelong passion. The Révolution.

A sudden sound, a shadowed movement rising from the floor, made a startled scream rise to Scarlett's throat. Just as she was about to let it out and into the room a hand clamped tight over her mouth.

"Scarlett, it's me."

Christophé's image rose above her. She stared at him, her eyes still wide as he released his grip on her mouth. "Where did you come from?"

"I was here, in the room, waiting for you to wake up." He looked down, flushing a little. "I heard steps coming toward the door and hid beneath the bed."

Scarlett gasped. "You were under the bed this entire time?" She quickly tried to remember all that had been said.

"Yes." He looked grim as he settled next to her and reached out for André. He looked down at the baby, clutching him close to his chest, and then impaled Scarlett with those, pleading, light-blue eyes. "You cannot stay here, Scarlett. It isn't safe."

He was right. Robespierre was feverish, mad with the Révolution. One misstep and she or her mother or sister could be in danger of the guillotine. No one was safe. Not even André.

Especially André.

"Yes." She pressed her lips together. They had no money, no means of escape, only this day-by-day survival. "But how?"

Christophé took up her hand with his free one. "Come away with me and Émilie. Once I have found her, and find her I will, we will go to England. I have friends there."

"Friends that will welcome a widowed woman and her child? What of my mother and Stacia? I could not leave them behind."

Christophé turned and sank down onto one knee, her baby clutched protectively to his chest. Oh heavens, what was he doing?

"Scarlett, will you be my wife? Will you allow me the great honor of being André's father?"

Scarlett gaped at him, on his knee, holding her son like it was his son. "To save us?" She leaned up, melting at the desire and longing in his eyes. But he hadn't said anything about love. "Are you doing this to save us?"

"Yes! All of us. From the moment I saw you at the grave-yard, when you turned and looked at me . . . you were so afraid and fierce and . . . all that is lovely. I knew I had found it." He reached for her hand and kissed the backs of her fingers. Her heart sped up, "Color," she reminded him. "The first word you said to me. It was . . . color."

Surprised pleasure lit his eyes as understanding flowed between them. "The dawn in your hair. The color of your lips. Your name. You are my great discovery."

"Oh, Christophé." She scooted to the edge of the bed, dropped to the floor in front of him, and reached for his shoulders. She wrapped her arms around him and leaned her face into his neck, the baby nestled between them.

He rose, lifting her with him, laid André on the bed, and then pulled Scarlett into his arms. As his lips lowered, his husky whisper brushed her face. "Come away with me?"

Scarlett leaned into his kiss. She was overwhelmed with the feel of his lips pressed against hers, his stubbly chin and cheeks rubbing the delicate skin around her mouth. Her hand touched his head where the dark hair was growing back. She wanted to tell him how much she loved him, all the sides of him. The intense scientist who could be lost in a starlit night or the splitting rays of light. The gentle soul that grieved and yet believed in something greater than the here and now to carry them. The man who fought to find his sister, who wouldn't give up until he did. The man that looked at her son, his adversary's great-nephew, and yet wanted him as his own. This man had decided to love all of them, and she knew as sure as the sun would set and rise and set and rise that he would do so every day of their lives.

She kissed him back as she'd never kissed Daniel. But then, Daniel had never kissed her with such abandonment and freedom. Daniel had never blocked all thought except that of her.

She opened her eyes a little as Christophé kissed her, finding herself straining toward something she wasn't at all sure existed. But she found exquisite satisfaction as she looked close, intent on his features. For there was no denying the truth.

This unbelievably complicated, brilliant, and beautiful man . . . wanted her.

Only her.

⟋⟍

CHRISTOPHÉ TRIED TO hold back the roar of blood that pounded like the sea and vibrated the tiny bones of his ears. He tried to temper the enchantment of her scarlet lips moving over his. He tried to bring reason into the equation so that he didn't overwhelm her. He envisioned the stars through his telescope, their blurry diffraction of light, but could only equate it with the sensation of his spinning mind. His arms gripped her. Behind his closed eyes he saw sparkling, swirling colors in hues that he knew were not possible.

He saw a heavenly kind of light.

His breath was ragged as he inhaled the womanly scents of a body meant to give sustenance. He delighted in her rounded, full curves and lushness, like a garden. Life. Like the Garden of Eden in flesh and bone. He stilled with the thought, knowing a sliver of God's thoughts when He'd made woman. What perfect, female, beautiful creatures they were.

"Scarlett." He took her more fully into his arms, reaching out to feel the contours of her shoulders, the slope of her back, her gown slipping down to reveal a rounded shoulder, unabashed grace in the light of midday. It was the time of day when people were honest. And in that light he sat back and stared at her, devouring her womanly perfection with the warmth of his gaze and touch. There was nothing flawed here. His Scarlett. His own special color.

She let him look at her, turning pink, and then caught her lower lip between her teeth. "Yes. I will marry you."

He felt happiness flood his whole face and throughout his body. He let out a joyous laugh, knowing. She would be his. She would come away with him and follow him to a life of a new sunrise and sunset. He didn't know how. He could not fathom how. But he would find a way.

He would save them all from this inglorious bloodbath they called *Révolution*.

Chapter Twenty-Five

The man named Jasper, as he insisted Émilie call him, tucked her into the bed in his spare bedchamber. He was a little awkward in the way he pulled the blankets up to her chin, patted her arm several times and asked if she needed a light, the door open or closed. His spectacles fell low on his nose as he watched her, treating her as a child or a frail invalid. She assured him she needed nothing.

She was used to the dark.

He padded out, turning toward her one last time with concern weighing his bushy white eyebrows. "Well, good night, then, my dear Émilie." He edged out of the door. "Tomorrow you will see your brother."

He left her with that thought. It brought a sob to her throat, but she'd grown so used to suppressing such things that she was able to force it back into the quiet rise and fall of her chest. The room flooded with darkness. But she wasn't afraid.

Robespierre had taken her that day. Taken her into a much deeper darkness than any light could dispel. He'd rescued her, or so he had insisted in a quiet hiss in her ear, over and over as his carriage conveyed them to his house. Once there, she had expected the nightmare to continue. What nightmare, exactly, she didn't know.

Before this daytime horror, she'd dreamed in the pastel colors of a girl wanting to become a woman.

Since it, since the hiding place—as she thought of her and Christophé's hidden hold that night and day—her nightmares had been of spiders crawling about her room and then in her bed. Or the one where her mother cried out and she'd been unable to reach her, some heavy, water-laden air keeping her from moving. Or the one when Jean Paul cut himself and bled all over their dining room carpet . . .

But she had found a secret. It was a magic prayer of sorts, like a faded memory, a long-forgotten song God had sung to her before she was born. It was the only thing that had kept her feet moving forward each day, and her eyes able to close each night. Tonight it was habitual and the usual comfort. But tonight, she realized, it had come true.

> *Our Father, who art in heaven,*
> *Hallowed be Thy Name.*
> *Thy kingdom come.*
> *Thy will be done,*
> *On earth as it is in heaven.*
> *Give me this day my daily bread.*
> *And forgive me my trespasses,*
> *As I will forgive those who trespass against me. As I will forgive*
> *   Robespierre.*
> *And lead me not into temptation,*
> *But deliver me from evil.*
> *For Thine is the kingdom,*
> *and the power,*

and the glory,
for ever and ever.
Amen.

She had changed it up a bit. But she didn't think the Lord minded. She knew He heard her prayer every night. It was why Christophé had come back to Paris.

"Thank You," she whispered into the pillow, unable to keep a tear from trickling down her cheek. "Thank You, God of my strength."

∽

THE MORNING BROUGHT Jasper with a tray. She'd spent so many years serving Robespierre, becoming his personal housekeeper and all that she learned that meant. Making sure his shirts were freshly ironed; his breakfast hot and waiting as he entered his private salon, where she faded in the background, hoping he wouldn't try to engage her in conversation so that he might assuage his guilt and convince himself of his moral ground. The endless errands she ran with messages clutched, burning hot in her hand, messages she refused to read, reminding herself that the God of her prayer would save her and not any notion of her own. She delivered his messages, set his meals on the table at exactly the right time, had his clothes freshly pressed and then, day after day, minute by minute, waited. Her only personal activity was to pray each day, each moment, when she first saw his face, that she might forgive him.

He must have seen it in her at times, for there were brief moments when the haze would lift from his shuttered eyes and he would look at her with such fear. Those were the times he banished her from the room and then avoided her for days. But he never banished her for long. And she never failed to serve him to the best of her ability. Even at her tender age, something, some woman part, knew that she had become his life. She was the one that kept him afloat when the madness threatened to take over. She was the one that listened and tried to love him, her enemy, as Christ loved His. She became his shadowed cross to bear.

And he, hers.

Now, this day, they would go back. She was terrified, if she admitted it to herself. There had been that moment of freedom as her feet were flying out beneath her, as she ran from the marketplace and the beautiful woman with the red lips calling her to come back. She had imagined herself one of Christophé's kites, bright and free and high enough in the wind that no one could catch her.

The feeling hadn't lasted long, though. It soon grew dark, and the citizens of Paris, ever watchful, were gazing overlong at the young girl in a servant's dress who looked lost.

The memory of the kite had taken her to the street where she and Christophé had hidden in the bushes . . . where he had promised to return, but hadn't . . . where she had not been able to find the red door. She thought him captured by Robespierre and somehow, somewhere, dead and buried. But Jasper said Christophé was alive. And he seemed the kind of man who knew what he was talking about. She knew God had helped her find this place where she was now being served breakfast from an old, wondrous man who acted as if he moved too quickly she might break into shattered glass.

He didn't know how strong she was. He didn't realize that she knew the source of her strength. He could not realize that she'd grown up overnight and no longer thought like a child.

And he must not discover it. They would expect a reunion where she was small and helpless and thankful and bereft of any knowledge of how to take care of herself. She must slip back into the role of little sister as she feared Christophé wouldn't know her otherwise. As she took up the honeyed bread and drank from the cup of chocolate, she decided that she could give them that. If only for a time.

"We will go now?" She asked Jasper as she drained the pretty teacup with rosebuds dotting up and down its sides.

"Yes. There is a washbasin on the side table if you would like to freshen up. As soon as you are ready."

"Are you not afraid we will meet Robespierre?"

Jasper looked down at her and reached out a reassuring hand to pat her shoulder, but she saw fear in his eyes. "We will be careful."

"There is a back stairway. I could show you."

"Yes. That would be helpful." He passed a thin-boned hand over his chin. "Do you suppose we should attempt a disguise?"

Émilie's eyes widened at the idea, a feeling of excitement spiking through her. Dress-up had been one of her favorite games as a child. "What did you have in mind?"

Jasper looked about the room then walked over to a large armoire. "This belonged to my parents. I never removed it and now I think I know why." He angled a grin over his shoulder. "There might be something amidst their old things for this play-acting show."

He threw the door open, and dust and mothballs billowed into the air and rolled onto the floor. "Come, child. Let's find our treasure."

Émilie bounded from the covers and walked over to take a look. She grasped hold of a black, lace-ruffled gown. It would be too large, but with some pins might make the journey to the house. "We are in mourning. Wearing the Republic's cockade proudly, of course. You are my grandfather, and I think"—she looked up at him—"that with a hat like this one"—she reached inside and dragged out the ancient item—"you are here for the funeral of my mother, your daughter."

She clasped the old dress to her, warming to the subject. "I will have this hat, as it has a veil and"—reaching down, she grasped something and held them high—"these very high heels to increase my age. My brother, John, is staying in a house on the same street as Robespierre and, if discovered, we have come to the wrong house. You are taking me back to Lyons after the funeral."

Jasper chuckled. "And what are our names, my little actor?"

"Montclaire." She stated with a sure smile. "It's common enough and not of the nobles."

Jasper looked down at her with a gleam in his eyes, and she knew in that moment that he realized he had underestimated her maturity.

"You will be Reginald Montclaire, and I will be Ann-Marie." She grew suddenly serious. "But we have no papers."

"Perhaps we will have papers," Jasper assured her. "I am not without certain hidden talents as well." They smirked at each other in glee. "Just give me a few moments to work my magic, my dear, while you change into your new identity."

ↄↄↄ

STACIA STRODE INTO Robespierre's sitting room in a fine, high-waisted, jade-green gown and sat gingerly on the edge of the silken cushions of a chair. She put her hand, aware of the pose of drama, to her forehead and let out a great sigh.

Scarlett peered at her. "It didn't go well, either?"

"Pompous jackanapes all around." Stacia blurted out about the men from the soireé. Their mother gasped and then tried to hide her smile behind her hand as she followed Stacia into the room.

Their mother shook her head, setting her curls dancing. "Stacia, you must never speak so. It's not befitting a lady."

Stacia smirked at Scarlett, but spoke to her mother. "There was no other way of putting it and you know it was true, Mother."

Her mother settled into another chair, arranging the skirts of her best dress. It was a lovely lavender costume, but of the old style, with a bodice that made their mother's bosoms nearly burst from the neckline. Thankfully she'd stuffed a fichu in the center to lessen the effect. "Yes, well, nevertheless . . ." She let the comment trail off, as if not knowing how else to describe the soiree they'd attended in the attempt to find Stacia a husband.

"Tell me everything. I've been cooped up in this house for days and desperately need the diversion," Scarlett demanded with a desperate look at Stacia.

"The men!" Stacia began. "They think of nothing but this Révolution. Do I not look pretty tonight?"

"Indeed, you do."

"I could have been a nasty bug on the wall for all they noticed. Not that I really cared. There was no one, and Scarlett, I mean not *one* of them that I would even care to dance with."

"Was there dancing?" Scarlett looked dreamy-eyed at the thought.

"Of course not," Stacia resounded. "Only talk and eating. And more boring talk." She fell back against the cushions. "This was my third time out in Parisian society and I can only say that it is sadly lacking. My expectations have fallen to a new low."

Scarlett shook her head, feeling genuine sorrow for her sister. When she'd come to Paris it was a fairyland. The balls, the dinner parties, the opera. Yes, the opera. "What of a play or the opera house? I have heard that while they've closed down all the churches, the opera is still alive and well. You could try that."

Stacia groaned. "The actors will be killing one another in the name of the Révolution. Of that I'm sure."

"Well there isn't anything to be done about it." Their mother spoke in an even tone. "We must make the best of any opportunities. It has been so kind of Robespierre to give us all of his social invitations and insist we go in his stead." She turned toward Stacia with uncharacteristically stern briskness. "It is what the world is at present."

Stacia pouted. "Yes, but Scarlett was so lucky."

Stacia's words hung heavy on the air. Scarlett knew they were realizing that Scarlett had not been so lucky in the end.

"Oh, Scarlett, I beg forgiveness. That was thoughtless of me."

Scarlett only waved her sister away. It didn't matter. The past was over, and the present was set to lead her to a wonderful future. Dare she tell them of her engagement? Her newfound happiness?

Just as she was deciding that it might be the right time, there was a slight knock at the door. Scarlett, being closest, rose to answer. Who could be calling at this late hour? Robespierre was out for the night, and Christophé was sound asleep the last time she'd looked in.

She opened the door and blinked. It was Jasper, Christophé's friend, she was sure, but he was dressed so strange, in a costume only the elders wore, as though he'd borrowed his dead father's clothing. There were even moth-bitten holes on his jacket! "Jasper, is that you?"

"Yes. Scarlett, my dear. You look wholly recovered."

Scarlett opened the door wider and saw that he was with a young woman who was entirely veiled. How odd! Peering over her shoulder, Scarlett stared, round-eyed, at her mother and sister. "I am feeling much better, thank you. Please, come in." She nodded to the lady as she passed, wobbling a little in a pair of shocking-blue, laced-up, high heels.

Scarlett could not help a smile as, upon seeing Jasper, her mother rose from her seat, all aflutter and allowing Jasper to grasp her hands tightly in his. "Jasper, whatever *are* you about? You look . . . astonishing!"

Scarlett exchanged laughing gazes with Stacia.

Jasper bowed low over their mother's hand, lingering it seemed, and causing their mother to blush from chest to forehead. "I have brought someone, dear lady. Someone for Christophé to meet."

"Christophé?" Her mother's voice was like a squeak in the room. She looked at Scarlett and then the veiled lady. "I daresay you don't know, Jasper."

He straightened to his full height, which was still rather short. "Know what, my dear?"

Suzanne pursed her lips together and then whispered, though they all heard her: "Scarlett loves him. You shouldn't be bringing another woman around."

The veiled lady turned her head toward Scarlett, and then slowly lifted the black lace.

They all gasped.

"Émilie!" For a moment, Scarlett couldn't move, then she turned toward Jasper. "You *found* her."

"She found me, my dear." Jasper turned toward the girl and gazed at her with all the pride of a father.

Émilie reached out and touched Scarlett's arm. "Do you truly love my brother?"

Scarlett could only stare at her. She was speaking! And she sounded so like him, the way her tone lifted on the word "truly," the way she tilted her head and stared straight into Scarlett's eyes. She really was Christophé's sister. Scarlett had been right. Until this moment she'd hoped and prayed that she was, but she'd been a little afraid. What if she'd been wrong?

"Yes." Scarlett looked down and then around at the carpet, and then back up at Émilie. "I love your brother."

The room was silent for a long moment as Scarlett and Émilie stared at one another, each communicating their love for Christophé St. Laurent. Then Émilie reached out for Scarlett's hand. "I'm so glad."

Jasper looked around at the ladies in the room and cleared his throat. "We might not have much time. Where is he?"

Scarlett blinked. "Upstairs. Sleeping." She reached out and grasped hold of Émilie's hand, imagining Christophé's face when he saw her. "Come." She led the girl from the room, motioning Jasper to follow them. "Even in disguise, you are not safe here. Let us hurry."

Chapter Twenty-Six

Christophé was curled onto his side, a shaft of light from the nearly closed curtains illuminating his hand up under his cheek. He looked as sweet as André . . .

Scarlett crept further into the room and sank down beside him. His wound was healing nicely; he'd had a resurgence of appetite the past two days, and she had seen to it that he ate well and often. His color was coming back. He was almost, he said today, ready to start the search for Émilie.

Love for him overflowed in Scarlett's thudding heart as she leaned over his sleeping form. She wanted to just stare at him, watch him sleep. But she would have the rest of her life to watch him and grow old together. Now Jasper and Émilie waited on the other side of the door and she was so glad. So glad that she would be there when he first saw his beloved sister's face. She leaned over his peacefulness and kissed him lightly on the cheek. He barely roused. She tried again, this time placing a chaste peck on his mouth and whispering his name.

He turned onto his back, his eyelids fluttering open. "Scarlett?" His eyes changed, turned dark and intense as his arm reached out to drag her toward him, across the bed and against his chest.

She couldn't help her laugh and nestled her face into the curve of his neck. "You must wake up, my dearest. I have the most wonderful surprise for you."

"Feeling better?" He breathed the words more than spoke them against her temple, pressing a kiss there.

She laughed and pushed against his chest. "Unruly man!" Suddenly serious, she leaned back. "You have visitors." She rose up onto one elbow amidst the rumpled covers, gave him a quick kiss on the lips, and then scooted away. Standing beside the bed, her gown, the one she'd not been able to wear in the last six months, settled back around her now-slim hips and legs. She clasped her hands behind her back. Christophé was looking at her as if he would like to devour her. She turned his attention toward the door with a wave of her hand, calling out, unable to keep the glee from her tone . . .

"You may come in."

∾

ÉMILIE HEARD THE words as a heartbeat. *You . . . may . . . come . . . in.* Her feet seemed rooted to the floor. Fear had, at last, overtaken her and she began to shake uncontrollably.

What if they were all wrong?

What if it wasn't him?

Jasper looked down at her. He must have seen her stricken eyes because he leaned down to put an arm, somewhat awkwardly, around her shoulders. "It will be all right, Émilie. Come."

His whisper reminded her of the prayer she said each night. In heaven they would all be together: Mother, Father, Jean Paul, and Louis. And someday, Christophé and she. She realized the reason she was no longer afraid to die. If she died she would see God . . . and her family. Some days she had longed to give up trying. Many days she had wondered what she might do to rile Robespierre so that he took her, hands bound behind her back, to the mounting steps of the scaffold. But it never seemed to matter. Robespierre had a place of suffering on earth for her; she was a used-up rag that he could wash himself with and thus make his world right again.

Now was no time to be afraid. Now was a time to be glad.

At Jasper's urging she took a step in the wobbly, borrowed shoes. Then another and another and another.

Four steps to see his bed and tousled blankets.

Another and another.

Two more to see his shadowed face.

Another and another and another. And then . . .

He was before her, the dream of his face come to life.

Her brother's eyes were like blue crystals. Jean Paul's eyes had been brown. Louis's blue, but not so blue as Christophé. Everywhere their mother had taken them as a group of children, Émilie could remember strangers stopping and staring at Christophé's other-worldly eyes. They were of the purest blue, like the azure in a peacock's feathers she'd once seen in the king's own garden, light and bright at the same time.

She took another step as the memories of their childhood rushed over her. He was so still. She wondered if he breathed. Another step, and then the crystal of his eyes changed, darkening to brilliant sapphire, suspicious and afraid. He looked to Scarlett.

Scarlett took hold of his hand.

Émilie reached up and grasped the front of her veil, pulling it up. She took off the wig. She shook out her golden hair and then raised her gaze to his.

She saw the shattered recognition, how he struggled to believe.

"Émilie?"

The sound of his voice broke through the hardness in her throat. Her face crumpled. Silent sobbing shook her shoulders. She cried, really cried, for the first time since soaking his shirt in that dark, hidden room.

He seemed unable to move, and she was afraid again, afraid something would take him from her as the last time. Then she threw caution to the nether regions and rushed forward, hurled her body into his arms. She peeled away the unfeeling glove, reached out and touched his cheek. Then her fingers grazed across his bristled hair and scalp.

"You cut your hair."

❧

THE SPELL AROUND them broke.

Christophé's chest heaved. His strong arms gathered her close. His quick breaths sounded like the wind in the stillness around them. "Émilie." He said her name like it was the last name God ever gave to the created.

He pulled her tighter into his arms. "They said you were alive, but I dared not believe it. Not until I saw you."

She cried into his shirt and then looked up into his eyes. Her voice was the soft, confused voice of a child. "Christophé, why? What harm had we done? What sin?"

What could he tell her? He could tell her of the poor and their wretchedness, their hollow bellies and huge, hungry eyes. He could tell her of the hovels across France, the dirt and the ignorance and the hopelessness. He could explain that the people had great cause to overthrow a corrupt and sordid government. He could explain the reasoning behind their righteous anger gone to madness, but he could not tell her why they hated him, or a twelve-year-old girl who had only known the bosom of a family's love.

Christophé lifted her face and saw the tears on her cheeks. His heart ached with the knowledge that she would never be the same. She would not grow up as she should have—safe, loved and accepted, *safe*. He looked around the room, saw Scarlett's hand at her mouth, her tears overflowing, saw Jasper's joy and sorrow making his body rigid, melded like a chemical compound ready to burn. He felt gratitude that he'd found these two, intense thankfulness that he knew their love. That was it. Wasn't it? It came to him as a blinding light.

Love. It was the only thing they had to cling to.

He held Émilie's thin frame against him. "Émilie." He pulled her closer, holding her and holding her, stroking her golden hair. The only one of the St. Laurents with such hair. "You will never be alone again. I promise you. I promise you."

Christophé looked up at Jasper over Émilie's head. "We must leave. I won't have her staying here."

Jasper reached a hand into the air, his face set with determination. "You and Émilie will come home with me tonight."

Christophé looked at Scarlett as he rose from the bed. He gathered his few belongings as he spoke. "Scarlett has agreed to be my wife. We will all go to London as soon as it can be arranged. You will come with us, Jasper?"

"I don't know."

"He will find out your part in this. You have nothing to gain by staying here."

Jasper looked down and flushed. "Actually, I do. There is a certain woman I wish to know better."

Christophé looked at Scarlett and then back toward Jasper. "What if the lady in question decides to come along with her daughters? What then?"

Jasper stood up straighter, taller. "If she does, I will be hard pressed to stay."

Scarlett looked from one man to the other, and he saw comprehension dawn on her features. "Scarlett, you must speak to your mother and sister. Prepare them, my dearest, for within a week, we sail for England."

Scarlett looked back and forth between the men. "What of André? Do you really think he can make the journey?"

"As long as he is in his mother's arms, he will not know, nor care, what country he is in. We will be safer in England."

Scarlett nodded. "I will go and tell them."

"Urge them to come with us. We will find a way."

SCARLETT SHUT THE door behind her and made her way back to the sitting room where her mother and Stacia waited with the baby. She heard André's cries before entering the room and felt a pang of guilt that she hadn't been there to take care of him. Perhaps he was hungry. He seemed forever hungry.

She was feeling much improved since the birth, and so glad to be able to fit into some of her earlier dresses, but still so new at mothering that it was hard to leave him in another's care for even a few minutes. She turned the knob of the door, feeling the milk come to fore at his wailing, and stepped inside.

She stiffened as she entered the room.

Robespierre was there. Standing right there, holding her child against his shoulder. He looked up as she entered, looked long into her eyes as if he knew all that had gone on in his house. "Scarlett! There you are. We've been wondering what could be keeping you."

Scarlett swallowed hard, saw the nervous expression on her mother's face and Stacia's raised brows, and then rushed over to André. "Here, let me have him. He must be hungry." Her heart was racing so that she didn't know if she could feed André or not, but she grasped her son's flailing body from Robespierre's arms as quickly as she could.

"You have been gone a long time, Scarlett. We were only attempting to soothe him." Robespierre regarded her with stern eyes.

"I do apologize." Scarlett glanced at her sister to further judge the mood of the room. Both her mother and Stacia looked white and strained. Scarlett thought for a moment, then turned from Robespierre and sank down into a chair without offering any excuse for her long absence. Then she simply began to unbutton her dress.

The move had the desired effect. Robespierre turned abruptly away, facing the fireplace, most ill-at-ease.

Scarlett took the moment to full advantage. "Why, Uncle, I feel as if we haven't seen you in days. Whatever is the news? I'm so confined here in this house. Do tell me something diverting." She exchanged a conspirator's look with Stacia and helped André find his dinner all the while covering herself with a blanket. She was sure to allow the sucking noises to fill the room.

Robespierre did not turn back around.

"The Committee of Public Safety has decided upon a festival." He paused and gave them a glacial glance of self-satisfaction over his shoulder.

"What is it for?" Scarlett met his look with one of polite curiosity.

His voice filled with a certain degree of pride as he expanded on the topic. "The Festival of the Supreme Being. It is tomorrow. I would like you all to attend."

Scarlett suppressed a chuckle. "Supreme Being? Is that God's name now?"

Robespierre fidgeted at the fireplace. "The atheists wish to abolish God. I shall bring Him back to His full glory. It will be an elaborate celebration of our continued belief in a Supreme Being." He glanced around at the ladies. "They've made me the leader of it, I suppose."

"Oh, that must be a terrific responsibility!" Stacia was a master of pretend, mock concern fairly overflowing her words. "Citizen Robespierre, you are so rarely to be found at home. How do you get any rest?"

"Only doing my duty." Robespierre turned back toward the fire. Scarlett sent her sister a warning glare behind the man's back. He was distracted and possibly mad, but he wasn't anyone to toy with.

Stacia pressed her lips together in acquiescence. Then, changing tactics, she launched into a detailed description of all the social events that Robespierre had passed along to them, thanking him profusely and begging him to join them at some future date when he might be available. Scarlett's mother joined in with enthusiastic bursts of detail, clearly unsure of her part in this particular drama, but playing it well all the same. Scarlett tried to keep the shocked laughter from escaping her chest. They just might pull this off. The man looked trapped in front of his own fireplace.

Finally Robespierre turned, his fingers massaging his temple as if he had a headache coming on. "I'm off to the Jacobin Club, then."

Scarlett almost cheered at his abrupt declaration.

He bowed at the three women, not looking directly at Scarlett or her half-covered chest, and then strode as fast as was decorous from the room.

The three women were hard pressed, despite the danger of hidden guests upstairs, to suppress their glee at their success as he fled the room.

As the door closed behind his slim form, they stared at one another and blinked, suddenly as silent as mice. Their mother rose and, as calm as any aristocrat, rang for tea and refreshments as none of them had eaten much that day. They waited in suppressed stillness as the laden silver tray was delivered. The tea was poured, and they all settled back into their chairs. It was well past bedtime, but they each knew that there would be no going to bed early tonight. They needed to discuss the astounding events of the evening.

As soon as the new serving woman, hired since Émilie's disappearance, left the room, they sipped their tea and ate sweet bread and crackers, cheeses and thinly sliced meats, olives and pickled beets. After the silent, ravenous feast, during which they'd avoided one another's eyes, they finally looked at one another and burst out talking.

"They are still up there now," Stacia began. "Should we leave the three of them there all night?"

"They should leave as soon as Robespierre is safely at his club. They are going back to Jasper's house." Scarlett kept her voice to a low whisper.

Stacia gripped her hands together. "Oh, Scarlett, Robespierre gave us such a fright! What were we *thinking* to keep Christophé here as long as we have?"

"We had no choice. Everything will be fine if we can manage to get him and Émilie back to Jasper's house undetected." She stopped, thinking. "Christophé might need a disguise."

"Do you really think he can walk the distance, Scarlett?" Her mother's worry made her few wrinkles more pronounced.

Stacia looked at her mother. "Mother, go up and ask them if they will need a carriage. Scarlett can't move a muscle or André will wake and start crying again. I will come up with a costume for Christophé."

"Yes, very well." Their mother rose from her chair, taking her lavender skirts into her hands. With slow and graceful steps, she left the room.

"Mother looks nervous," Stacia stated in a low voice. "She never acts like that."

"I think she is nervous for a good reason." Scarlett looked at her sister, allowing the glint of knowledge to reach her eyes.

"Whatever do you mean?"

"I do believe . . ." Scarlett paused. How to put it fully into words?

"Yes?"

"Well, I do believe that our mother is in love."

"In love? You can't be serious. She hasn't shown the slightest desire to look for another husband since Father died."

"I know. Perhaps she hasn't found the right man . . . until now."

"You mean Jasper?"

"Well, it's certainly not Robespierre."

Stacia let out a laugh, then stopped. "But he's so . . . he's so . . ."

"Old?"

They both pressed their lips together to keep the laughter and shock from escaping.

"I really don't think he's above ten years older than Mother. What worries me more is that he is eccentric."

"What do you mean?"

Scarlett waved her free hand in the air. "A scientist."

"What's so wrong with a scientist? Mother could do worse. Why, Father never had anything much of a job."

"Yes, I know. But Jasper has never been married and well, he just seems odd to me."

Stacia laughed. "Odd like Christophé?"

Scarlett looked at her sister and grimaced. "I suppose so. In a way. I don't know; I can't describe it. Maybe it's just such a new thought. Mother remarrying."

"Will you remarry, Scarlett?"

"Perhaps." Her voice must have softened when she said it because Stacia immediately perked up, brows raised.

With a mock sigh, Stacia placed the back of one hand against her forehead, her head thrown back. "Oh, Christophé . . ."

Scarlett glared at her. "He's different."

"Oh, yes. He *is* different. And very, very good-looking."

Scarlett wet her lips, turned her head, and tried to explain. "He is . . . he is . . . brilliant."

"And as lovely as a Michelangelo statue." Stacia finished with a grin. "You don't have to explain. If he turned those startling eyes on me like he does on you, I would be lost too."

"It is more than that."

Suddenly serious, Stacia agreed. "You love him, I know. Are you afraid? Afraid it will turn out like it was with Daniel?"

Scarlett took a long, deep breath, held it and shook her head. "What I feel for Christophé, and what he feels for me, is nothing like it was with Daniel." She looked up at her sister. "He has asked me to marry him."

"At a time like this?"

"Yes." Scarlett looked down at the sleeping baby. "He wants us all to go with him to London. I said yes."

Stacia gasped. "And you didn't tell me?"

Scarlett shrugged. "Until we found Émilie, I didn't really know if it would ever come to be. He had to find her first."

"And now that he has?"

"He wants us all to leave as soon as it can be arranged. They are preparing as we speak. I haven't told Mother yet. She may be discovering the truth of it now."

Stacia looked as if someone had shaken her. "I cannot believe you would leave France."

"We have no choice. Robespierre is mad! We risk our lives every day, living here. And it is too dangerous for Émilie and Christophé to stay. You and Mother have to go back to Carcassonne or come with us."

"But we don't know anyone in London. What will we do? Where will we live?"

"Christophé says we will find a way. I believe him."

Stacia looked about the room. "Well, I *have* always wanted to see London."

Scarlett motioned her sister over to her chair. Stacia sank down to sit at her feet and put her chin in Scarlett's lap, right next to the babe.

"I can't imagine going without you." Scarlett stroked Stacia's hair.

Stacia closed her eyes. "You won't have to. I won't leave you."

Chapter Twenty-Seven

The morning of the Festival of the Supreme Being promised to be a perfect day—bright and sunny, the sky of a blue that brought happiness to faces, clouds so thick and fluffy that they looked good enough to eat.

Scarlett rose early and shook her mother and sister, who shared her cramped bed. "We have to attend the festival. Come on, Stacia, time to wake up."

Stacia groaned and rolled away from Scarlett's hand. "Do we *have* to go?"

"Yes," Scarlett said a degree louder. "We have to seem to be giving our support to Robespierre. So get up!"

She watched her mother struggle awake. They'd been up late helping Christophé, Émilie, and Jasper dress in costume for the walk back to Jasper's house. Émilie would hardly let go of Christophé's hand, and Christophé had been the same, looking at his sister often, as if to ascertain that she was really there. It was quite late when the Bonham women had laid their heads on their pillows and even then, they all found it hard to sleep. Scarlett knew her mother and sister struggled with the same worry for the fugitives, wondering if they'd made it back to safety.

Finally they were up and ready to go. Scarlett was out the door first, holding her son close, wrapped in a blanket despite the heat of the July day. Soon Stacia and her mother followed her outside, and then the three women walked toward the Champ de Mars.

It wasn't long before they were jostling elbows with other people on their way, the crowd growing thick and noisy.

"Look," Stacia cried, pointing. "Do you see that?"

"Good heavens." Their mother squinted. "What is it?"

Scarlett strained up onto her tiptoes. "It looks to be a mountain, or something close to that."

"Someone made that?" Stacia gaped at her.

"Well, it does look realistic. Look at the outcroppings of rocks and trees."

"Come on—" Stacia took off, weaving through the crowd— "let's get a better look."

The closer the apparition grew the more they could tell that the giant spectacle was only plaster and wood and paint, but at the top stood something impressive. As they gained a space in the square, they saw that it was a massive statue of Hercules.

"Gracious heaven be told," Scarlett's mother murmured.

"I believe heaven knows." So—Scarlett felt her heart go cold—were they to worship Hercules now as their god? If so, why didn't God strike them all dead with a thunderbolt?

She gazed about her. Perhaps He was planning to do exactly that . . . and perhaps this was not at all the place to be.

"Look!" Stacia pointed again. "There's another statue. Isn't it the Statue of Liberty? Like the one we gave America after they won their freedom from England?"

Scarlett craned her neck around the tall man standing in front of her. It was, indeed. She didn't know the meaning of all the symbols, but her fear grew. It was a mockery, of that she was sure, and it would prove a mockery to all of France in the end.

A sudden sound behind them caught their attention. They turned, and a group of robed choristers, singing a song Scarlett had never heard, approached in a long and wide line. The crowd parted as the word "Marseillaise," a newly composed hymn to the Supreme Being, rang through the square. Young girls dressed all in white came before and behind, like a sign of innocence. They carried baskets of flowers and fruit, smiles wreathing their cherubic faces. There were flowers everywhere, gracing costumes and coiffures and the landscape around them. The crowd swelled both in numbers and in hearty self-congratulations. They were a republic now. They had freedom.

The deputies of the Convention marched to the summit of the mountain. The music rose to roaring. They all waited, speechless, as the music resounded around them and then ended with a sudden final flourish.

Then silence. Complete silence.

Suddenly Robespierre appeared at the top of the mountain. Applause broke from the people, and cries rose around them.

"Long live the Republic . . . long live Robespierre!"

"He is the king!"

"A priest!"

"He is a god."

Chills skittered across her nerves at this last cry, but Robespierre's voice, thin and weak, drew her attention before she could comment to her sister.

Her uncle's sorry voice always made Scarlett wonder who would listen to him at the Convention or the Jacobin Club. But something about the man stopped them all. The crowd stilled as if a saint was in their midst. Their bodies strained forward to hear the diminutive man in his robin's-egg blue coat, yellow breeches, and three-colored sash of red and white and blue and white, tell them all how to take their next breath.

Robespierre finished his speech and then, taking up a flaming torch, he set fire to a gigantic paper image of atheism. As it burned before their eyes, a man came forth from the flames. His blackened body shook but as the smoke cleared in the light of the bright day, Robespierre proclaimed him Wisdom.

The new symbol of their god and nation.

SCARLETT TURNED AND fled, jostling through the crowd, tightly grasping the now-wailing André to her chest, trying to break free to open air. The baby's cries helped to part the crowd, some glaring at her, many complaining with rude comments, but she didn't care. She had to get her son away from this madness. She continued until she reached the place where the crowd dwindled to only a few children playing in the street.

She took great gulps of air, not realizing that the cold on her cheeks was the blowing of the breeze against her tears. Stacia and her mother were soon behind her.

"Scarlett, what is it? Is André well?" Her mother sounded as distressed as Scarlett felt.

Stacia came up next to her and touched her wet cheek. "Scarlett . . ."

Scarlett struggled for the words. She saw the celebratory crowd around her and motioned them all to continue walking. After another block and then another she slowed. Her mother's eyes widened with every step they took.

"A carriage. We must find a carriage."

Stacia ran ahead, in search of one. After a few more minutes, Stacia was able to round up a carriage. Stacia gave the man Robespierre's address.

They climbed in, sweaty and labored, settling themselves against the comfortable seats. No one dared speak. They all knew that the coachman might hear Scarlett's words, and none of them wanted to discuss the festival in a public place.

"We can't go back to his house." Scarlett looked at her mother. "Do you remember where Jasper's house is located?"

Suzanne looked out onto the passing cobblestones, at the houses and the street signs, for a long moment. "Oh, I do believe it is the next street."

Stacia rapped on the window, causing the driver to stop. "We've changed our minds, good citizen. Please, take us to Rue Vivienne."

The man shrugged, turned the vehicle around and continued driving.

"Scarlett, what is it?" Stacia studied her, her face, taunt with fear.

Scarlett could only shake her head and look out of the window, hoping, praying to arrive at a place of safety.

They arrived at the street, Suzanne looking closely at the houses so as to direct the driver. "There," she said triumphantly. "The house with the red door."

They rapped that they wanted the driver to stop, stepped down, and paid the man, who tipped his hat to them. He seemed to Scarlett to be watching them too intently. Stacia tried to distract the man by smiling up at him and motioning toward André. "He's to see his grandfather for the first time. Such an exciting day!"

The man, sharp-eyed and broad browed, seemed mollified and slapped the reins, sending the horses cantering off.

The three women made their way to the door. Suzanne took the lead, her hips swaying, determined, toward the red door. She knocked hard, three times. And then three more.

Jasper opened the door like he'd rushed to it. His face changed from alarm to delight when he saw Scarlett's mother. But then he noted their somber faces and quickly motioned them to come in.

"Is something wrong?"

Her mother looked ready to burst into tears at Jasper's question. Stacia stood mute. Scarlett finally spoke. "Where is Christophé? I have to speak to him."

Jasper took them into the parlor which was clean and tidy. Christophé had turned from the chair at the desk, stood when he saw them, and rushed across the room toward Scarlett. He immediately took her into his arms. "What has happened?"

Scarlett burst into tears.

Christophé looked up at Stacia and then their mother. "What is it? Is it Robespierre?"

Scarlett reached up and grasped his shoulders, her face pressed against his chest. "I'm afraid. Robespierre has gone mad. Today at the festival, it was such a mockery. He acted as though he thinks he is a god."

Jasper intervened. "Come. Come and sit."

They all sat down, Émilie pouring them each a glass of water and pressing it into Scarlett's hand. André had fallen into an exhausted sleep, but Scarlett clutched him to her chest all the same. Her arm ached with the tension of holding him.

Christophé reached for him. "Here, you rest. Let me hold him for awhile." He gently took the baby into his arms and sat next to Scarlett on the settee. "Tell me."

The words and all the fears tumbled out. "We went to the festival. He's renamed God as the Supreme Being. He claims it is to bring down the atheist, but it isn't. He wants something. Something he can never have on his own. Do you understand what I mean? I used to think he was eccentric, back when I first married Daniel. I used to think he might be a little crazed. But now. Oh, Christophé." She shook her head, lowered her chin, and stared at her fiancé as she never had. "He will destroy himself. And anyone in his household or associated with him will go—" she shook her head as fresh tears rose to her eyes—"to the guillotine with him."

She grasped Christophé's arm. "We have no more time. We have to escape now."

❧

NOW SHE KNEW Robespierre as he knew him. Now she knew Christophé's daily fear. He looked to Jasper, who inclined his head. They were ready.

"You're right. You cannot go back." Christophé's gaze swept to include the others in the room. "Not any of you. A ship to London leaves in a few days. We will travel to the harbor in Le Havre tomorrow."

They all stopped and looked at one another. Scarlett's mother looked at Jasper. "We're leaving France? Will you be coming with us?"

Jasper rubbed his chin. "If you won't be convinced to stay here with me and become my wife."

All three women gasped, but unlike her daughters, Suzanne's gasp was of delight. She put her hands to her cheeks. "Are you asking me to be your wife?"

Jasper walked forward and took her hands in his. "I suppose I didn't do that very well, did I? You would think a man my age would know better than to just blurt it out like that. But yes, Suzanne Bonham—" they all watched as he leaned forward and held her astonished gaze—"will you become my wife?"

Scarlett's mother nodded, her face blossoming with color. "Yes, I will." She leaned forward. "But we'll be married in London in a proper church."

Jasper gave her a little kiss, as though to seal their agreement.

"Great heavens!" Stacia fell back into a chair in a perfect imitation of her mother. "What will happen next?"

"Jasper and I will be going for a little walk in his garden." Their mother sounded positively giddy. She took her betrothed's arm, and Jasper's smile grew into a grin.

Stacia must have sensed Scarlett would like to be alone with Christophé, too, for she turned to Émilie. "Could you show me the house? Let's take on the task of finding sleeping places for everyone."

When they all left the room, Scarlett leaned into Christophé's shoulder.

"Are you well?" Christophé put an arm around her.

"I'm better now that I'm here with you. It was just that I've never seen it so clearly before. I'm afraid Robespierre will find us, or worse, we will all go down to the grave with him." Her body shuddered. "What of André? He is his blood relative. If they guillotine Robespierre, they will try to destroy anyone related to him."

CHRISTOPHÉ LAY THE baby on a cushion on the floor. He turned and took Scarlett into his arms. He didn't have any more words of comfort for her. He didn't know what promises he could make and keep. Truthfully, all their heads might lay in the executioner's basket by next week. All he had was his arms to enclose her. His head to lean towards hers. His cheek to press against her soft cheek. His lips against her yielding, seeking mouth.

Lips the color of her name.

Thy will be done.

Chapter Twenty-Eight

Christophé woke in the middle of the night to a silent, peaceful shot of moonlight crossing his face. He rose, careful not to disturb Scarlett and the sleeping babe between them. She looked so peaceful with her eyes closed and body slack as she lay curled onto her side, her hand just touching André's toes. And Emilie. Having her back . . . he could hardly contain the jolt of joy that shot through him when he thought of it. He reveled in the feel of family. His family.

Rubbing his hand across the short-cropped hair, he turned toward the window and the open curtains. He padded across to it, pulled the curtains further aside, and grasped them in each hand. Leaning forward, he pressed his face against the glass, watching the condensation form and recede, form and recede. How did breath have such vapor? How could it cling to a pane of glass? Did any of that matter anymore?

Scarlett was right. Robespierre had, this day, crossed a line that would likely mean his demise. He saw it as clearly as if he was reading about it in some history book from the future. The man's true agenda had finally been revealed, and both he and Scarlett and all they loved hung, like hapless spiders on the thinly spun webs glowing in this moonlight, suspended, waiting time's accounting sheets.

He pressed his closed fist against the glass and stared out. "God help us." He wanted to pound his fist. He wanted to rail at the time of their birth. What if they'd been born before . . . during the time of Voltaire and Rousseau? What would they have been then? Would he have ever known Scarlett? His mind played tricks on him, wandering into paths he'd never considered before. What if they'd been born fifty or a hundred years from now? What would their lives have looked like then?

It was the reason he was alone, he realized. Thoughts like these. There had never been anyone very much interested in anything but the problems of the day, the here and now. Except for Scarlett. She might not understand all his thoughts, but she listened, really listened, and thought about what he said. She understood something in him that no one else had.

He turned from the window and the moon's cold light. He walked over and stared at the woman sleeping there. Nothing had happened between them. Nothing of a marital nature would until they were wed by clerk or priest. Still, the blanket had fallen off her legs. His gaze traveled up the length of her toes and ankles and then calves. Her skin was pale, glowing in the moonlight. The sheets and her nightgown, the same one she'd worn when he had met her in the graveyard of Carcassonne, clung around a newly slim waist. Her arms were curled up, one toward André and the other under her cheek.

Her hair. His gaze traveled over the strands of her hair as it caught the moonlight in a vision of fire and embers, making him slowly sit down and then reach for a strand. He held it up, a careful move, so as not to wake her. It felt like silk between his fingers. He turned and rotated the strands into the light, watching how the colors changed. Fire and earth melded together in a single strand of hair. His chest heaved with the beauty of it.

"Christophé?"

She sounded afraid, and with everything in him, he didn't want her to ever sound so again. He dropped the lock of hair and leaned close. "The moonlight woke me." He leaned close enough to feel her breath over his face.

"Oh." It seemed all she could say.

He smiled.

He'd never been the seducer. He'd never tried to convince a woman of anything, save his mother, who he often tried to convince the necessity of having taken apart some clock or destroying some household apparatus to figure out how it worked. "I didn't mean to wake you."

Scarlett sat up, whispering as he did so they wouldn't wake André. "But you did." She lifted her face.

Her lips stood out as they always did, red in any light. He felt a slow melting take over his limbs, imagining that even in the dark they would glow. The color of her lips defied the science of light.

He leaned toward them, unable to help himself. "Scarlett."

She adjusted her position enough to lean across the sleeping baby and closed her eyes. As his lips reached hers, he felt her melt, let the worries and tension of the day's events fade away.

"I love you." She said the words against his lips, making him feel them more than hear them. He'd meant to say it first. He had asked her to be his wife and knew, in his heart, that he loved her from the moment he'd first saw her. It seemed unfair that he'd forgotten or misplaced those words and not said them. Saying it back now seemed too small. Words could never tell her how much a part of him she felt.

Instead, he cupped her cheek, feeling each molecule of silk glide beneath his thumb. As he breathed in her breath he knew her oxygen, the recently found fuel of fire. He allowed it to kindle and burn, turning the sparks within his heart into a blazing flame.

A sound escaped her throat as they kissed. He was shocked by how it resonated within him, as if there was a language only she could speak and only he could hear. He had not known the power of one woman's love.

When the kiss broke off, they leaned together, his forehead resting against hers, the sound of their mingled breathing loud in the room. He tried for words. "You are my life now."

It was bad. It wasn't the first "I love you" or the poetic words his heart strained to offer to her. It was too broad a stroke, not at all the words that told her she'd given him all the colors in the world like a prism never could. But it was all he had. It was all he knew.

"Oh, Christophé." She raised her arms to his shoulders, wrapping her hands around his head, and brought his cheek next to hers. He closed his eyes, reveling in her femininity—the grace in her movements, the softness of her skin, the softness of her form pressing against his chest, so much softness and yet such strength. Strength in her voice and convictions, strength in the way she took care of everyone around her, strength to love him just as he was. He wanted to kiss her again but knew that roar of blood in his ears was a sign that he should stop.

Scarlett must have sensed the change in him. She'd been married before and must know the constraints on a man's resolve. She let him go, but softness rested in her eyes.

"If we move André to the cradle Jasper brought in, we could sleep side-by-side for the remainder of the night."

Christophé didn't need to be asked twice. Tomorrow they might be chased down. Tomorrow they might be captured. Tomorrow they might be imprisoned.

Tomorrow they might be struck down by the guillotine's blade.

Tonight.

Tonight.

They would sleep in each other's arms.

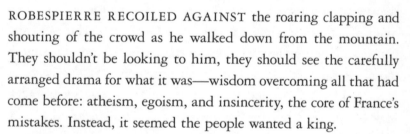

ROBESPIERRE RECOILED AGAINST the roaring clapping and shouting of the crowd as he walked down from the mountain. They shouldn't be looking to him, they should see the carefully arranged drama for what it was—wisdom overcoming all that had come before: atheism, egoism, and insincerity, the core of France's mistakes. Instead, it seemed the people wanted a king.

A god even.

The fact that it felt good and right when he looked down at their upturned faces, at their longing for fathering, was not to be considered. He would ignore it as he'd ignored so many other emotions since his mother's death and father's abandonment. He could not save these people, though he tried. He could only direct them; point them to the one and only hope they had.

The Law.

The next day he would give a thundering speech at the Convention about ridding the party of snakes and conspirators. There were those among them that didn't love the purity of the law as they should. These evil fiends had personal gain in mind— power, wealth, and a rise to infamy. He called out his enemies by name for the first time. A part of him knew this naming was born of fear. That these men were conspiring not against France, but against him. But he had become very good at squashing conscious truth and pretending first to himself and then, more easily, to everyone else that they were enemies of the nation. His greatest enemy, Fouché, and his supporters would come to their end. Fouché would know the voice of the people.

Robespierre left the Convention and went home, a surety that he had done the right thing uplifting his mood. The house was quiet. Good. Scarlett and her family were taking his suggestion and inquiring about rooms for rent in the area. Or perhaps they were visiting his sister, Charlotte, for advice on where to room. Charlotte might even offer to take them in. He sincerely hoped so. The Duplays would like the return of their daughter's room, he was sure, although they said nothing.

Shaking off the concern, he set out for a long walk in the Marbeuf gardens by the Champs-Elysees. The streets were now filled with summer dust, but he hardly noticed. His mind was clear of all but the cadence of his stride in the night.

∽◦◦∽

THE NEXT MORNING Christophé and Jasper were down in the laboratory, leaning over the freshly written passports. They were perfect, the ink dry.

"Do you think it will work?"

Jasper held up and studied the work in the dawn light. "They are my best work to date. Now we only have to rehearse the story with the women and prepare for the journey to Le Havre."

"We leave tonight?"

"Hmmm, if nothing impedes us."

Christophé paused, looking at his old friend. "You don't have to come along, you know. I think you and Madame Bonham might be safe here together."

Jasper shook his head. "Don't think I haven't considered it. But no, I'm an old man. I've lived my life. I would rather risk the scaffold helping you than hiding here. And besides, if Robespierre discovers Suzanne is here, he would force the truth from her." He rubbed his chin and made a face of admission. "Quite easily, I'm afraid. There is no one safe anymore."

"Scarlett is convinced Robespierre will fall. Do you think so?"

Jasper gathered up the papers and pushed his glasses back on his forehead. "She has good reason to believe it. The Festival of the Supreme Being is only the latest sign of his madness. The numbers who hate him are growing by the day."

"I want to champion his enemies, Fouché and that crowd, but they are all atheist. Fouché is bent on taking God and church from the nation."

Jasper put a hand on Christophé's shoulder. "There is no side of good left in France. They will destroy each other."

The men made their way upstairs to the main floor, where they found the women in a flurry of activity of cooking and packing necessities for the journey. The baby was crying in his cradle, which had been moved into the sitting room from Christophé's bedchamber. Christophé went over, picked up the babe, and buried his nose into André's soft hair. The memory of holding Scarlett throughout the night rushed back over him. He looked down at the child and felt a fresh pang of fear and sorrow. What if they were caught? What would they do with a child that traveled with aristocrats and was the blood relative of Robespierre?

André had quieted and only stared at him from slate blue eyes, his tiny fists waving as if to catch Christophé on the chin.

Scarlett called over to him from the counter where she was kneading bread dough. "Thank you for quieting him. We are trying to pack as much food as we can for the journey."

Christophé walked over to her and kissed her cheek, smiling at the smudge of flour on her chin. He reached up and rubbed it off with his thumb. How beautiful she was! They gazed into each other's eyes—until Stacia giggled, breaking the tension.

"No more love gawking, you two. We have work to do."

Christophé leaned over and kissed Scarlett, a quick peck on the mouth, but a public declaration that he didn't care what any of them thought. He had the most intense understanding that these could be the last moments of their lives, and he wanted to soak in each one.

Scarlett's eyes told him she understood all. "Have you and Jasper finished the papers?"

"Yes. The man missed his true profession. He has the most astute hand for forging documents. They look authentic."

"What are our new identities?" Mrs. Bonham queried from another flouring board.

Jasper came through the doorway and paused, his eyes lighting on the older woman. "You, madame, are now Lucille Marie Burlier." He bowed at her. "My wife."

She dimpled at him and cocked her head. "Have we been married long?"

Stacia and Scarlett exchanged amused glances.

Jasper took up his role with a side nod, all serious intent. "Oh, yes. A very long time. You harangue me with your nagging and incessant chattering."

Scarlett's mother broke out in laughter. "And you, *Citizen* Burlier, try my patience daily with your interests in science." She sighed dramatically. "You are always so distracted!"

All three women burst out laughing.

André turned his head at the sounds and wrinkled up his face, but did not cry. Christophé jostled him the best he could to keep him content, feeling the happiness of the moment wash over him. He looked up and caught Émilie's gaze. She had been washing pans and was standing stiff and silent as they all joked. Her eyes reflected pain.

Christophé knew her thoughts. He had them too, at times. A gaping hole that opened at his feet when he thought of his family. He'd found love again and that had helped heal him, but Émilie was still fresh from the grip of Robespierre. He had still not heard everything that had happened to her since that night of disappearance.

Scarlett must have seen the exchange of glances as she walked over and took André from his arms. "Go and talk to her. She needs you."

Christophé gave her a quick nod, communicating his thankfulness. He walked over and touched Émilie on the shoulder. "Come with me."

She looked up and over her shoulder at him. There were tears in her eyes.

He took her hand and led her from the now quiet room. As they walked away, he heard Scarlett ask in a bright voice, "Tell us, Jasper, who are Stacia and I to be?"

Chapter Twenty-Nine

Christophé took Émilie to the back door and led her outside. Jasper had an overgrown garden in the small yard behind his house. A long time ago, he'd explained to Christophé that he grew his own herbs for his medicinal concoctions and potions. He didn't trust anyone else with the task. Now, in the middle of July there were thick clumps and rows of mature plants, mostly green, but a few flowering on either side of the narrow path that wound through his garden.

Toward the back of the garden was a wooden bench, painted red. "Émilie, what color is that bench?"

She stared at it and then back at him. "Green."

He pressed his lips together and looked down. "And the plant here?" He reached over and pulled the leaves closer to them so that she could see it.

"The same, though a little duller in color."

Christophé turned toward her and leaned his head into his hands. "I failed you."

It was a whisper, but loud enough for her to hear.

"No. I failed *you*. I'm sorry . . . but . . ."

He looked up and saw that she was fighting back tears.

"I tried! I really tried. I walked up and down the street. But it was dark and I couldn't find it, Christophé. I couldn't find the red door in the dark."

Christophé stood and brought her into his arms. "I should have known!"

"Known what?" Émilie demanded through her tears. "You had to go back. We didn't have the money Father left for us. There was nothing."

"Oh, Émilie. I should have known so much." He didn't say that now he knew how to travel on three silver francs. That he'd learned to hide and charm and work very hard. He didn't tell her that he'd really just been afraid. How could he tell her that when she looked at him like some kind of savior?

Instead he led her over to the bench and sat beside her. Holding her hand, he spoke quickly. "Your sight is not the same as most people's, Émilie. What you see as green is sometimes red. And there are many shades of green, which you see as yellowish or brown."

She looked up at him. "I know. I didn't know at the time. I should have, there had been signs all along. But I didn't know it then. I'm sorry."

He touched her thin cheek with the back of his finger. "It's my fault."

Émilie shook her head back and forth. "You were only trying to save us." Her eyes looked as strong as glittering diamonds.

"Émilie, tell me. What did he do to you?"

Émilie looked away, out over the garden. She sat very straight on the bench, her breath coming in and out with effort. Her lips were pressed together, her chin up.

"Tell me." Christophé demanded in a soft voice. "Tell me everything that happened after I went back to the chateau."

"There's nothing to speak of. I've forgiven him."

"*Forgiven* him?" Christophé rasped out the words. "Forgiven him of what?" He stood and paced, unable to stop his movement in the face of her still form. The desire to hunt the man down and kill him rose so strong that he had to clench his hands into fists and his jaw shut. But he'd promised God not to take the path of revenge. He'd promised to trust Him.

Still, he had to know. He would not let her bear this burden alone. "What did he do?"

Émilie's chin went up another notch. "He took me to the place where he resides—the Duplay home. I never saw them. He hid me in an adjoining room to his. I had a bed and food." She paused and looked off into the distant sky. "He bade me to serve him his meals. Gave me money sometimes to go the market to get him certain fruits and vegetables, when the Duplays weren't around. Sometimes he would have me sit at the table with him. I didn't speak. He just looked at me."

She stopped for a moment and seemed to gather herself. "I wrote out his correspondence. He said my handwriting was . . . clean."

"Clean." It came out a broken whisper. "What did he mean?"

Émilie looked down and then back up toward him. "He said I had something he did not. He said I had faith. So . . . I think he meant clean in the way Christ makes us clean." She shook her head. "But I don't think he knew what that even meant. He only loved one thing aside from his strange love for me. The law."

Christophé sank. He knelt at her feet and put his head against her knees. "Oh, God. He was making you his savior."

Émilie's hand brushed over the bristled hair of his scalp. "He didn't hurt me." She paused; the silence growing with the only sound of Christophé's shaking breaths. "He asked me to do everyday things. To play with his dog."

Émilie reached out and touched Christophé's arm as he leaned against her, his head bowed. He could not look at her. "I failed you."

Émilie's hand patted his back, as if she'd become the parent in this moment. "Jasper told me. You thought I was guillotined. He must have planned that. I am sorry for the girl that died in my stead."

"How did you . . . survive?" Christophé backed up a little to look into her eyes.

She shrugged, an unconscious movement. Christophé held very still waiting for her next words.

"I didn't speak. He understood. He didn't ask me to. Not ever. I prayed . . . constantly to forgive him. But I never spoke aloud. He didn't make me speak."

Christophé blinked, trying to comprehend it. "How could you forgive him?"

Something came into Émilie's eyes as he looked deep into them, like a blink of heaven, a flash of eternity. "When you didn't come, when I realized that you couldn't save me, I knew that only God could."

Christophé's voice was a harsh grating in the peacefulness of the swaying garden vines. "And will He save us, Émilie? Will He? For I fear I no longer know."

Émilie's bittersweet smile lit her eyes. "God brought you back to me. I didn't think that was possible. And He brought you Scarlett, didn't He?"

Hope, or the hint of it, stirred within him. Yes, God had done both. And now . . . He needed to do the impossible.

Get them out of France alive.

༺✦༻

THEY WOULD LEAVE that night, as soon as it was fully dark, dressed as a bourgeoisie family. The patriarchs—Jasper and Suzanne—with their three daughters, son-in-law, and first grand-child were on a scientific errand. It wasn't much of a cover, but it would have to do.

They were leaving France on a business trip as Jasper and Christophé, astronomers with a new discovery, had letters of invi-tation, albeit fake letters, to the London Royal Society for science. They'd packed their telescopes and many journals outlining all of Christophé's notations over the last few years. They'd packed little else, aside from the food stores the women were insistent upon, some clothes, and their false passports.

Dinner that night was a huge affair, all of them feeling a jovial energy laced in anxiety. Had Robespierre noticed the miss-ing women yet? His schedule was so erratic, with long hours at the Committee of Public Safety, the Council, and the Jacobin Club, they couldn't be sure he had even been home to notice.

After dinner they dressed in their new identities: traveling costumes of sturdy shoes and plain dresses for the women, the homespun of the working class for the men. Christophé wore his stocking cap, the long red one of the Patriots low over his brow. Jasper wore the tri-cornered hat and powdered wig. Each man carried a walking stick. What the women didn't know was that the bottom of the stick hid the point of a blade. They might not be able to carry weapons, but Jasper and Christophé had their defense well planned should they need it.

Evening and time to depart came quiet and soft. A gentle breeze caressed their hair and faces as they hoisted up their bags and skirted through the narrow streets toward the eastern edge of the city. Traveling at night had its advantages, but also the added fear of the patrols. If they could just escape Paris, they might have a chance.

Christophé looked down at Scarlett, his heart swelling with protective love and pride. She had made a makeshift sling to carry André by knotting his blanket around her neck. She explained to him in low tones that, should the need arise to feed him or quiet him, she could easily unbutton her dress and continue walking. As he looked down at the little bundle, he silently prayed the child would not give them away.

Jasper led the way, keeping to shadows and the soft places in the light. The four women brought up the middle, with Christophé at the end of the line. They made their way quickly and silently around the ghostly buildings of old France. They passed through the ruins of palatial homes and gardens, monstrous churches and cathedrals and elegant hotels. Then they tread through the back neighborhoods of the city folk with their apartments, two- and three-storied houses, cafés, and shops. As they neared the edges of the city, the landscape gave way to the more rural feel of farmland, the houses getting further and further away from each other.

Scarlett was becoming increasingly winded and had dropped further behind. Christophé could tell that she was trying to keep up with Stacia, but now they could just make out the back of her striding figure. More alarming was the sudden stops she would make, bending down a bit and breathing hard.

Christophé came along beside her. "What is it?"

She didn't pretend to know what he was asking. "I am bleeding again. I thought it was finished. It must be the walking."

Christophé motioned toward the babe. "Give me the child."

She stopped but fear tightened the skin around her mouth and eyes. "I can't continue at this pace." He could tell that she didn't like it, but they both knew that she had to rest.

Christophé whistled, a bird-like call, and then reached for André, adjusting the sling around his neck. André woke, blinking in the night air and looking around as if he would know what had changed his world.

"He will cry. I know it." She looked up at Christophé, alarm lighting her eyes. "What will we do?"

Christophé took the baby up against his chest and rocked him, looking down at the downy hair and soft skin. He leaned over and gave Scarlett a kiss. "We will rest awhile."

The others had heard the whistle and came back. "Is everything all right?" Suzanne's eyes in the moonlight held concern.

"Scarlett is tired. We have to rest." André awakened, decided he did not like to be so confined, and began to wail in earnest.

Jasper looked around them. They were standing close to a grouping of houses. "We should find a safer place." He looked to Scarlett. "Can you hurry a little longer?"

She grasped her skirt in her hands and nodded.

After several more minutes of walking, they saw a lone farmhouse. It sat in a hollow in the land, quiet and peaceful with light flooding from its windows. Jasper came up to Christophé and pointed to it. "I don't like how Scarlett is bleeding. We could ask for shelter for the night."

"It would be better to sleep out in the open, but I agree. They look awake and she needs a bed if we can get her one."

Leaving the women in a small stand of trees, Christophé and Jasper approached the farmer's door. It was an old door, he thought distractedly as he watched his hand curl into a fist and knock. The door opened and he saw the frightened face of a man peer out from the crack of light. "What do you want?" The man scratched at his cheek and then chin, while staring at Christophé.

"Good citizen, we are in need of shelter for the night."

"What do you think? Out traveling at this hour? You could be anyone. Why would I let you into my house?"

"We are scientists traveling to London. Another two days and we will reach Le Havre to board a ship. We have papers."

The man opened the door a little wider. "Let me see them."

Jasper pulled the papers from his overcoat pocket and handed them over to Christophé. Christophé found his and Jasper's in the pile and passed those over to the man.

The man looked to be reading them, but Christophé could tell from the way the man's eyes scanned the documents that he could not read.

Christophé and Jasper exchanged sudden glances. They'd both seen it.

A tall shadow just behind the man.

Christophé backed slowly up as Jasper put a hand, low and waving back, toward the women.

The man saw their actions and filled their silence, dropping the passports on the ground. "Yes. Yes. Everything looks to be in order." As he said the words his hand, the one outside the door, waved them frantically away.

Christophé took a few running steps back toward the door to pick up the papers. His fingers grasped the pages, wadding them into his hand as he turned to run.

The man talked to them as if they were still standing in front of him. "You may stay. But I don't want any trouble. Come in." There was a thread of panic in his voice.

Christophé shouted over his shoulder. "We'll be back after we gather our belongings. Thank you, good citizen."

When he reached the women, he grasped Scarlett's arm.

"It's a trap!" Jasper rasped out the words, stopping in front of Suzanne. They could see the man standing where they left him, waiting for them. "Someone has been following us."

"Oh, heavens!" Mrs. Bonham squeaked. "What shall we do?"

"Run," Christophé commanded softly. "Hurry."

As they turned away from the house and ran from the road, they plunged into a thick copse of woodland. A sudden commotion sounded from the house.

"*Run!*" Christophé shouted to all of them.

Émilie stumbled and fell. Christophé turned back, scooped her up into his arms, and followed the flying feet of Scarlett and howling cries of André. A bullet whizzed by his ear but he grinned. He couldn't help it.

He didn't know Scarlett could run like the wind when she had to.

Chapter Thirty

Jasper had Suzanne's hand grasped tightly in his as they rounded the thick brush and undergrowth of the forest. The dear lady was doing her best, but he knew she wouldn't be able to keep up their reckless pace much longer.

The pursuit was on. They could hear their adversaries coming.

"There, do you see that?" Jasper paused as the others caught up. He pointed up into a tree with easy climbing branches, lots of them.

"Up you go, madame."

"Into the *tree?*" Suzanne gasped, turning shocked eyes toward him. She looked up and up at the swaying, leafy branches.

"I have faith in you." He stared at her feeling his heart in his eyes.

Suzanne looked at him for a second and then planted a big kiss square on his mouth. Turning from him, she hoisted her skirts up and grasped the lowest limb. Jasper clasped her around the hips, able to feel their lush curves beneath her skirts, and lifted with all his strength. She gasped and let out a little squeak.

And even that sound was music to Jasper's ears.

CHRISTOPHÉ AND THE other women caught up with Jasper, all of them breathless as they watched in silent hope as Suzanne reached for the next higher branch, her shoes sliding against the slick bark.

"You can do it, Mother. Hurry!" Stacia whisper-screamed her support.

Stacia was next. Then Émilie, as lithe and agile as most children. Scarlett looked at Christophé with fear in her eyes. "I'm afraid. What if I drop André?"

Christophé took hold of the sling and quickly adjusted the fabric so that André was completely ensconced. "I will be right behind you. Now go."

Scarlett scrambled up the first two branches. Her foot stretched for a far branch on the other side of where Stacia, Émilie, and her mother clung. It slipped, causing a yelp to sound from her throat. Christophé started to come up behind her but then they all heard a great crashing sound behind them.

Overcome with fear, Scarlett scrambled for the branch, this time aiming for a knot in the wood to help steady her. With a mighty step, hanging onto the branch overhead, she landed on the stout limb.

The sounds of men shouting and the rustle of the bushes broke into their little clearing. Scarlett looked down and saw that Christophé had two choices. He could leap up after her, which might give them away, or drop to the ground to protect their hiding place. Her heart beat in her throat so that she felt like choking as she watched him weigh the options and then drop from the branch and walk over to stand with Jasper, away from them.

She watched as a dozen men surrounded them, rifles pointed at their chests.

"State your names, citizens!"

Scarlett's brow knitted in anxious thought. The booming voice sounded vaguely familiar.

Jasper and Christophé stood erect, chins up and spines stiffened as they were surrounded. Jasper spoke first. "Mon Dieu. We go to London for science. We have done nothing wrong. See?" He pulled out the passports and Scarlett's heart chilled—those were the papers for her and the women.

Jasper must have realized the same, for he looked to Christophé, who quickly pulled the wadded papers from his pockets. "We have passports for travel to London."

The leader spat. Scarlett suddenly recognized him from her hiding place and took a long quivering breath. Henri Vonriot, one of Robespierre's supporters in the Convention. Suddenly it all seemed to Scarlett madness and hopelessness. They would be caught. Christophé and Jasper would be imprisoned. They might all be imprisoned. What story could they conjure to explain false passports, a sudden trip to London, and hiding in a tree?

The men circled around Christophé and Jasper, while Vonriot reached for the papers. A long moment went by while he smoothed them out and studied them. Scarlett held herself very still as one man looked around the area and then up. André started to move. Scarlett prayed as never before, begging God for peace to flood her and the babe. As she relaxed so, too, did André.

The leaves were thick, their clothes were dark, but Scarlett knew that if the man looked closely enough, he would find them.

"Qu'est-ce que c'est?"

Other voices joined the questioner, and Scarlett looked down. A finger pointed up into the tree. She blinked and blinked again, numb now.

There, just below, was a malevolent gaze staring straight into her eyes.

❧

IT WAS 8 Thermidor, according to the Révolutionary calendar, a sunny day just before noon. Robespierre rose from his seat in the packed national Convention hall to give the speech he had labored over all night. It was time to strike.

He could feel their eyes upon him as he stepped up to the rostrum. His hand rose to find his green spectacles buried in his white powdered wig. He shook the glasses free, settling them on the bridge of his nose, cleared his throat and began.

It took two full hours to say everything he had to present. His words were slow, laborious, and carefully meted out with just the right note of reproach toward the Convention members for their neglect at snuffing out the conspirators. He didn't like to think of their end, how they would die, he only considered them an evil that must be sponged away from the virtue of the people. He paused after an especially weighty sentence to raise his spectacles and meet each man's eyes, as if he were able by just looking at them to see the truth in their nature and name them enemy or friend.

The end of his speech became more personal. He rebutted the title *dictator,* as some had secretly called him. His was a life laid down for his country. Those that called him names were vipers and snakes and must be punished.

He paused to look about the crowded room of friends and foes, but before he could go on someone shouted out, "We must examine the accusations made toward these people you mention. We need a careful and rigorous examination!"

Robespierre was taken aback. He had always been able to convince them to the point of clapping, stomping, cheering heights for anything he presented to the Convention. It was why he sweated and struggled so over his speeches. To make certain they were perfect and unquestionable. He felt a slip of fear, like a dark shadow, pass over his body. Rallying, he blasted the man for his audacity.

A small group began to clap. Just as Robespierre was prepared to allow his lips to curve into the semblance of a relieved smile, another man stood, Bourdon de l'Oise. "I demand proof before any names are publicly announced."

Robespierre struggled to sustain his calm—this was Joseph Fouché's friend, both names on his list of conspirators.

A third man strode up to the rostrum and moved Robespierre aside. *"This* is our enemy," he bellowed. "Judge him! Judge Robespierre!"

Robespierre turned and walked out of the hall.

The next day Robespierre went back to the Convention ready to name names. Saint-Just, his right hand for the last few years, had agreed to be the one to read the list. Robespierre watched with satisfaction as the young man took the rostrum. Working together, they would convince these men of the conspirators and then . . . then Robespierre would be safe.

But as Saint-Just launched into the demands for punishment of such evil, another man rose and rushed the stage, demanding to speak. Saint-Just yelled back, but the president for the day rang his bell with such force that every time Saint-Just opened his mouth, no one could hear him. Finally Saint-Just gave up.

In a panic Robespierre watched as several other men, one after the other, spoke against them. When he rose to make his own way to the front to defend himself, he was shoved aside. When he tried to yell out his request to speak, the bell rang and rang and rang, until finally, he gave up too.

Suddenly someone stood and said the words Robespierre hadn't allowed himself to consider he might ever hear. "Arrest Robespierre!"

Robespierre watched as his place in the universe swayed, groaned, and then crashed down around his head. It was gone—all of his power and authority and strength. He watched as if from another place as the men voted to arrest Robespierre and Saint-Just.

Hours later Robespierre sat in a stupor in an upper room of the Hotel de Ville. There were several men in the room—Lescot-Fleuriot, Payan, Couthon, and others—who still believed in him. They took turns pleading with him to make an appeal or raise up an army to fight.

He sat there and stared at the scarred wooden table and the quickly written pages they had drawn up for him to sign. How could he sign them? He was without authority. The law—the very law he had painstakingly written almost single-handedly over the last two years, the law that he had breathed out of his own mouth in speeches and small gathering talks—that law said that he was accused of treason, without the ability to defend himself, without recourse. Just as the thousands of others who had been accused and guillotined without proof or defense. And the law said the penalty for his sin was death. A penalty he himself had doled out more times than he could count.

How could he now take the coward's way of signing his name on a document as if he were still a deputy of the Committee? To do so was to spit in his own face and call himself the greatest of liars.

He looked around at the men who were willing to fight for him and felt nothing but disgust. They were as children, begging for a reprieve from punishment. Robespierre loved the law. Worshipped it. It kept him safe so long as he could keep each letter of it. Now . . . he realized his god had turned on him and abandoned him.

Just as his mother and father had.

The men in the room turned as they all heard a commotion coming up the stairs. Philippe Le Bas, a look of terror on his face, pulled out a gun, raised it to his head, and shot. The men jerked, fell back, cries coming from their throats as the force neared the door. Augustin, Robespierre's younger brother, turned, ran, and jumped through a window. Gobeau raised a stiletto, turned it on himself, and plunged it into his chest.

Robespierre lifted the pistol that he always carried with him to his mouth. As the door burst open, he, too, escaped in the only way left to him.

He pulled the trigger.

Chapter Thirty-One

ndré was miserable, going in and out of fits of sobbing, cries that made the men look at Scarlet as if they might, at any moment, use the saber on the end of one of their rifles to silence him. Christophé's anger burned within him each time they eyed her.

Every time the babe began crying, Scarlett panicked, slowed to jostle him, to take him from the sling to hold in different positions. The guards had tied all of their hands except Scarlett's, as she was the only one allowed to carry her son. Christophé could tell that the added weight and walking all night, combined with the fear of what was to come, had such a crushing effect on her body that she could hardly keep her trembling legs from collapsing.

And then the worst. The bleeding had increased so that she left a dripping trail in her wake.

Christophé saw the blood and started to speak, but then stopped as they all heard horses approaching. The soldiers backed them off the road, their rifles aimed and ready. When they saw the uniform of the Patriots, Vonriot ordered the men guarding them to lower their weapons.

The riders dismounted and approached. "Henri Vonriot, lay down your weapons. We have a warrant for your arrest."

"What?" The startled man pushed forward. "By whose authority and on what charges?"

"By the authority of the Convention. Robespierre has been arrested, along with Saint-Just and all of his followers. You are to come with us immediately."

As the commander of the small force spoke, all the blood drained from Vonriot's face. Scarlett looked at Christophé, eyes wide and panicked.

Christophé shook his head slightly, stilling her.

Vonriot looked at his men, pulled a pistol suddenly from his belt and raised it to his head.

The crack of the shot jerked through Christophé's body. He saw Scarlett jerk, and André's frightened wails filled the woods around them. The officer looked momentarily shocked, and then disgusted. He motioned for his men to gather the weapons of the others.

"Who are these prisoners?" he demanded, looking at Stacia for an extra moment.

One of the other officers under Vonriot spoke up. "We have their passports here. They say they are scientists on the way to London for a scientific meeting." His voice shook, and Christophé wagered the man thought he might be going to one of the many prisons in France now.

"Why did you arrest them?"

"We have reason to believe the passports are forged."

"Let me see the papers."

The officer took his time looking them over. "They appear authentic to me." He pointed to Christophé. "Explain yourself and your business."

Christophé launched into his practiced speech, almost yelling to be heard above the crying of the baby. When he finished, they all waited while the man weighed his words—but his gaze kept swinging back to Stacia.

"You will go with us to Paris where we can look into the authenticity of your tale."

Scarlett struggled against tears at the officer's pronouncement. She glanced up and caught him looking at her with clear concern. "You will ride with me," he said in a tight voice. He looked around at his men. "Untie the prisoners and use the bindings on the soldiers. We will send someone back for Vonriot's body."

Soldiers came to help Scarlett onto the man's horse, hoisting her to sit in front of him sideways, practically on his lap. One of his arms supported her, keeping her from falling. She looked down from the height and noticed Christophé looking at the man like he would like to land a solid punch on his pretty face. She quickly looked away, afraid of what might happen next. As she watched, her mother was lifted, with some huffing and puffing from the soldier doing the lifting, onto another man's horse. Émilie was assigned to a young, thin man's care—the soldier looked barely older than she. Stacia climbed nimbly onto the horse of a handsome, young man, who promptly wrapped one of his arms around her waist, clearly pretending it was because she might need his aid to stay balanced.

Scarlett did not miss the glared warning the commander gave the man.

If she wasn't so terrified of what might come next, Scarlett would have allowed the bubble of hysterical laughter to escape her throat. Instead, she held on to the horse's mane with one hand and André with the other, and prayed she wouldn't fall off. As they started back down the road to Paris, the man behind her asked, "When was the last time the poor little fellow ate something?"

Scarlett looked up over her shoulder. The man looked to be in his early thirties. He had short-cropped, dark hair, hazel-green eyes, a square chin and dimples when he smiled. Well, he hadn't exactly smiled, but she could tell he would have dimples if and when he did. She pressed her lips together. "I'll not feed him now. On a horse, with you looking down over my shoulder."

"Suit yourself. I just thought it would make for a quieter ride." There was underlying laughter in his voice.

"It hasn't been that long. He will not starve." Suddenly she frowned and looked back at him. "You sound as if you know something about children. Do you have children?"

"Three. My wife died some time ago. I am raising them alone." He shrugged and grinned down at her. "As you can imagine, I have had some experience with babies."

"Where are they now?"

"Tucked away at home. My sister keeps them when I am away."

"What is your name? Perhaps we've met." Scarlett needed to know if this man knew or could easily discover her relation to Robespierre.

"No. We haven't met before. I would have remembered that. My name is Antoine Laroche. But what of you? Who is the father of this squalling babe?"

Scarlett remembered their fake passports and the story they'd all memorized. "My name is Scarlett Burlier." She gestured back to Christophé, who was working hard to keep up with the horse and them. "That man is my husband." She looked up at the man behind her, hoping her face wouldn't betray her. "He is a great scientist. His mind is . . . a natural phenomenon."

Antoine cast a brief glance back at Christophé. "Were you really going to London for science? No one thinks of those things anymore."

"Do you think so?" Scarlett dimpled. "Well, there is one other reason." She pointed toward Stacia. "My sister is unmarried and looking for a husband. She hasn't had any luck in Paris, so we thought to look in London."

"Doesn't she like French men?"

"Of course! But French men are only enamored of the Révolution. Few seem to care about love these days."

"There are some who care about family and love."

"Really?" Scarlett let her eyes widen. "And might you be one of those men?"

"I might be." He cast a long glance at Stacia, and Scarlett felt a spark of hope.

"Perhaps I should introduce you." It certainly couldn't hurt their cause to have this man interested in her sister.

"Perhaps you should." He smiled, showing perfect white teeth and looked down at Scarlett.

He did, indeed, have very nice dimples.

"Tell me of the arrest you spoke of. I know so little of politics, but I have, of course, heard of the famed Robespierre."

"His time as ruler is over." There was satisfaction in Antoine's voice. "He will be taken where he has sent so many others."

"Where is that?" Scarlett knew, but needed to hear the answer.

"To the guillotine."

⟨∽⟩

THE LEADERS OF the Convention stared at the carnage in the room.

At one time they were a united force, building a new government, a new country. Now four men, those who'd chosen to follow Robespierre, lay on the floor, bleeding horribly. Two had escaped through the windows, so they would have to search for them to see if they were still alive. One man sat in a chair, his eyes wide with horror.

Robespierre didn't know how it could have happened. He was still alive. The bullet that was aimed for his brain had turned somehow, maybe a jerk of the pistol as these men burst through the door. He couldn't think. He didn't know anything except unfathomable pain.

His jaw was shattered, blood spurted from his chin to drip in a long line down his neck. He couldn't talk, couldn't swallow, he could barely breathe as pain and panic washed over him in waves of unremitting fear.

The men surrounded them and took stock, lifting the maimed from the floor. Saint-Just stood to one side, the only one of them uninjured, still pristine in his gray breeches, white shirt, and waistcoat. The *Angel of Death*, they called him. He alone stood perfect as if, indeed, he possessed otherworldly powers.

Robespierre was heaved up and carried by his wrists and ankles to a table where they laid him. Time made no sense as he lay, in and out of consciousness, for what seemed like hours. At one point, he thought a face bent over him and mockingly commented, "There *is* a God."

As the morning sun slanted through the tall windows, two surgeons came in and bent over him. They mumbled between themselves and then one took up a long, thick needle. One of them cleaned his face then opened his mouth and yanked out the loose teeth. Robespierre groaned with the agony as they held his mouth open and began to dig for the lodged bullet in his jaw. Why they would bandage him up only to cut off his head, he didn't know. For the first time, he thought of all the men and women he had personally sent to the guillotine, what their last moments might have been like.

His body shook uncontrollably while they did their work. He couldn't look at them and he couldn't close his eyes, so he only looked up and stared as hard as he could at the plaster ceiling of the room. Finally he heard the bullet drop into a metal cup. Fresh blood gushed down his face, which the surgeon staunched with wads of linen. His entire skull felt ready to burst as they wrapped strips of bandages around his head, from under his chin to the top of his head, to hold the jaw in place.

He couldn't talk.

His voice, that which had been the phoenix of his life, was ruined. There would be no hope of salvation now. If only they had let him speak! It was the only thing his father had given him. Oh, if only they had let him speak.

It was his last thought as he fell back into unconsciousness.

⌇∽⌇

THEIR PARTY OF soldiers, prisoners, and suspects turned onto the Rue Saint-Honoré. Scarlett had dozed off and came awake with a jerk, realizing that she was leaning against Antoine's broad chest. He pointed ahead of them. "Look."

Scarlett stared at the masses of people running to fill the street. She straightened in her seat, peering ahead. "What is happening?"

"Do you see the carts up ahead?"

She nodded, swallowing hard, recognizing a familiar light-blue coat. They were taking a group to the guillotine.

"Who is it?" She asked, but she knew.

"Listen to the crowd."

"Death to the king!" A woman near them shouted, her face a mask of hate. "Death to Robespierre!"

More insults were being shouted by everyone around them. The crowd was growing moblike with wild-eyed faces and rage-screaming voices. It seemed the whole world was aflame with hatred. Scarlett turned back and looked for Christophé. He was right behind them, looking exhausted but intense. Their eyes met. He pressed his lips together and motioned his head toward her.

"Let me down!"

"It's not safe. You could be trampled."

Scarlett ground her teeth. She wouldn't care about being trampled if she didn't have André. She wanted to be with Christophé! Looking over to Stacia, she shouted. "Will you take André?"

Stacia nodded, wide-eyed, looking afraid to do much of anything. Scarlett turned to look at Antoine. "I must walk this part with my husband. Please, take Stacia. I know she will keep André safe."

He looked at her for a long moment and then agreed with a signal of his hand. He stopped their troop and waited while Stacia and Scarlett dismounted. "It's not the right time, my dearest. But—" she gestured with a hand toward Antoine—"he is a good man. I have a good feeling about him."

Stacia's eyes grew wide. "You must be insa—"

"I know." Scarlett pressed a kiss upon Stacia's cheek. "Don't let anything happen to André."

Stacia approached the man's horse. Antoine had dismounted and offered Stacia his hand. Scarlett watched as Stacia reached for it, grasped it, and then took a sudden bright breath as the tall man hefted her up without any of Stacia's aid, to land perfectly in the saddle. Stacia settled herself as Antoine climbed up behind her. Scarlett handed up the baby and watched while Stacia placed him into the sling.

Émilie had dismounted and took up Christophé's other side.

Scarlett turned to Christophé, grasped his face between her hands, and leaned up to kiss him. She knew not what might happen next. All they had was their combined breaths, their skin touching, their lips pressing.

Christophé broke free first. "How are you? Are you still bleeding?"

Scarlett grasped his hand and turned toward the square, where the guillotine sat like a giant bloody statue. "No. The rest did me good."

They pushed their way through the throng of cheering, shouting people.

She stopped toward the front and saw them. Carts, one with four men, one with six. Her gaze locked onto Robespierre. His clothes were torn. The blue coat that he loved so much was ripped and dirty. His stockings were around his ankles as he climbed out of the cart and stood with four other men. They all looked terrible, their faces, their dissembled clothing, all except one, Saint-Just. The Angel of Death looked exactly as he always had.

Scarlett clutched the front of her dress as she watched Robespierre. His face was shattered, bruised and bleeding, swathed in cloth like a mummy. She couldn't tear her eyes away.

The scaffold stood huge in the mid-afternoon sun. She watched as a crippled man, mumbling and incoherent, was carried up the scaffolding steps to the platform. He was strapped to a board, which took many minutes, as his twisted body couldn't be pressed flat against it. His body sidewise, they slid him onto the guillotine, positioning him under the blade. Scarlett turned away, clutching Émilie's hand, leaning on Christophé for support as the sound of the blade whooshed though the air.

A great cheer rose from the crowd.

She swallowed hard as the executioner raised the dead man's head.

It was a play to them, wasn't it? Scarlett looked at the manic faces around her. "God, Your creation! Oh, God, what have we done?"

Christophé's arms encircled her, and she shivered against him.

The next man was led up the steps. Saint-Just. He lifted his head and glared at the screaming crowd, who roared afresh when his young, angelic head was held high in the air.

Robespierre was last.

Scarlett pressed her fist over her mouth as the executioner removed his robin's-egg blue coat. He tossed it into the crowd. They raised their hands to grasp at the souvenir. Next, he ripped off the bandage around Robespierre's head. Scarlett could see the jaw fall open, as though unattached. She gasped and pressed her body into Christophé's. "God, have mercy."

Émilie stood straight and tall. She didn't move. Her face didn't change. Scarlett watched as the young girl disengaged herself from them and walked forward. As though sensing something of import was happening, the crowd in front of them parted. She walked until she was in the very front.

Scarlett looked at Christophé. "What is she doing?"

Christophé looked down, tears in his eyes. "She is telling him that she forgives him."

Scarlett began to sob quietly into Christophé's shoulder.

AS ROBESPIERRE WAS strapped to the board that would slide him beneath the blade, he looked one last time into the crowd. These were the people he had fought so hard for. And now, they hated him. There was one face though . . .

One face that didn't hate him. His gaze locked with that of a young woman.

As the crowd roared their approval of the Master of Terror going to his death, Émilie St. Laurent stared into his eyes. As the insults flew all around him, he held to her sweet, innocent face, her righteous faith in something he, until this moment, had not been able to grasp.

She blinked, and he suddenly knew.

What had he done? In the name of freedom? In the name of finding his solace? To be loved? For that was what it had really been all about. *What had he done?*

Forgive me! he cried within as they leveled his body and slid it under the blade. *For I have sinned!*

Émilie turned her face away. She didn't need to see the final moment, didn't want to see retribution. As the crowd roared their approval of the beginning of the end to Terror, Émilie St. Laurent turned away from them, knowing that at the end he had understood. Somehow, she was sure. A little sob broke from her throat. Someday, in heaven, she would see her family, they would all be together. It was her prayer that Robespierre, too, would be there. Forgiven.

Finally whole.

Émilie looked up but she didn't focus on the crowd of hate around her. She didn't listen to their screams of jubilation at what they thought was a new freedom. No. She saw the light shine down on a man and a women, her brother and his beloved, and she knew that, somehow, they were all going to live. They were going to live . . .

And love each other for a long, long time.

Epilogue

Six Months Later

Scarlett walked down the aisle of lavender-strewn flowers and bright leaves, arm and arm with Émilie. They were dressed alike—simple, white muslin gowns that flowed from high-waisted ivory ribbons. The only difference was that Émilie wore an interwoven twine of ivy leaves in her hair, a green crown, the hue of which she could see. Scarlett's crown was interwoven with blood-red roses that cascaded down her back in a leafy red train.

A symbol of all they'd known and seen.

Christophé stood at the front with the magistrate they'd hired to do the ceremony, as France had no church. Christophé wore his only suit of black breeches, a black tailcoat that fitted him none too well, and white stockings, shirt, and stock. But his face.

Scarlett grasped hold of Émilie's arm as she looked at her beloved's dear face.

"He has never loved anything like he loves you."

Émilie's whispered words caused her to falter in their walk, their silken, red slippers touching as they turned, for a moment, toward each other. Scarlett looked down at her soon-to-be sister-in-law's young face and saw the mercy of God.

She exhaled a sudden breath on three words: "And I, him."

Émilie handed her off to her brother, gave them both a long, happy glance, and then went to her chair in the front, beside the newly married Jasper and Scarlett's mother, now Suzanne Montpelier. Stacia sat beside Antoine; they were never very far from each other these days and already hinting at a wedding of their own. Stacia was young to become, overnight, a mother to three small children, but Scarlett had already seen a side to her sister that showed she could take on the task. It helped that she seemed to have an inborn love for the motherless children and got along so well with Antoine's sister.

Scarlett turned from those happy thoughts toward the man beside her. She thought back on all her dreams. As a young girl, as a young woman, as Daniel's bride even. She hadn't known. She had never truly grasped finding her other half . . . until now.

Christophé reached for her hands. He held them tightly, as though afraid. She looked up and commanded with her eyes that he look at her, really look at her. Standing there, while the magistrate began the words that would make them man and wife, she willed him to see the truth of her heart.

The truth of their forever.

His hair had grown. His face was shaved, but he still had the dark shadows of a beard on his cheeks and chin. As the man of the law spoke, she memorized this moment and each fleck of color in his startlingly beautiful blue eyes, each line just starting to form around his eyes, each movement of his face as he said the vows. With everyone watching them, she allowed her gaze to rove with love over this man God had given her.

The magistrate's speech talked of man and wife and the law that would bind them together. But all Scarlett could think of was Christophé's prism and the colors he had shown her. She broke then, crying a little as she spoke the words when they were demanded of her, but knowing . . . knowing that this man was the light in her world. She thought back on the stars in his heavens, of the microscopic world that thrilled him, the scratching of numbers and mathematical signs that she would never understand, but that gave his eyes a blazing light of passion. He would only and ever be all that brought her a new and glorious world, one she'd only been able to imagine. Until now.

She remembered his first word to her—*color*—and then she thought back on her father and the name he had given her.

And then, she considered God and how He planned it all.

CHRISTOPHÉ SAW COLOR everywhere. His vision was overly bright today. He saw the red in her lips. He saw the white of her gown, knowing it to be so pure that the color blurred away into nothing but brightness. He saw her glorious hair, and in her eyes he saw her love. He repeated his lines, not knowing what he said, not caring, as long as what they spoke made her his, forever.

He was so glad to grasp her hands and say the words of his heart out loud for everyone to hear. "I love you."

It wasn't raining.

It was sunny and bright in Jasper's garden as a new day dawned for them. For France. The bloody Terror was behind them. A new day, full of possibilities, stood before them all. And it was filled with hope.

As Christophé and Scarlett took the sacraments of Communion, drinking from the cup of His blood and eating from the holiness of His broken body so that they might live, they stood in unison under an azure sky.

"Thy kingdom come." Christophé's gaze glowed as he stared into her eyes.

"Thy will be done." Scarlett's beautiful lips curved.

A bird screeched above their heads, and they both looked up.

They all looked up.

And there, in the clear blue sky . . . arched a bow of color.

A perfect rainbow.

The promise of a future filled the air and all their hearts. Scarlett and Christophé gazed into each other's eyes, knowing . . .

God's blessing, a sanctification, a benediction, a healing, and a future.

It was a great day indeed.

Christophé looked back up at the arch of color, saw each hue as a calculation, then looked at his wife's face . . .

And saw the dawning of a new day for them all.

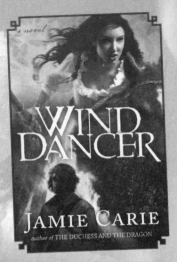
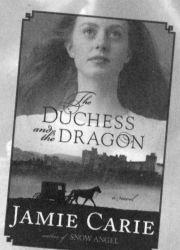